When North
Becomes South

A Novel
by
Becky Bronson

Rebecca Bronson, Publisher

Rebecca Bronson, Publisher

Westford, MA USA

www.beckybronson.com

Printed in the United States of America

Library of Congress Control Number: 2020909031

First Printing, July 2020

ISBN 978-1-7348551-0-4

Cover Image by Arek Socha from Pixabay

Cover Design, Graphic Design, and Illustration by Joanne Kenyon

*To my father who taught me to reach for the stars
and my mother who gave me the gift of writing*

Table of Contents

Prologue
The Superstorm
November 11, 2021

A major superstorm arises within the sun, jettisoning off huge particles of hot, molten gas. These flare-ups happen often. In fact, a smaller one occurred ten years prior, though the effect on Earth was minor and most of the damaging particles eventually disintegrated in the vast reaches of the universe. This time, however, there is an unfortunate confluence of events. The storm is exceptionally strong and due to the alignment of the planets, the mass of radioactive particles heads directly for Earth. The storm also lasts for two full days, bombarding all parts of the planet continually with radiation as it rotates. Added to this, accelerated changes in climate during the past ten years have spawned numerous major storms that destabilized much of the infrastructure humans have built, especially in coastal areas and flood zones near rivers.

As the particles hit the outer stratosphere of Earth's atmosphere, their interaction with the magnetic field causes massive disruption of power grids around the world. Moreover, the magnetic field has been shifting slowly for ages, and this barrage of galactic radiation tips the scale. Earth's magnetic poles have been slowly on the move—and suddenly, this storm causes the migration of the magnetic poles to accelerate. Scientists on Earth had been predicting this shift, thinking it would most likely take centuries, but the force of the storm changes all predictions. *On the planet Earth, north is soon to become south.*

Chapter 1
Ten Years Earlier

Laurie sighed out of sheer exasperation. After two full days with no power, she was truly at her wits' end. School was canceled, and her bored boys were fighting again—their latest argument over a stupid game of Monopoly. She had to get out of her house. Thankfully, her neighbor Jenny was home. She could see Jenny's car in the driveway from her bedroom window. Deciding that Brendan and Josh were old enough to fend for themselves for a bit even without any electronic babysitters, she called to them as she walked out the door.

"Brendan, Josh! I'm going across the street for a little while. "Find something to do separately!"

The moment of silence upstairs indicated to Laurie they must have heard her. Hopefully, they wouldn't kill each other while she was out.

Jenny answered the door as soon as Laurie knocked. Dressed in a sharp pants suit, she looked ready for a job interview. Laurie, in her sweatshirt and jeans, felt rumpled by comparison.

"How are you holding up?" Jenny asked as they exchanged a brief hug.

"It's been brutal, having both boys home and no electricity. And since our neighborhood well doesn't have a generator, no power means no water either—so no showers. Thank goodness I have short hair!" She ran her hands through her short, curly brown locks. "My kitchen sink is piled high with dishes. Yesterday, we thought about going to a movie, but all theaters were closed. Then, we considered going out to lunch but couldn't find an open restaurant they would both enjoy. The two of them can't seem to agree on anything these days. Honestly, I never thought having teenagers would be this tough!"

Jenny smiled sympathetically. "I know. My kitchen sink isn't quite as bad since it's only the two of us now, but we did once have four kids living here and I remember those days well!"

"How did you survive?" Laurie asked. "I feel like everything we do is wrong. The two of them are constantly getting into trouble. We grounded them both for the past two days for drinking at a party last weekend. Though right now I don't know who that grounding is punishing more—me or them. I wish I could send them to friends' houses!"

"They do grow up eventually," replied Jenny. "And then you'll really miss them. Mark my words."

"What I'm really going to miss is you. I can't believe you're moving! Who am I going to run to when things get crazy at my house?"

"You'll be fine," Jenny assured her. "And you can always call me. We do have the technology to stay in touch these days."

Laurie teared up as she looked at her friend with her perfectly coifed hair and chic clothes. They were so different, yet they had managed to form a bond that had lasted for years. She remembered when they first met. It was shortly after Laurie and Stan moved into the neighborhood. Somehow, Laurie had managed to lock herself out of the house, and Jenny saw her trying to pry open the basement window. Jenny ran over to help and together they managed to open the window just wide enough for Laurie to squeeze her petite body through. It was the start of a friendship that lasted over fifteen years. Jenny had been there for her through so much, from the birth of her first child to her boys' recent forays into teenage-hood, and Laurie dreaded the thought of new people moving into this house that felt almost like her second home.

"What's with this power outage, anyway?" Laurie asked. "When it started, we thought it would last only a few hours, and it's been two days." She paused and bit her lip, recalling the rumors heard from other neighbors. She couldn't get a clear answer from anyone. One neighbor thought the power company was having a huge strike, while another said they heard a massive meteorite had landed in New York City! "Have you gotten any updates? It's so annoying when we can't even watch the news."

Jenny smiled. "I talked to George down the street. He's been on his ham radio nonstop for the last two days and said this is a pretty widespread outage that affected most of the east coast. He thinks things should be back to normal later today. Apparently, a solar flare messed up electrical grids up and down the coast, from Canada all the way to Florida."

"Wow," said Laurie. "That's kind of scary."

Jenny nodded. "It could have been worse, though. Even though a huge geographic area was affected, damage was minor, and everyone should be back online soon. Power to major cities is already up and running and it won't be long before we're back in service. George knows a lot about this kind of stuff, and he isn't too worried. He has quite an amazing communications setup in his house."

"I know. I've seen it and it's impressive." Laurie replied.

"Maybe Brendan and Josh would be interested in seeing it in action."

"That's actually not a bad idea!" exclaimed Laurie. "George runs the ham radio club at school and Brendan thought about joining it, but none of his friends were interested, so he didn't sign up. But maybe they could spend a little time with George today. The problem is if I suggest it, neither of them will be interested. You know… teenagers!"

"I have an idea," said Jenny. She picked up her phone. Luckily, though cell phone service was out, landline communications still worked, at least locally. After a brief conversation, she turned to Laurie and gave her a thumbs up.

"George says he'll come by your house in a little while and invite the boys over. Maybe they'll take him up on it. You never know."

Laurie rose to leave and gave her friend a hug. "Thanks, Jenny," she said. "You always seem to find a way to make things better."

Back at her house, Laurie was relieved to hear silence, and nothing seemed out of place. If the boys had had a blow-out, at least no furniture was destroyed. She decided not to say anything to them about George. It would probably be better if they thought the idea came from him. They both knew him, as he had lived in the neighborhood longer than they had. His wife had died recently from cancer, and many neighbors had been reaching out to him for the past few months. Brendan and Josh were aware of that and had gone with Laurie several times to deliver him meals when his wife was sick.

There was a knock on the door, and Laurie welcomed George in. She had always had a soft spot for her neighbor, who she thought looked like an absent-minded professor, with his bushy gray hair and wire-rimmed glasses. She called up to the boys. Josh came down first, looking slightly disheveled in an old t-shirt, his long straight sandy blond hair masking his eyes. "What's up?" he asked, before looking up and seeing George. "Oh, hi Mr. Morgan."

"Hi Josh. I was wondering if you and your brother might like to come by my house for a little while to help me with some communications work. I'm a little overwhelmed right now—this power outage has me crazy. I could use another set of ears."

"Really?" asked Josh. "I'll go."

"I think I'll pass," Brendan said from the stairway, curling his lanky body around the railing. Though two years older than his brother, he and Josh looked like twins with their dad's narrow face and blond hair. Brendan's hair was close-cropped, however, and he had Stan's bright blue eyes, while Josh had Laurie's deep brown ones. And right now, those blue eyes narrowed with irritation. The truth was he wanted to learn about ham radios. In fact, he had wanted to join the ham radio club at school, but his friends had talked him out of it, calling it dinosaur technology. Not wanting to be teased at school, he'd abandoned the idea, though he felt a little guilty since George was his neighbor. Yet if he went now and his friends found out, they might make fun of him even more. Plus, he'd have to deal with his younger brother's annoying and never-ending enthusiasm. It was probably better to let Josh go alone. At least his brother would be out of the house for a bit.

Laurie shrugged. One out of two wasn't bad, she thought. At any rate, the house would be quiet for a little while. Maybe by the time Josh got home, power would be restored, and life could go back to normal.

Chapter 2
One Year Before the Superstorm

L aurie awoke as usual at 5:30 a.m. and tiptoed into her meditation room, which had once been Brendan's bedroom. Dressed only in a loose t-shirt and lightweight pants, she pulled a soft fleecy blanket around her and settled down to meditate. While fully expecting a wave of calm to wash over her, today she felt uncomfortably flat. Funny how she felt smothered by the familiarity of it all. For years she had prayed for normalcy in her life. As a parent, ordinary often seemed entirely out of reach, especially when her two boys were undergoing their wild teenage years with constant bickering and getting into trouble. Thankfully, Brendan had matured and outgrown that phase. And Josh? With an effort, Laurie pushed thoughts of her younger son aside. No amount of worrying about him now was going to make a difference. Meditation usually helped when those thoughts started veering out of control.

There was a time when she used to crave a peaceful structure for her life, but now that she had it, that peaceful life seemed suffocating. Surely, she didn't want to go back to the mess that had been her life ten years ago, yet being stuck in a rut was no fun either. Where was the balance? Contemplating this, Laurie focused on her breathing and simply sat. And after a dull, run-of-the-mill meditation, she picked up her tablet and wrote down what she was grateful for. Even that felt ordinary:

I am grateful for shelter from last night's torrential rain.

I am grateful I have the time and space to meditate each morning.

What else was there? As far as she could see, that would do for today.

Briefly, she scanned Brendan's room, observing all the trinkets from his childhood: sports trophies, autographed baseballs and photographs of famous sports figures, stuffed animals, and even artwork from his high school days. Brendan had told her she could use his room to meditate, but he didn't want her touching any of his things. Looking around, she wondered how he would feel about all those things when he came home in a few months. After being away for two years, would he be ready to pack all his childhood memories away? She wasn't sure, though thinking about him coming home made her smile. At least she had something to look forward to.

Dimly in the background, she heard her husband, Stan, as he got up to begin his day. He would be going off to work soon. Usually, Laurie felt energized after her morning routine and would go downstairs to see him off. Today, however, she felt exceptionally tired, so she decided to sit for a while longer and let her thoughts wander.

Laurie's predictable days felt so mechanical, like many of the things in the house. Everything was controlled by some device to the point where she now felt utterly bathed in a virtual reality. She had a smartphone, a smart TV, a smart kitchen. Hell, even her bathroom was smart! The toilet seat opened when she entered the bathroom and the toilet flushed itself when she was done. She wondered if kids these days even knew how to flush a toilet. Sinks turned on automatically. Food was prepared quickly and easily in her kitchen—all she had to do was press a button. Robots vacuumed her house, mopped her floors, took out the trash and performed all the other little tasks of the day. If she needed something, she simply ordered it by pushing a button (or speaking aloud to her smartphone), and it would magically show up on her doorstep within a day.

As a recently retired teacher, and with Brendan now living far away, Laurie had looked forward to having time to herself. Yet suddenly, for the first time in her life, she felt completely useless. For years, she had a place to go each day, a reason to get up every morning. A school and students who depended on her. That structure supported her, especially a few years ago when Josh disappeared. This past year, however, continuing to teach had been difficult. As more and more technological advances were added at the school, Laurie's job was slowly replaced by computers. She saw the writing on the wall and decided it was time to take the leap into retirement before she was forced out. At least she could retire on her own terms.

Whenever she doubted her decision, she would look at an old comic strip which she kept on her desk. She had seen this about ten years ago and never imagined how true it would become. It showed a university professor lecturing to a class of 100 students. On day two, there were 99 students and one recording device. By the fifth day, there were 70 students and 30 unoccupied seats with devices, and by the eighth day, about 90 seats were devoid of students. In the last panel—day ten—the professor was absent. There was simply a podium with an electronic speaker, and 100 empty seats with recording devices. And in today's world, she realized, so much learning was done online that lecture halls and classrooms were almost obsolete. Yes, the time had come when the physical presence of students and teachers together was no longer needed.

While working, Laurie appreciated all the mechanized help. Who wouldn't want a robot to vacuum for them? She had other, more important things to do with her time. But now… she wasn't sure if this truly benefitted her. Maybe it made things easier, but it certainly didn't make her feel any better about her life.

A year ago, shortly after her retirement, a major pandemic swept the globe, shuttering many small businesses and forcing everyone to distance themselves physically from one another. Staying apart helped slow the spread of illness, and thankfully, no one close to her became seriously ill. A vaccine was rapidly developed, and the virus now appeared under control; however, the social effects of it still lingered, making her feel even more isolated. People had changed their habits and were slow to return to life as it had been. She used to go to a Yoga class regularly, and now practiced alone at home, occasionally watching online videos provided by her teacher. She no longer had coffee with friends or socialized in groups. Aside from her husband, she had little contact with the outside world.

In large part due to that isolation, Laurie had a habit of constantly checking the news on her smartphone. She knew it was an unhealthy addiction, yet she found it impossible to restrain herself. Glancing now at her phone, she scanned the local headlines. Sadly, there had been a horrific car accident overnight. The driver (apparently drunk) was killed instantly. She recognized the name—Reginald Lamprey. Reggie, the boys had called him. He had been a Boy Scout leader years ago and involved in some kind of sexual misconduct scandal, but nothing was ever proven. She had a brief flash of a memory— Josh once referred to him as "Wedgie" and she had chewed him out, telling him he shouldn't judge people based on what was clearly gossip. Josh had run off in tears. She couldn't recall the details of what happened with Reggie, though she remembered his wife divorced him about six or seven years ago. And now here he was, dead from driving drunk. What a sad tale.

Continuing her obsession of reading the news, she moved on to the national headlines. The President was once again cleaning out his cabinet and had fired Leonard McFay, Director of the Environmental Protection Agency, who had only been on the job for six months. No surprise there. It seemed like every day another position was up for grabs. Yet Laurie thought it was an unfortunate change, as McFay seemed like someone capable of standing up for the truth. Laurie had heard him speak at a climate change rally six months ago, shortly before the pandemic struck. He had impressed her with his breadth of knowledge and ideas about what individuals could do to minimize the effects of climate change, even if the government denied it. He was a passionate speaker, and she recalled feeling grateful he was in such a position of power at the time. And now, the government was shutting him down.

When North Becomes South

Laurie felt her body tense up as she looked at her phone, yet she couldn't stop reading. The country was in chaos, especially at the southern border where a new wall was being erected to keep immigrants out. Police brutality was everywhere, and no one truly felt safe going out. Even in her quiet suburban neighborhood, kids rarely ventured out onto the streets as it was too dangerous. Instead, they holed up in their basements and pummeled each other long-distance with violent video games. She briefly thought of seven-year-old Diego, the little boy who had recently moved into the house across the street. She met his parents in passing a few weeks ago when they were unloading their things, and Diego barely seemed to notice her. Being a teacher, she tried to engage him in conversation, but he was completely immersed in whatever electronic game he was playing.

Just a few days ago, a short-term power outage in town had put people on edge. This was one of the things scientists had been warning about, and Laurie found the general silence about what caused it and how widespread it was unsettling. Diego's mother, Sophia (with a last name she couldn't pronounce), came to their house to ask if they had also lost power and was worried it would go on for a long time. Diego was with her, tugging at her shirt, trying to pull her away.

"Diego, you can live for a few minutes without your game!" Sophia snapped at him. "It'll still be there when we get home." Laurie was surprised at her command of the English language. Sophia's dark features were clearly Hispanic, and Laurie had assumed she had not lived in the States for long.

"But the battery is low!" he whined. "What if I can't charge it?"

Sophia turned to Laurie. "I hope power comes back soon. I'm trying to get him out to walk around the neighborhood. He can't seem to occupy himself without his device!"

Laurie flashed back to a day ten years ago when power was out for two full days and her boys were at each other's throats without their electronic gadgets to entertain them. She smiled at Sophia. "I completely understand," she said. "My two boys used to be glued to those screens."

"I didn't know you had children," said Sophia. "I never see them around here."

Laurie hesitated. How much of her life story did she want to reveal? "I have two boys," she began. "They are both older—not children anymore and not living here with us. My oldest son, Brendan, is working in Africa, teaching. He's been there for about a year and a half."

"Wow!" said Sophia. "That's amazing!"

To Laurie's relief, at that moment, the power came back on and everything in the house turned on at once. She could hear the coffee pot, the vacuum, the furnace and the refrigerator. Even the toilet flushed! Alarms beeped everywhere, indicating the need to reset timers.

"I'll tell you more sometime over coffee," said Laurie, turning back inside. "Right now, I need to get my house back under control! With all this technology, I'm afraid the house might self-destruct if I don't recalibrate everything!"

Quickly they exchanged phone numbers and Sophia promised to invite Laurie over to her house soon. Laurie closed the door, thankful she didn't have to explain about Josh, though she had to admit the small connection with her new neighbor felt good. Perhaps she and Sophia could find some common ground and become friends. She thought of that now as she sat in Brendan's room reading the news.

The interruption of power a few days ago had only lasted about two hours, and Laurie was grateful for that. But now, as she continued to read the news, a chill went down her spine as she scanned an article about Venezuela, now in its third day of a country-wide power outage. In a series of photographs, the report detailed complete devastation. Whole neighborhoods completely dark. People lined up to collect drinking water, while there was massive looting of retail and grocery stores. There were lines at the gas pumps, and traffic jams at intersections where police were ineffectively trying to direct traffic. Hospitals were without electricity, with patients, relatives, doctors and nurses walking the hallways using candlelight. Could that possibly happen here? she wondered.

The entire world was on the brink of disaster, teetering on the edge of possible nuclear war. North Korea refused to slow down its frequent testing of intercontinental ballistic missiles, while Russia, Iran, and the U.S. continued to build up their nuclear arsenals. All semblance of humanity seemed to be going down the toilet—and it might not even be a very smart toilet, Laurie thought wryly. At some point, it may decide to overflow, and then what? She took a deep breath and shook her head.

Her thoughts drifted to her son, Brendan—half a world away and living a vastly different kind of life in an extraordinarily different kind of place. A place where kids didn't even know what a flush toilet was....

Brendan

Morning was a busy time in the village and Brendan always woke early, even on the weekends when there was no school. Roosters crowed, dogs barked, children ran and squealed, and women chatted with one another as they shouted to their kids to stay nearby. Brendan's house was nearby one of three community wells in town that supplied water for many families in the area. Each morning, kids as young as five years old would line up to take their turns with the hand pump, gathering their buckets of water for the day, stopping every ten minutes or so to let the water level recharge. Such a simple ritual, yet vitally important.

Brendan smiled as he sat on his porch watching the local villagers. "Wait small!" called out a woman to her little boy who was jumping up and down in line. Brendan loved that statement. It meant "be patient" and carried so much more meaning than the English phrase. The boy finally reached the head of the line, stood on his tiptoes, and stretched his arms up to reach the pump handle, then hung for a moment, using the full weight of his tiny body to bring the handle down. Brendan recalled the first few times he attempted the task of water collection. The neighbor kids laughed at him, and quickly fired him from that job, saying he was spilling (and therefore wasting) too much water. This was a major sin in the village, especially during the dry season. After that, he hired two of his young neighbors—Theo and Ezra, both seven years old—to collect and haul water for him, paying them each an enormous price of eight cents per bucket. He enjoyed watching them now as they delivered four full buckets of water to his doorstep. He dropped a few coins into their outstretched hands, and they scurried off.

Whatever water they collected would be used to do laundry, to cook, bucket-shower, and flush their toilets. At least they had reasonably clean well water and were not forced to get water from the swampy river a mile away. Small improvements over the past few years had made a huge difference in this little village.

Brendan lived in the tiny West African country of Loscoaya. Two years ago, after graduating from college, he wanted to do something important and meaningful in his life, and he also yearned to experience a new culture and a completely different way of living. As he explored some options, he stumbled upon a program run by TeachAfrica, a U.S.-based company with a mission to bring education to all the African nations. Intrigued by what he read, he put in his application on a whim, never dreaming he would be accepted. But when the acceptance came, it felt like a doorway into something fresh and exciting in his life, and he decided to take the leap.

Thus, he landed in Loscoaya as a high school physics teacher. He wasn't paid much, though at least he had housing and enough money to live the way the local people lived. In fact, his standard of living was slightly higher than most of his neighbors. He lived alone in a simple mud-brick house consisting of two bedrooms plus a living room, a tiny bathroom and a covered porch with a coal pot that doubled as a kitchen.

"Hiya Brendan!" He turned to see Anna, his 17-year-old neighbor. Graceful as a swan, she carried a full bucket of water on her head, and another in her hands.

"Good morning, Anna," he replied. Before he left for Africa, his dad had given him some advice that Brendan took to heart. "When you arrive in your village, the first thing you should do is find a mom," his dad had said. "Find someone in the village you can go to if you have any kind of problem. If you're sick or lonely or confused, a mom will help you get through the tough times."

Brendan had done just that. He wasn't sure if he found his "mom" or she found him, but either way, Anna's mother, Talah, had taken him under her wing and the entire family had embraced him, including him in their daily lives. Each night, he was warmly welcomed at their family dinner table, which was always crowded. As with many families in the village, numerous relatives lived in a house slightly bigger than his. They were lucky, though, because they had a generator which they ran every other evening for about two hours. Shortly after Brendan moved in, they connected the generator to his house by running a wire through the woods. So, even though he didn't have running water and electricity like back home, he did have water brought into his house (happily delivered each day by Theo and Ezra), and some "current" (the local word for electricity) for a few hours every two days— enough at least to charge his phone and laptop. It was a win-win situation, as Brendan paid them a small amount for the gas for the generator, the food, and their work to cook dinner each night. In return, he didn't have to cook over coals which he found exceedingly challenging. Additionally, he had a group of people to enjoy dinner with each night.

Anna sat with him as he watched the early morning activity. Numerous neighbors walked by, greeting them with a cheery "Hiya!" and "G'mornin'." Brendan loved the friendliness of the townspeople, especially since he knew the pain many of them had endured in recent years. The country had suffered through over a decade of civil war, and though the war ended almost fifteen years ago, many scars remained. Then the Ebola virus struck, and everyone in the village knew someone who had come down with the deadly disease. Now, they were striving to rebuild their lives, and this tiny remote village was enriched by the continued contact of the people with their land and community. Brendan saw this highlighted in the way the women banded together to start a gardening club and share in the workload, allowing them to plant more produce which increased everyone's standard of living. Talah had been instrumental in getting that organized.

Anna noticed him watching a group of young boys working together to collect six buckets of water and load them onto a wagon. "They work hard, eh?" she commented.

"They certainly do," he replied. "Even after being here almost two years, I am still amazed at how hard the kids work—even the littlest ones."

Life was so different here! To an outsider, it looked primitive, and back home this town might be considered a slum, but here in Africa, it was just the way life was. The villagers planted and harvested native plants to sell at the local markets and planned their lives around the seasons—rainy and dry. Children as young as eight years old learned how to handle tools, such as hammers, to build with, and machetes to chop down trees, and they knew how to survive on the land. Brendan marveled at that.

He had come here to teach physics but quickly discovered his job involved much more. He had his work cut out for him, as the children in the village had little schooling. For years, the country had been wracked by civil war, leaving most adults illiterate as they never had the opportunity to go to school. This meant the children had no real support for learning at home, at least for book learning. Yet, Brendan discovered what they lacked in scholastic skills, they more than made up for in Earth expertise. It was a culture rich in lore and understanding of how to survive in the bush, despite the fact that it would get extremely poor marks when it came to an understanding of Western technology.

Brendan came from a completely different world. He was rich in technological knowledge but had little experience with survival skills. He had grown up in a quiet suburban neighborhood in the United States and never had to worry about basic necessities of life. While that occasionally embarrassed him, the local villagers generally embraced his presence and helped him every step of the way.

"My banana and pineapple plants are starting to grow," he said to Anna. "I could never have done that without all your help."

"I know," Anna teased. "It is easy for us, but we could see when you came here you didn't have any idea how to do that. You don't have the talent—how do you say in America?—the green thumb."

Brendan laughed. He knew about technology, but when it came to gardening, he was completely at a loss. Life here *was* less complicated in many ways. However, while Brendan enjoyed the simplicity, he recognized that simple did not mean easy. People struggled in countless ways. Many people barely subsisted on what they sold at the markets, and while the houses were sturdy for the most part, the tin roofs on most houses typically didn't last more than a year or two. During the rainy season, this was one of the wettest parts of the world. Leaks were common as it was hard to get good quality materials to build anything, let alone a sturdy roof.

And people got sick. A lot. Since his arrival one-and-a-half years ago, four villagers had died of things Brendan would have considered minor illnesses back home. Malaria was as common here as influenza was back in the States, but deadlier, especially since there were no hospitals in town. On the positive side, however, the remoteness of the village had its benefits. Miraculously, the pandemic that swept the world six months ago had skipped over their little village. Brendan had read news accounts of the disease and been terrified it would wipe out the entire town, because when people got sick, they often reverted to treatment with traditional medicine involving ancient herbal remedies or even religious rites. Sometimes this worked and sometimes it didn't. After seeing many people's difficulties of struggling with sickness and losing loved ones, Brendan wondered where the balance was between the old ways and modern advances of Western medicine.

As he thought of the myriad of ways in which technology changed things, Brendan struggled with the nagging thought that perhaps the 'Western way' of doing things wasn't always the best way. There was something to be said about a quiet little village with no real roads going through it (and thus no cars and no pollution or noise from the cars). Everyone walked everywhere, and because of this, everyone knew everyone else.

His thoughts were interrupted as Anna stood and replaced the bucket on her head. "I need to get home soon or my Ma will be wondering what happened to me. Enjoy your Saturday!"

Brendan watched her go, grateful it was Saturday, and he had the day off. As a teacher here, Brendan often got frustrated and occasionally wondered if it was worth the effort. He loved teaching and especially loved the personal interactions he had with his students. However, while most were certainly smart and capable, they lacked discipline and had a hard time setting priorities—his priorities. School simply wasn't important to them. Often, students would skip classes, saying they had other things to do. Sometimes the excuses were legitimate, such as needing to care for a younger sibling or an ailing parent. He knew some of his students lived in difficult situations with abusive parents or relatives, and they had enormous pressure to tend to family business rather than school. But other times, Brendan got the impression they didn't show up because they simply didn't feel like it. From Brendan's perspective, they had an extremely narrow view of the world, and he desperately wanted to change that, yet after being here for almost two years, he wasn't sure how much he could do. He was starting to think about possibly extending his service with TeachAfrica for one more year, wondering if it might make a difference for at least some of the students. For the bulk of them, however, he feared it wouldn't matter.

When North Becomes South

Briefly, Brendan thought of home. Although he felt comfortable here, he missed his mom and dad enormously. And when he thought of home, he thought of Josh as well. What had happened to his little brother? At times Brendan felt guilty about his lack of attention to Josh, even though he was away at college at the time and there was nothing he could have done to help. But still, he wondered if he could have been more responsive to Josh when they were both home for Christmas. In hindsight it was clear Josh was suffering, but how was he to have known? Brendan shook his head, trying to clear it. Thoughts of Josh always turned into this slippery slope. On one hand, he felt guilty, and on the other, he was angry at Josh. And if he had a third hand—well, he just felt downright sad and confused and wished they could have a resolution. Was Josh even still alive?

Josh

Josh woke with a raging headache and a wet tongue licking his face. Rolling over, he looked around and for a moment was completely disoriented. He was lying on a sand dune and couldn't for the life of him remember how he got there. He must have been drinking, as evidenced by the empty beer bottles beside him, but who had he been with? And whoever it was, why had they left him there to rot? At least Amigo had stayed by his side.

His trusty dog was the only constant in his life. He had picked up Amig as a scrawny stray puppy off the streets three years ago, an act of compassion that was the best thing he'd done in recent years. Having the responsibility of a dog gave him some semblance of control over his life. Plus, he felt he and Amigo were kindred souls—loners trying to make it on their own.

Stumbling to his feet, he made his way over to the bushes and threw up. That helped a little, but what he really needed was a reviving dip in the ocean. Luckily, the tide was high so he could get himself to the water's edge quickly, and once there, he dove in to wash off the dirt and crud of the previous night. Amigo dove with him, wanting to play, but Josh was in no mood to entertain the dog.

It bothered him that he had no memory of how he had ended up at this stretch of beach. Getting drunk was one thing, but getting drunk to the point of not remembering was something else altogether. He admitted it scared him a little. Maybe it was time to start reforming his ways.

This was not a foreign thought. He had been contemplating changing his lifestyle for a while now, but somehow never quite felt motivated to stop drinking. It helped him forget what a loser he was. He had a minimum wage job as a janitor at the local border patrol housing facility. As long as he did what he was told at work, his life was his own. At least that was what he told himself. In reality his life sucked, and deep down he knew it. He stood up in the water and turned to his dog.

"What do you think, Amigo," he asked. "Are you as tired of this life as I am?" Amigo simply shook the water off his fluffy body and stared back at him with big soulful eyes. Four years ago, Josh arrived here hoping to live the dream, and now that dream had become a nightmare he couldn't escape. He was a college dropout. He had no real skills to speak of. He had moved from one menial job to another eight times in the last four years and had gone through countless brief liaisons with women. Nothing stuck except Amigo. It was a transient existence and he had absolutely nothing to show for it. It was probably time to make some changes in his life.

That thought terrified him and was the reason he had remained here for so long. Where would he go? Could he possibly go home? He ghosted his parents and was sure that must have devastated them. He had done everything possible to cover his tracks, and more than once had hoped they presumed him dead. How could he possibly go back and ask their forgiveness? To do so, he would have to reveal why he left, and he didn't think he could face the shame of that.

When North Becomes South

Quickly he gathered his meager belongings and set off with Amigo along the beach to the rooming house he called home. It was about a three-mile walk, and he figured the exercise would do him some good. The dip in the ocean had cleared his head a little, but what he really needed was a nice long shower, clean clothes, and a strong cup of coffee. He dreaded charging up his phone, because he was certain there would be some nasty messages on it from whoever had ditched him last night. Another reminder of being a loser.

He rented a sparsely furnished room in a dilapidated building. As he entered, he thought it looked barely lived in. In truth, he spent little time there. Mostly, he was at work, or at the beach, or out partying. This room was simply a place to sleep occasionally, get cleaned up, and store his few possessions.

Looking in the mirror, he decided it was time to completely shave off his beard. Maybe that would help him start a fresh life. After a hot shower, he fed Amigo and walked to the local coffee shop for breakfast. It felt good to get cleaned up and go for coffee rather than reach for another bottle. He wondered why he didn't make that choice more often.

As he entered the café he was greeted by Steve, one of the local firefighters. "Josh, it's good to see you. I was hoping I'd find you here. Do you have a few minutes to talk?" Steve asked. Though his first instinct was to decline, Josh reminded himself he was thinking of turning over a new leaf. If he was serious about reforming his ways, he needed to start by cultivating a few friendships here. He had played the lone wolf game for so long it was hard to even think about new relationships, but here was an opportunity to at least practice.

He sat down at the table with Steve, and Amigo dutifully lay down by his side. Josh first met Steve several years ago when Amigo was a puppy. Josh had enrolled Amigo in a scent-training class and Steve had been in the class as well. Amigo was one of the star students. In fact, the local police department had tried to get Josh to turn the dog over to them so they could use him as a drug and bomb-sniffing dog. Especially drugs. In this southern California town close to the Mexican border, drugs were rampant, and Amigo would have been a great asset to the department. Josh refused, though he had no doubt the dog would have been amazing in that role.

"Good to see you still have Amigo," said Steve. "Have you done any more training with him?"

"No. I just did the class for fun," said Josh. "I had just gotten him, and it seemed like a good way to get to know him."

"I remember how great he was in class. You know, we need more search and rescue dogs in the fire department. We're looking to start a new training soon. Would you consider joining in? It'd be good training for you as well—it could even lead to a job."

"Thanks, but I can't afford it right now," said Josh. His first reaction was annoyance, but then once again, he remembered he was considering making some changes in his life.

"Well, they're really pushing this new training program and want to get it up and running soon. There may even be some scholarships available. Think about it and give me a call if you decide you're interested. Here's how to reach me." He scribbled his phone number on a napkin.

Josh pocketed the number. "I'll think about it," he said, reluctant to commit right away. If he was honest with himself, he had to admit that more than once in the past few years, he had considered training as an EMT and working with Amigo as a search and rescue dog. That was something he could see himself doing with his life. Maybe this was a sign that life could change.

As Steve left, Josh looked at Amigo. "Well, now that was interesting! You may have launched me into a new career! What do you think?"

Amigo wagged his tail in response and nuzzled Josh's hand, looking for food. Josh looked down at the dog. Could he actually do this? He did feel ready to make a change. He had been hiding for too long, and it was time to make a move. Acting on impulse, he stood up and ran after Steve.

Chapter 3
Six Months Before

A knock on the door startled Laurie. Odd, she thought. She rarely had visitors these days. She peeked out the window, surprised to see her neighbor, Sophia. They had chatted about getting together for coffee months ago when the power briefly went out, but it hadn't happened yet. Laurie felt a twinge of guilt about that. Sophia and her husband, Alejandro, were from somewhere in South America, and as far as she knew they both worked full time in the city. Just the other day, Stan told her he saw Alejandro outside while taking out the morning trash and Alejandro mentioned Sophia was pregnant.

Sighing, she walked to the door. Opening it, she saw Sophia darting back across the street to her house, looking like a scared rabbit. *Strange,* Laurie thought. *I wonder what she wanted. And what is she doing home on a weekday?* As she started to close the door, she noticed a small piece of paper on the ground. *Who uses paper anymore?* she wondered as she bent to pick it up. Hand-printed on the paper was a neatly written note: *Can you come to my house for coffee this morning? About 10:00?* Clearly, Sophia hadn't wanted to talk to her. She simply delivered the note and left. Laurie shrugged, then turned to look across the street. Sophia was staring at her from her living room window. On impulse, Laurie smiled at her and gave her a thumbs up before quietly closing the door.

She sent a quick text to her husband, Stan. *Going to our across–the–street neighbors for coffee this morning.* Stan replied immediately: *What, the survivalists?*

Chapter 3 ~ Six Months Before

Laurie smiled. Yes, that is what she and Stan had jokingly nicknamed their new neighbors, after recently observing them digging in the backyard. It looked like they were putting in some sort of storage house and a private well, even though water was supplied to the entire neighborhood from a community well. Every day they received deliveries of basic goods. As far as Laurie could tell, their basement must be filled from floor to ceiling. Well, this will be an interesting outing, she thought.

As she walked across the street, Laurie thought of her friend Jenny who had moved out of that house almost ten years ago. How many countless times had she and Jenny casually visited each other? She missed that. Since Jenny left, she had not truly connected with any other neighbors. Occasionally, she walked around the neighborhood with another next-door neighbor, Lisa, but she hadn't done that for quite a while. This isolated life had a way of creeping up on her. Maybe it was time to change.

Well, here goes, she thought as she knocked on Sophia's door. *Time to stop being such a recluse!*

Sophia opened the door and quickly ushered her inside. She was a small woman, and though she was casually dressed in a loose-fitting sweater and jeans, Laurie could see the slight bulge of her belly. Laurie debated saying something, then decided it would be better to wait. Instead, she looked around at the room. It was not at all what she expected. The front entryway had been completely re-done, much different from Jenny's layout. But that was not the most surprising thing. What shocked Laurie was the sight of multiple shelves packed with stuff. All sorts of things—paper towels, toilet paper, canned goods. It looked like a small grocery store. Maybe Stan was right, and they really were survivalists. Spellbound, Laurie gazed around the room. Sophia laughed, "You must be wondering why we have all these things." It was exactly what Laurie was wondering, but she didn't want to seem so obvious about it. "I promise I will explain in a few minutes. But first come in and I'll get you some coffee."

When North Becomes South

As she entered the kitchen, Laurie was amazed to see there were no devices or electronics around. No screens or monitors or any of the other technological gadgets that covered the walls and countertops of her house. She watched in fascination as Sophia set about making coffee, measuring out everything carefully and doing all the little jobs that were automated for her and Stan. Sophia seemed quite at home in the kitchen. Laurie thought of her own kitchen and how little time they now spent in it. Cooking for herself and Stan was a thing of the past. Why work at it when robots could do it for you?

Laurie turned and went into the living room. "We have very few devices in our house," Sophia continued. "No robotic coffee makers or other gadgets. That may seem strange to you as we're both scientists, but I can explain a little. Come in and meet Alejandro."

Sophia's husband seemed to materialize out of nowhere. Laurie was a bit startled as she hadn't seen him when she first arrived, but there he was, quietly watching them from the corner of the room. He was a slight man with short, cropped dark hair. She wondered what he was doing home during the daytime. In fact, she had been wondering that about Sophia as well, since she knew they both worked full time.

"Alejandro, come greet our neighbor!" Sophia pulled him up from the sofa. Turning to Laurie she explained, "He is a little shy at times. He thinks his English isn't good." Alejandro smiled at her, nodded and held out his hand.

"Nice to see you," said Laurie stiffly. She felt a little foolish as she had only met him once before and barely would have recognized him as her neighbor.

Sophia set the coffee down in front of her. "I bet you're wondering why we have no electronics in the house." What Laurie was really wondering was whether Sophia had some magical powers and could read her mind. This was the second time Sophia had verbalized her exact thoughts. Laurie nodded slowly.

"We are both scientists and worked for the National Oceanographic and Atmospheric Administration. We have no devices in our house because we are worried about being monitored."

"We are afraid," Alejandro spoke slowly and deliberately. Laurie was surprised at how good his English was, though he had a thicker accent than Sophia. "We learned some extremely unsettling things that the government doesn't want made public. But we feel strongly that people need to know these things in order to prepare."

"What things? Prepare for what?" Laurie asked. She and Stan had joked about it, but once again Laurie wondered, were they survivalists?

Alejandro continued, "It has to do with the work we were doing for NOAA. You may have seen some news reports about changes in Earth's magnetic field. We don't want to get too much into it right now, but we have a meeting planned for tonight and have invited a select group of neighbors we hope we can trust. Your neighbor Lisa thought you and your husband would be interested. Will you come?"

Laurie knew Lisa slightly as they occasionally walked together when the weather was good. Lisa's kids were now in high school and active in the scouting program Josh and Brendan had been part of. While they hadn't developed a strong friendship, Laurie at least felt Lisa was a decent person.

"I think so," said Laurie slowly. "I need to check with my husband, though. I'm not sure if he can come or not."

"This meeting—it is secret," said Alejandro. "You can't tell anyone about it or talk about it in your house. And definitely don't text, call or email your husband about it."

"But how am I supposed to bring my husband about it if I can't talk to him?" Laurie asked.

"You can talk to him—in person, and outside. Your house and phone and computer—they are all ears, all the time. Everything you do and say inside could be monitored. And we do not want this meeting made public, at least not yet."

"But we're talking here," said Laurie.

"Yes, and look around you," Alejandro countered. "Do you see any devices? Any computers or TVs? This part of our house is a safe zone. We have none of those things. Not even a cell phone in here. The only cell phone in use in our house is Diego's and he can only use it in his room or outside."

Laurie flinched as she thought of the cell phone in her purse. And once again, Sophia read her mind.

"Don't worry about your phone. It isn't *you* they are concerned with monitoring, it's *us*. And anyway, it's not like your phone would be actively recording us right now. But it is possible other devices in your house may be turned on without you knowing it in order to get more information about us, especially if they know you have visited here. And believe me, they are quite interested in getting more information on us."

"Why?" asked Laurie. "Who are 'they'? Have you done something wrong?"

"It depends who you ask," replied Alejandro. "Come tonight and you will get more answers to your questions. You will come, yes?"

Laurie nodded slowly, wondering how she was going to surreptitiously communicate all this to Stan. It certainly was a bizarre invitation, and she wasn't quite sure how she felt about it. She was a little hesitant to get involved, though it did promise to be an interesting evening and it might even add a little excitement to her life. At any rate, she had a little time to think about it and decide if it made sense to go.

"Good," said Sophia brightly, rising and handing Laurie a slip of paper. "Here is the address. It's an old warehouse. There is a large lot in the back. Park there and come in the back door. And remember, do not speak of this meeting in your house. We don't want to be shut down before we have a chance to get started."

As she left the house, Laurie glanced back and saw Diego peeking out from an upstairs window. Smiling, she waved at him and he glanced at her momentarily, then immediately looked down. She was quite sure his attention was on his electronic game and she wondered if he ever put that thing down. From her time at school, Laurie knew it was getting harder and harder for parents to manage their kids' screen time and she felt sad that Sophia and

Alejandro had to deal with that on a daily basis, though at least they seemed to have firm boundaries about where he could use it. She supposed that was a good thing. Shaking her head, she walked into her house.

Brendan

As a high school physics teacher, Brendan had the challenging job of making his subject matter accessible and interesting to his students. Lately, he'd been feeling they were not engaged with the classwork at all, so he decided it was time to try something new. They were studying electricity and magnetism, and he wanted to run a lab. This was especially challenging in a West African public high school, where the classroom consisted of a blackboard and a bunch of student chair/desks. With no fancy lab equipment at all, Brendan had to use considerable ingenuity to come up with an experiment which would be doable with the minimal supplies they had and would also capture his students' attention.

He remembered his Boy Scout days with Josh. One of their earliest projects was to build a compass, and he thought he could do this using some basic materials he was able to scrounge from his house and the town. First, he needed something to act as the compass needle. A sewing needle was easily obtained from the village tailor. Then he needed something to magnetize the needle. He would have liked to use a magnet. A refrigerator magnet would have been perfect. Unfortunately, in his remote village, there were no refrigerators. There was a local man who sold nails, and he decided to try that. Since he wasn't sure it was truly made of iron, he did a trial and to his delight it worked beautifully. He gathered the rest of his supplies: a bowl, some water and a small leaf to float the needle on. He wanted to use a cork for this purpose but couldn't locate one anywhere.

When North Becomes South

The day before in class, he had taught his students several different methods of determining the direction north using the sun and their shadow during the daytime, and the stars at night. He then gave them a homework assignment to figure that out using both methods and see if they matched. He intended to start today's class by getting that information from them. Motivating his students to do homework was next to impossible. They rarely did it and when they did, it was usually sloppy and clearly done last minute. For this project, however, they couldn't wait until the last minute, as one of the techniques involved looking at the stars. Fingers crossed, he walked into the classroom hoping maybe this time at least some students had remembered to do the assignment.

To his surprise and delight, many students had done the homework and were excitedly talking about it as he walked in. They already had a good consensus of which direction was north. After moving all the chairs aside, Brendan placed his materials on a small stool in the center of the room and started to magnetize the needle by rubbing it down with the iron nail. The room fell silent, save for a few bees buzzing around an open window. Carefully, he passed the needle around to let a few students share the work. It had to be stroked at least 50 times in order to work correctly.

Then he gently placed the magnetized needle on the floating leaf, deliberately lining it up so it would point south, and they all watched with rapt attention as the leaf began to turn.

"It's moving!" exclaimed Janice. She was one of his most outspoken students. "Look—now it's stoppin' almos' at north!"

"It's magic!" said another. It wasn't quite pointing north, but it was close. As far as Brendan was concerned, it was close enough to declare the experiment a success. He explained to the students that it didn't point to "true" north because the magnetic poles and the actual north and south poles of the earth didn't quite line up.

"Why don' they line up?" asked Ian. "What's the point of havin' a compass point north when it's not actually north?"

Brendan was a bit flustered. First of all, his students rarely asked that kind of question. Maybe it was because this was hands-on learning and they were more involved. And second, he hadn't thought much about that particular question before.

"I'm not sure why they don't line up. But that's a great question, Ian. I'll research it and let you know what I find out."

"Wha's research?" asked Jenn. "I don' know what that means."

"Research is when you look at books and what other people have done to get more information," explained Brendan patiently. Sometimes it surprised him how many holes there were in his students' academic background. *Baby steps*, he reminded himself. That was what teaching here was all about.

Josh

Josh looked at his compass. He was completing the last of five supply drops, leaving bottles of water in the desert to help migrants who had made their way across the border from Mexico. Each one was at a specific spot he and Steve had mapped out. He wished he could use the GPS on his phone, but Steve was worried about surveillance if they used their phones. So, the cell phone was off for now, and he had to rely on good old-fashioned methods. The first spot was a half-mile walk north. Then he traveled a mile east to the second location, three quarters of a mile north-west for the third and another half-mile due west for the fourth, before making his way south again. At least he had learned how to do this in Boy Scouts years ago. Thinking of Boy Scouts gave him a moment of panic, but he quickly pushed that aside. Right now, he had a job to do. He felt like he was doing something useful with his life by helping others. Even though these people had crossed the border illegally, he didn't think they should be left in the desert to die from dehydration.

He looked around to find a suitable hiding spot and carefully placed his last gallon jug of water under a bush. Then he and Amigo started the hike back to his car. Hopefully, they could get there without being spotted by any patrollers. This was his sixth trip to the desert and so far, it had been smooth sailing. He had a script prepared if stopped, but he had yet to use it.

"Damn," he muttered under his breath as Amigo gave a low growl. Peering ahead, he could see the border patrol police in the distance. They were searching for illegal immigrants and didn't take kindly to those who helped them. It looked like he would have to use his script after all. Hopefully, all would go according to plan. At least they hadn't seen him *before* he made the water drop.

Best to be proactive, he thought. "Easy Amigo. Let me handle this." He took a deep breath to steady himself. "Good morning, officers!" he called out. "Boy, am I glad to see you! I was just out taking a short walk with my dog here, and he started going crazy. He's a scent dog, you know, and he has an amazing ability to track people. I'm sure he saw a few who may have crossed the border illegally."

"Which way were they going?" asked the agent.

"That way. I'm sure of it." He pointed west in the opposite direction of his water drop. Migrants would be coming through here later, and the further he could get the patrol away from this area, the better. The agent looked at him skeptically.

"We just came from there and saw no one. And what are you doing out here, anyway?" The officer stared at him with glassy eyes. *Mean eyes*, thought Josh. He glanced at the partner, a big, burly man with a walking stick that made Josh shudder. The stick jogged something deep in his memory, leaving him with an eerie sensation. He shook his head, trying to clear the feeling away.

"Like I said, I was out walking my dog. He needs to run a lot. You must have just missed them. I'm sure they went that way." Once again, he pointed west.

The officers looked at one another, shrugged, and walked off in the direction Josh had pointed. As they left, Mean Eyes called back, "Take my advice, sonny and stay away from here. This is a war zone. Find somewhere else to walk your mongrel of a dog."

Amigo growled quietly and Josh turned to him. "Ignore him, buddy. He's just doing his job. Let him go."

Much as he hated to admit it, Josh was shaken by the encounter. A few hours later he met up with Steve to debrief. As he described the scene, Steve shook his head.

"I was figuring you'd get stopped sooner or later. The patrols have really picked up in that area. We're going to have to find some different places to leave supplies. But it's good Amigo was with you and they seemed to believe you. What a headache!"

Josh looked at Steve. This was the first real friend he had made in years and it bothered him that Steve was so upset. He wished he could be more help, but he was still new to this whole operation.

After his conversation with Steve several months earlier, he had enrolled Amigo in the search and rescue training course with the Fire Department. Amigo was once again a star student, and they managed to fast-track Josh's training as well. The department offered him a scholarship along with a small stipend for living expenses, which allowed him to quit his janitorial job at the immigrant detention center and enroll full time as an EMT trainee.

Over time, as he and Steve got to know one another, Steve told him of some volunteer work he was doing to help refugees who were crossing the border illegally. Steve was heavily involved with a vast network of people who were leaving supplies in the desert for migrants. He recruited Josh to do a drop, and after the first time, Josh never looked back. Finally, he had a purpose for his life. It was a small toehold, but every day he felt stronger. Occasionally, the old emotional wounds still surfaced, yet he felt he was in control of his life again and moving forward. Eventually, he knew he would have to fully confront his past, but for now, at least he had a friend he could confide in and was doing something important.

"So… what do you think, will you come?" Steve asked, jolting Josh out of his thoughts.

"What? Sorry, I was thinking about something else. Come where?"

Steve shook his head. "As long as you don't daydream on the job! I was telling you about a friend of mine who invited me to some sort of secret meeting tonight. He has some information to share about climate change, or the environment, or something like that. I'm not sure how much I want to get involved in whatever he's doing, but he seemed to think it important that I come with a few others from the Fire Department, especially the disaster relief people. Will you come?"

"Sure," said Josh. "I'll go."

"Great," said Steve. "I'll drive you there. It's at a remote location, and he said the fewer cars, the better. This sounds like something they don't want publicized much."

Josh was intrigued. So far, his friendship with Steve had opened several interesting opportunities in his life. Perhaps this would be one more.

Laurie

"Are you positive you have the right address?" asked Stan incredulously, looking at the dilapidated building. All the windows were boarded up, and paint was peeling off the rotting siding.

"Yes, I'm sure." said Laurie, pulling out the paper Sophia had given her earlier that day. "It's written right here. Sophia said it's an old warehouse and we should park in the back."

Stan frowned and scratched his head. It wasn't like his wife to be impulsive, but this whole thing seemed rash. He had only met Alejandro once briefly and wasn't sure he wanted to get involved in some nefarious scheme. "I don't know. This just seems strange to me. I can't imagine what it's about. Are you sure you want to go?"

"I am," replied Laurie. "I talked with Lisa this afternoon. She didn't know any more details than we do, but she's gotten to know Sophia a bit since they moved in, and she feels this is something important. She thinks both Sophia and Alejandro are incredibly smart. Apparently, they have extremely high-power jobs with NOAA. Which is weird because they were both home today. Lisa wondered if maybe they were laid off." While Laurie had been skeptical about the meeting earlier in the day, the conversation with Lisa served to make her more curious. She was surprised at how much she was looking forward to it and a little annoyed at Stan's reluctance.

"Great, so we get to be involved in some neighbor's labor dispute with the government. Just what I wanted to do tonight," said Stan cynically.

"Come on, I don't think it's about that. They didn't seem angry or upset. It's just a meeting!" Laurie pressed. "And besides, our neighbor Lisa said she thinks George will be there."

"Well, in that case, I'm in," said Stan. "Why didn't you say that in the first place?" George had been Josh's mentor all through high school, and no one was more devastated when Josh disappeared. For two solid years, George worked tirelessly alongside Laurie and Stan as they tried to track Josh down, using all his ham radio expertise and connections. He found it inconceivable that Josh had completely dropped off the radar, especially his radar. More recently, as Laurie and Stan became resigned to the idea that Josh might not surface and spent less time searching, they saw less of him. Yet even so, Stan always enjoyed talking to him. The two of them often bonded over house repair projects. They both felt they belonged in a past era when people got together to create and problem-solve with their heads and hands, rather than wasting hours in front of a computer playing games. As instructed, Stan parked the car in the back of the building in a large lot with about ten other cars in it, and they walked in the rear entrance.

"Glad you could make it," said Sophia, taking Laurie's sweater and leading them into the meeting room. Laurie recognized several other couples from the neighborhood, though she felt embarrassed Lisa was the only one she knew by name.

"I'm Sally," one woman said. "I live two houses down on the other side of Lisa." Sally had jet-black hair and a narrow face and seemed to be in her mid-forties. Laurie wondered how it was possible she barely knew this person who had lived so close by for several years.

The back door opened, and there were voices in the hallway as Sophia greeted the newcomers. More neighbors entered; people Laurie recognized but couldn't really place. Rachel and Tim lived near Lisa as well, just two houses down from her. Laurie strained to think about the house and couldn't say whether she ever saw any kids there or not. She was thinking not.

The only other person Laurie knew was George. She looked around the room and noticed Stan and George engaged in conversation. With a quick apology to Lisa, Sally, Rachel and Tim, Laurie crossed the room to join them.

"Hi Laurie! Good to see you!" George enveloped her in a big bear hug. He looked the same as always, despite his bushy hair being a bit whiter. He peered at her over the top of his gold wire-rimmed glasses. "I've been thinking about the two of you lately, wondering how you are doing."

"Good to see you as well, George," Laurie replied. She felt a momentary pang of guilt. He had been so kind and helped them through so much grief, yet they hadn't ever acknowledged him for that. The pain was still there, and Laurie was surprised at how even the slightest trigger could overwhelm her. Still, she was glad to see him, even if it reminded her of an open wound.

"You know," George was saying to Stan. "I keep thinking about that last night I saw Josh four years ago. I know we talked about it a lot, but I can't seem to get it out of my mind."

Stan nodded. They had rehashed Josh's last few days repeatedly, and he couldn't get it out of his mind, either.

"He came over to my house," George continued, "and when he walked in, he looked like he had seen a ghost. I think there were a few other people there and I had a small dinner planned to say goodbye to him. Josh didn't last more than five minutes before dashing off. It was strange. And then the next day, he was back to school...."

Laurie thought back to that night. She, too, had noticed Josh had seemed spooked when he returned from George's house, but he tended to be moody, so she brushed it off as normal. He retreated to his room mumbling something about packing. Then, as George said, the next day he was on his way back to college. In hindsight, it was so easy to think about what she could have said or done differently, but she reminded herself none of that made a difference now. She looked at her other neighbors, feeling a little envious at how they all seemed to have perfect lives. And they all knew each other, or at least it seemed that way. Before she could reply to George, she heard Sophia across the room.

"Well," Sophia announced brightly. "Shall we start?" Taking a deep breath, she brushed her long dark hair out of her eyes. "I'm going to dive right in. We don't know any of you very well, and we called you here tonight because we need your help. Alejandro and I moved here recently to work as research scientists for NOAA, and we both just got fired." Laurie gasped silently and noticed the looks of surprise and confusion from others in the room. Everyone sat with rapt attention.

Sophia held her head up without losing her composure, and continued, "We lost our jobs for a variety of reasons. They told us they had to let us go because we are here on green cards and not yet naturalized American citizens—and it was a government grant with a small quota for green card holders. That may be true, but we believe it was also because we were tracking something the U.S. government doesn't want made public. We were designing a new satellite to study and monitor the Earth's magnetic field. The project was recently canceled due to lack of government funding."

Stan sat back in his chair with his arms crossed and scowled. Laurie glared at him to keep quiet.

"We'd like to show you a recording made by Leonard McFay, the former director of the Environmental Protection Agency. He made DVD copies so people can view it in small groups, and starting tonight, it's being shown by scientists all over the country in groups just like this. McFay is a brilliant man."

Indeed he was, thought Laurie. She had only seen him once, at a climate change rally several months ago, and remembered him as a passionate speaker with a lot of practical, down-to-earth ideas. She was glad to know he was still out there lobbying for the protection of the environment, even if he wasn't working for the government.

Laurie glanced again at Stan who sat up and leaned forward in his seat as soon as McFay's name was mentioned. He, too, had been impressed by the man, and Laurie could see Sophia now had his full attention.

As she watched her neighbor, Laurie was struck by Sophia's quiet confidence. She recalled thinking Sophia was a bit timid and shy when they first met, but here in front of this crowd Sophia seemed to take on a new persona. At just over five feet tall, she was a diminutive woman, but somehow managed to appear much taller. The only hint of nervousness was her habit of touching her hair.

Sophia went on to describe McFay. "He was educated at Harvard and was the first African-American man to be the head of the EPA. We believe he was let go in part because of his race, and to some extent because of the message he is delivering. We are part of a group of scientists trying to educate the public, and with the way in which science has been vilified recently, this is the best way to get this information out broadly.

"This can't go on social media yet—so please don't share it. I know you are probably wondering why. Why all the secrecy? It is important you understand. We believe the government is not currently acting in the best interests of the people. The government does not want people to know this, though we are not exactly sure why." Laurie felt extremely uneasy. Could it really be true? In some ways, it sounded like something out of a science fiction movie, yet she was drawn towards Sophia's openness. She glanced at Stan, who was shaking his head. He once again looked skeptical.

Sophia continued, "Perhaps they are concerned that this knowledge will cause widespread panic. Perhaps it's simply because there are those in high places who don't believe in science. But whatever the reason, it's been made clear to us this information is not meant to be dispersed publicly. What you're about to hear is shocking, and I'm sure you'll have a lot of questions, but please just watch to the end and then we'll try to answer your questions as best as we can. All we ask is that you keep an open mind."

The video began with an African American man sitting with folded hands at a large desk, looking directly into the camera. Leaning forward, he spoke slowly and deliberately with a slight West African accent that sounded faintly British.

"To my fellow Americans and anyone else out there listening: In recent months, I have been made aware of a growing crisis affecting the world in ways we cannot even begin to imagine. As many of you know, the current administration has shut down all channels of environmental scientific research, and most of what I will be telling you is a result of work done clandestinely over the last few years with little funding. But it is nevertheless quite real." He paused and looked directly at the camera. "And extremely dangerous.

"During the past several months, I have been meeting with senior scientists from the Environmental Protection Agency, from NASA and NOAA, and with senior scientists from top universities around the country, as well as around the world. Because of the censorship of news over the past few years, much of this information has been kept under wraps, but it is time for you, the people, to be made aware, so you can prepare. The entire world is about to be hit with a calamity that is bigger and more potent than anyone can imagine.

"Some of you may be aware that during the past decade, the magnetic north pole of our planet has been slowly migrating south. You may already have seen small changes due to this. There have been increased power outages and more communication breakdowns as satellites struggle to keep up with this shift. In addition, the five-year update of magnetic north's location in relation to Earth's true north pole had to be issued a full year earlier, because during the last five years magnetic north shifted far more than anticipated.

"At first this seemed like an anomaly to scientists who thought it would eventually correct itself, but it now seems that is unlikely to happen. Our planet is on the verge of a magnetic shift, the likes of which has not been seen for *780,000 years*. Consider this: 780,000 years ago was before the appearance of the Neanderthal Man. It was pre-prehistoric. At that time, Earth's magnetic field flipped—magnetic north became south, and south became north. In the past 100 years or so, with our increased scientific knowledge, scientists have been able to determine that this type of flip has occurred hundreds of times over the lifetime of the Earth—averaging about 350,000 years between flips, and it seems the planet is overdue for another. This is not science fiction. This is real. And many scientists believe it is already beginning." Laurie glanced around the room, and realized that like her, everyone's eyes were glued to the monitor. She pinched herself to make sure it wasn't a dream.

McFay continued, "The scientific community is in complete agreement this is likely to happen and is a natural phenomenon that cannot be stopped. Many questions remain as to when and how long this will take, and those questions may or may not be answered in our lifetime. For a long time, scientists have been aware of this and predicted it would happen within the next 2,000 years. But now, with new developments, we believe this is more likely to start within the next 20 to 30 years." He paused for a moment to let that sink in.

"You may be wondering why this is such a crisis and what importance the location of magnetic north and south play in our lives. Scientists are still working this out, but one thing seems clear. The magnetic field around the earth protects us from many types of galactic radiation and other hazards. Comets, meteors, and even flares from our own sun are all deflected from our planet by this protective shield. Usually the shield is strong and capable of handling all this bombardment, but it is weakest at the magnetic poles. If the poles move, those weak spots move as well, leaving large portions of the Earth that were previously protected vulnerable to radiation. It is this that has us most worried.

"I am going to outline the things that should have us all concerned, and some things we can do to help us survive as a species.

"First and foremost, as the migration of magnetic north and south continues, the entire magnetic field of our planet will weaken. Some of you may remember that recently the aurora borealis was observed as far south as Ohio and Indiana for a short period of time. The aurora is visible wherever the field is weakest, and the appearance of the lights so far south is an ominous sign. As the magnetic field weakens, we will be exposed to more harmful solar and galactic radiation than ever before. For millennia, the magnetic field has been a shield of armor protecting our planet, but there are now chinks developing in that armor. A weakening magnetic field may mean that for a period of time, large portions of Earth may become uninhabitable." Once again, he paused momentarily, and Laurie shifted uncomfortably in her seat. "In other words, for some number of years—perhaps decades or even centuries—the surface of our planet may be unable to sustain life as we know it.

"Now, there is some disagreement among scientists as to how long and how much of the earth would be affected, and we may not know the answers until the process is well underway. It is possible there will be 'safe spots' but no one can predict where those safe areas will be. Everyone on this planet should start thinking about making a plan. Scientists have been working on ways to protect buildings and insulate people from dangerous radiation, and we need to consider how our lives will be changed if we are restricted from going outside. For instance, it may be that we will need to wear insulated suits any time we leave a protected building.

"Furthermore, as magnetic north moves, there may be problems with navigation. For instance, airplanes depend on compasses to chart their routes, and airport runways are like compasses on the ground. Runways are numbered based on their orientation to magnetic north. If that location changes, the runway numbers need to be changed as well, and several major airports in the past five years have already had to make those changes. It will be a nightmare to keep up with this.

"Additionally, as the field weakens and is disrupted, we may have difficulties with our NASA satellites, and see more random power outages across the grid. We need to develop and enhance new energy technologies such as solar and wind power and we need to do this fast. All houses and buildings with solar panels should be equipped with a way to access that power should the power grid go down, meaning we need to facilitate battery storage capacity for solar power. That is something tangible that can be done soon. Unfortunately, our current Government doesn't acknowledge this, so you as individuals need to do whatever you can.

"In addition to alternative power sources, we must devote a substantial effort to building up a subterranean infrastructure for the entire country. We will need ways to get from place to place without exposing people to the dangers of Earth's surface. This will obviously take many years to put in place, but it is a priority that cannot be ignored. And research must be devoted to putting insulation into cars, busses and trains so people can continue to move above ground.

"What can you do as an individual? Every house capable of supporting solar panels should have them. Houses should be insulated completely, and basements should be equipped with enough food and water to withstand a prolonged period of isolation for each family. How long is prolonged? Unfortunately, we do not know, but at the very least, people should be prepared to be cut off from all outside contact for a month.

"One other thing that will be disrupted is communication technology. We are urging everyone to have some sort of backup radio—solar powered if possible. Cell phones and the internet may well be unusable for extended periods of time. Think about how you will survive without your devices. If your house depends on 'smart technology' make sure you still know how to operate all the things your smartphones and devices now control."

At this, Laurie shivered involuntarily. She took hold of Stan's hand and squeezed it tightly. So much of their house was controlled by robotics. Did this mean they might lose all their modern conveniences? She turned her attention back to the monitor.

"I know this is a lot of material to digest in a short amount of time. I also know I will probably be vilified and attacked as an alarmist for making this speech. Believe me, I have struggled greatly about how to convey this information. I am doing this because I have talked with scientists all over the world, and 95% of them agree with these conclusions. Given we are already seeing more frequent interruptions of power and communications and experiencing a weakening of the magnetic field in the far northern and southern hemispheres, we cannot ignore this growing crisis. As individuals and as a united country, we need to prepare, and we need to devise ways to survive once this shift is fully underway. To do anything else would be essentially sealing the fate of mankind.

"I am sure you know there are people who don't believe in science who will say this is fake news. You can decide for yourselves whether to believe or not—that is your choice. For those who heed this warning, I am setting up an organization to provide education, counseling, detailed plans of action, and financial subsidies. But if you disregard this information and fail to prepare, it will be your own downfall.

"In recent years, there have been massive hurricanes along the coasts of our country, and authorities have ordered evacuations of major cities. Invariably, there have been people who have refused to go. I imagine there will be those who will feel the same about this message. But once disaster strikes—and it will strike—we will not be able to guarantee the safety of any citizens who have not taken the necessary steps to prepare themselves. If you go outside without insulation during a radiation superstorm, you will likely die. And radiation poisoning is a terrible way to die. We can't stop that from happening and we can't protect those who deliberately flaunt our warnings.

"Lastly, I urge you not to panic after hearing this. Obviously, we want you to be prepared, but we are not expecting anything to happen tomorrow. As I said earlier, this is still likely about 20 to 30 years away, and there will be warning signs along the way. However, the fact is, it is going to happen, and it is imperative to prepare now to ride out the storm once it hits.

"I hope to be able to keep you updated as much as possible. Use these warnings to sharpen your preparation skills. Get involved in your community and form action groups to help at the local level. Because when things really heat up in the stratosphere, all we may have is our towns and neighborhoods."

As the video ended and neighbors peppered Alejandro and Sophia with questions, Laurie and Stan slipped out, unnoticed. Both felt the need to process this privately, away from the crowd. Still holding hands, they walked to their car in stunned silence, trying to assimilate what they had heard. Laurie held onto Stan's hand tightly, grateful for his strength. His presence was like an anchor to her. Six months earlier, she had been on the verge of depression, reading the news and idly wondering what each day would bring that might be fresh and different. And now, it appeared their entire world was about to be turned upside down. Literally.

Josh

Josh and Steve watched McFay's recording, along with a group of people who called themselves the Southern California Environmental Police. Josh listened with rapt attention. Living in southern California, he was well aware of the effects of climate change and had seen numerous instances of how it was impacting life. But this seemed even more ominous. He closed his eyes and tried to imagine a world without the power grid. Without cell phones. Without the internet. Without access to clean water and electricity. Without all these—and added to that, it might be unsafe to travel outside. If this was true, it was downright terrifying. As he listened to McFay, and then to the discussion afterward, an idea began to form in his head.

"You know," he confided in Steve. "I have a lot of experience with ham radio technology that could be useful if normal communications are wiped out."

Steve looked at him. "Really? That's such a dying technology. There are very few people around here who know much about it. We've tried to get some of the guys at the Fire Department interested, but most of them haven't seen the need. They all think their smartphones are invincible."

Josh's eyes lit up. For a brief moment, he thought of his time with George. Aside from his last evening at George's house, he had very fond memories of those days. "I learned a lot from one of my neighbors when I was in high school. I used to spend all my free time at his house. I'd need a little money to put something together, but if I had a small budget, I could set something up in the department and train a few people." He hesitated, wondering if he had overstepped his bounds. "That is, if you think it would be useful…" he continued hopefully. Though he thought this might be a good opportunity and maybe his true purpose, he feared that it might fall through, and he'd be considered a failure. He pinched his arm to remind him of his promise several months ago to make some major changes in his life. Of all the people he had met recently, Steve was the most open-minded and he trusted Steve would take him seriously.

The recording sponsors urged everyone to stay vigilant. While they acknowledged this was a major threat, the bigger problem was lack of government action. It was unlikely they would be able to get any federal or even local government funding, so giving Josh a small budget might prove challenging. Yet they recognized the need for better emergency communications and agreed to try. As Steve, along with others in the group, promised to look into it and see what they could come up with, once again another piece seemed to fall into place in Josh's life. Perhaps he could do something useful and productive with his life after all.

Brendan

Dusk came quickly in West Africa, where they were close to the equator. One minute it was light, and the next it seemed the light was snuffed out like a candle. Because of the lack of power, meals were usually timed to be eaten during daylight, and Brendan was enjoying a late afternoon dinner with his adopted family.

Tonight, the meal was Brendan's favorite African dish: cassava leaf soup with smoked chicken. It was a delicious stew served with the typical staple of white rice. Brendan used to love rice; however, after his time in Africa he swore that once he was home, he would never eat it again. As they sat around the long table for dinner, the conversation ranged from Loscoayan politics to the squabbling going on in the women's gardening circle.

"All these women, they wan' a bigger share of food for their families, but they aren' doin' hardly any work," Talah said.

The problem was their "families" included many people. Often, several families who were either unrelated or distantly related to each other lived in a single house. It was hard to determine exactly what was meant by the term "household" and how much food each household should get, especially if only one or two people in the household were working at the gardens.

"Well, you may want a larger share soon as well, Ma," 26-year-old Anjali piped up. "We due to have another baby in a few months' time!"

That brought on a flurry of conversation, most of which Brendan couldn't follow. Sometimes, when the local people got excited, they reverted to their native tongue, and Brendan had absolutely no idea what they were saying. Clearly, they were excited about the announcement of the new arrival even though it would present the family with a new dilemma of where to put another human in their already over-full house. Tonight, as usual, they were crowded around the table on a motley collection of chairs. But they always seemed to have room for one more.

Small town problems thought Brendan. He thought of his suburban neighborhood back home and couldn't imagine such a conversation happening there, where it seemed like no one even knew their neighbors anymore. While his real mom had told him that wasn't always the case, it was certainly his experience. After college, he had moved home and worked for two years at a local grocery store. Often, customers told him they were his neighbors, yet he had no clue who they were because he never saw them. He imagined that now with more and more people back home getting groceries delivered, he would have even less of an idea of who their neighbors were.

After dinner, as Brendan walked to his house through the damp woods, past colorfully painted mud huts with chickens and dogs running free in the front yards, he once again thought nostalgically of home, glad he was planning a visit in a few short months. Even though he was comfortable here now, he missed his family and looked forward to being away from the village during the height of the rainy season. Aside from seeing his family, it would be good to take a hot shower, cook a decent meal, and easily wash his dirty clothes in a washing machine!

He was sure being away for two years had changed him. Still, he thought he would enjoy some of the comforts he wasn't able to get here... running water, electricity, hopping in a car to visit friends, movies, television, and of course food. He looked forward to all kinds of food that wasn't available here and walking into the grocery store where he had worked prior to living abroad. There were so many things he used to take for granted and now realized were simply conveniences he didn't truly need. While he got by fine without all those things now, he certainly intended to enjoy them when he was home.

Chapter 4
Three Months Before

Brendan awoke early and looked around his childhood room. It was exactly as he had left it two years ago, with a few small changes. His mom had used it as her meditation space while he was away and he didn't mind, though he was relieved she hadn't packed away his things. As he really looked, however, he wondered whether he truly needed all this. Why did he have all this stuff here, anyway? Maybe later in the day he would sort through and get rid of some of it. While he had always been a bit of a hoarder (he preferred the term "collector") and enjoyed the memories those things carried, it occurred to him that maybe he didn't need to keep them all. So many knick-knacks: the ribbons he had won at dog shows when he was a kid, sports trophies from his elementary school days, a collection of baseball paraphernalia— autographed photos and baseballs. And stuffed animals—he surely didn't need those anymore! Being in Africa for the past two years had turned him into a minimalist. Yes, he would take time later to peruse and purge his room. Maybe there were some things he could bring back to the village for his neighbors to sell at the market. After all, one man's trash was another's treasure.

Hearing his mom downstairs, he hopped out of bed and quickly threw on a t-shirt and jeans. He was hoping to go to the local grocery store to visit some of his friends. After college, Brendan had worked there for two years and it had been a major part of his life. He looked forward to reconnecting with some of his former co-workers. But first, his mom wanted him to meet their new neighbors who had important things to tell him. She was anxious to introduce them to him, though she was evasive about why, and when he pressed her, all she said was they were both physicists. That got his attention. He figured he would spend a little time across the street with the neighbors, then head to the store to see his friends.

As he reached the kitchen, he glanced outside. "What's with the backyard?" he asked. "Did you put in a well? And a chicken coop?" Smack in the middle of the backyard, looking totally out of place in this well-to-do neighborhood, was a well with a hand pump, and next to it a small shed with four chickens grazing in front of it and a large concrete shed that looked like a bunker. Brendan stared at it. It made absolutely no sense. The neighborhood had a community well servicing about 100 houses. They had even put in an emergency generator several years ago so the well would continue to run if there was a power outage. So, what was this well doing in the backyard along with chickens? And what was that building?

"I'll explain it all to you when we visit the neighbors," his mom said. "It'll make more sense to you then. Want some breakfast? We have some waffles in the freezer." Brendan smiled. It had been a long time since he had been able to simply take a frozen waffle from the freezer, stick it in the toaster and enjoy it a couple of minutes later heaped with butter and maple syrup. Small things he hadn't even realized how much he missed. How was it he had managed to go without waffles these past couple of years?

"Tell me about these neighbors," Brendan said, as he and his mom sat down for breakfast.

"Well," Laurie began, wondering how to talk about Sophia and Alejandro without revealing too much. She still felt a little self-concious in her house because of all the devices. "They moved in last year and I met them about three months ago. They're both physicists and have a lab in their basement. I think you'll find it interesting. Oh, and they have an eight-year-old boy and a baby due in about three months."

"Cool," said Brendan. "Did I tell you my neighbors also have a baby due? Their oldest daughter, Anjali, is pregnant. I don't know how they are going to manage—they already have seven people in their house and it's not much bigger than my house. But I guess they'll figure it out."

Laurie looked at Brendan and was overwhelmed with a mixture of pride, awe, and sadness. Suddenly her little boy seemed so grown up and yet, still so much a child. She wondered how he would react to what Sophia and Alejandro had to say. After watching the recording, Laurie had embraced their ideas immediately, though Stan was more skeptical. He believed McFay; yet after thinking about it for a few days, he wasn't convinced it was such a dire problem. When he researched it on his own and found little on the internet, he became even more wary. Sophia and Alejandro spent many hours talking with him, showing him all sorts of data they had collected. It was a hard sell, but once on board, Stan had helped to organize people in the neighborhood. Many of them were becoming the "survivalists" they had once mocked. What would Brendan think of that?

"Let's go see our neighbors," she said brightly. "They're anxious to meet you."

As they walked into the foyer of the house across the street, Brendan stared with his mouth agape. Like Laurie, he remembered the house from ten years ago when his mom had spent so much of her time there. But what amazed him was that the room was now packed floor to ceiling with stuff. All sorts of stuff: canned food, paper goods, boxes of food. These people had far more supplies than one household needed. What was going on here?

"Are they preparing for the end of the world?" he asked jokingly. When he looked at his mom, though, he had the distinct impression she didn't think it was a joke.

The door to the basement opened and Sophia appeared. "So nice to meet you, Brendan!" she exclaimed. "Your mom has told us so much about you."

Brendan turned to his mom. "What are all these things doing here?"

"I can explain," said Sophia. "But first come downstairs and meet Alejandro and see our lab."

With one more double take at all the shelves in the foyer, Brendan followed his mom and Sophia down to the basement, only to be stunned into silence again. The basement had been converted to a makeshift physics lab. Brendan was astounded at all the equipment they had, especially given what he had experienced during his time in Africa. What could they possibly be up to?

"I'm sure you're wondering what we're doing here," said Alejandro. "Probably the best way for me to explain is to first show you a recording. This has been shown privately across the United States during the last few months. It's not widely publicized on the internet because the government is still denying it, but we are trying to make people more aware of a problem. We showed it to your parents and other neighbors a few months ago. Since then, we have gathered even more information that I can share with you."

While Alejandro and Sophia set up the DVD of Leonard McFay, Brendan gazed around the room. He recognized quite a lot of the instruments and felt a little overwhelmed by them all. It was a far cry from the homemade compasses he had shown his students.

"What you are about to see may come as a bit of a shock," Alejandro began. "Scientists around the world are convinced this is happening, but as I said, the government here is doing its best to squelch all research and keep us quiet. We are 'conspirators' accused of trying to take down the government. Especially us, because we are immigrants as well. But we feel strongly that people need to wake up to this now or face devastating consequences if worldwide power grids and communications systems aren't prepared."

Alejandro started the video, and as Brendan listened to McFay, he began to feel more and more anxious. As a physics teacher, he valued science above all, yet he had a hard time wrapping his head around these radical shifts in the knowledge base. It was too much for him to process. How could north possibly become south? What did that mean for the world? He wasn't completely sure they were on the right track with the science, and he was a little agitated about that. But there was something more—something just below the surface of all this that he couldn't quite name. From what he understood from the recording and what Alejandro was telling him, there was a possibility this shift might happen within the next twenty to thirty years, yet they were stockpiling provisions now to prepare. For this reason, they had all sorts of food and supplies upstairs in their foyer. He wondered if the bunker in his parent's backyard was filled with supplies as well.

As the presentation ended, anxiety overwhelmed him. He felt suffocated in the basement and desperately needed fresh air. Was this what a panic attack felt like? With a quick apology, he dashed up the stairs and ran back to his house and the safety of his bedroom.

Looking around his room, he once again thought he had far too many things. Maybe it was a reaction to the stockpiling he witnessed across the street. Or maybe, living with less for the last two years had affected him in ways he couldn't imagine, leaving him with an aversion to all this stuff. At any rate, he felt a major compulsion to purge himself of whatever he could. In general, Brendan had always felt like he could calm himself by making a plan and acting on it. Perhaps if he busied himself now with the task of cleaning out his room, he would feel more in control.

For the next several hours he clawed through all his junk (at least it felt like junk), making four distinct piles. One to throw away, one to give away, one to bring back to Africa for his neighbors to sell, and one to keep here. At the end of that time, the number of items remaining in his room was miniscule compared to the other three piles. Then, Brendan felt ready to go out and see his friends at the grocery store. He was pleasantly surprised at how much lighter and calmer he felt.

He was totally unprepared for the shock he experienced when he walked into the store. After all, there was a small grocery in Troeburg, and he shopped there whenever he went to the Capital. But this store was at least ten times larger, if not more. Walking in the door, he was stunned by the sheer quantity of merchandise on the shelves. He had forgotten how much the store carried. The amount of food in this one store would probably be enough to feed his entire village for at least a month. And people in his village were often hungry because they didn't have easy access to food. He watched, spellbound, as people walked through the aisles filling their carts to the brim with goods, many that he thought would likely end up being thrown away. How had he worked here for two years and not been bothered by that? One thing was sure—it bothered him now, almost to the point of giving him another panic attack.

As he gazed around, he was immediately hit with the same unnerving feeling he had at Sophia and Alejandro's house. He desperately needed to get out. He backed out of the store, and spent a few minutes just breathing, trying to gain some perspective. He wanted to go in and see his friends. They all knew he was back in town and would be disappointed if he didn't stop by to visit, but he wasn't sure he was up to it yet. Maybe if he gave it one more day, he'd be able to walk in there without freaking out.

Slowly, he drove home and even that felt weird. He had not driven in over two years, and his mom had been nervous about him taking the car. But he figured it was only a five-minute drive and he could handle it. Once he pulled into his driveway, though, he completely fell apart.

Laurie came out and saw him hunched over the steering wheel. Gently she opened the door and was surprised at his angry outburst. "They've got it all wrong!" he cried.

"Who?" she asked, confused.

"Everyone! Your neighbors, the grocery store. Everyone! Why does everyone need so much stuff?!"

Uh oh, Laurie thought. Brendan hadn't seen the inside of the backyard bunker yet. It was even fuller than Sophia's foyer.

"They have it all wrong!" He was practically shouting now. And then it hit him—the source of that gnawing feeling he couldn't identify earlier in the day. "Mom," he started hesitantly. "How much toilet paper can you possibly save up? How much food? For how long? Across the street, they probably have enough food to last them for a few months at best, but if things unfold the way they are predicting, you could be *years* here without power. *Years.* And during those years, you can either barely get by and survive for a fraction of the time, or you can adapt. People here need to look at strategies to live with less, not hoard more! The idea that you can save up all these provisions for when you lose power for several years is crazy. It won't work."

Laurie was silent. This was the last thing she expected Brendan to say. She and Stan had completely embraced the survivalist culture, and she couldn't understand why Brendan would object to it. Of course, they needed to learn to live with less, but did that mean they had to go back to the dark ages? Collecting all sorts of things helped her stay sane and made her feel more secure. Now, Brendan was saying it was the wrong approach and that scared her.

"What do you mean, it won't work?" she asked hesitantly. "What do you think we should do to prepare for this?"

"I don't know, but hoarding isn't the answer." He was on the verge of tears. "Somehow people need to recognize they don't need as much. That they can get by without filling their shopping carts to overflowing. It's a whole lifestyle change, and it won't be easy here. People are going to suffer unless they learn to live completely differently." He got out of the car, slammed the door, and ran inside, leaving Laurie squirming uncomfortably on the driveway. She started to follow him but decided to let him be for a while. His words had completely derailed her and she needed time to process what he had said.

In his room, Brendan thought about what he could do that afternoon. Back home (funny how when he was *here* he thought of Africa as home, but when he was *there*, this was home), he would simply walk around the village for the afternoon and "sit small" with his neighbors, making small talk, listening to all the village gossip. That wasn't really an option here. But he did feel the need to understand more about what Sophia and Alejandro were doing. Perhaps he would research this a little first, then go talk to them again when he felt more prepared. He opened his laptop, glad at least he didn't have to explain the term "research" to his mom or anyone else here.

He had to admit it felt good to have so much information at his fingertips. He calmed down considerably as he began to read. There were vague references to possible "issues" with Earth's magnetic field, but most of those looked like they were on the fringes of science. And, for every claim of the magnetic field moving, there were about fifty claims debunking it. There was little real information out there. Brendan had been sure there would be whole websites dedicated to this topic, but the more he dug, the more he felt like he was hitting a wall. After spending about an hour making little progress, he shut down his laptop in frustration. He took a deep breath and decided to return across the street to look at the lab. After all, how else could he find out what were they really up to? He was still skeptical of the science, but at the very least, he might learn some interesting things to take back to his high school physics students. He recalled their fascination with the makeshift compass. It had been one of the highlights of the year for them. So, maybe he could bring back a few other ideas for practical lab experiments.

Alejandro welcomed him in and sat with him while he re-watched the recording from Leonard McFay. "It's been three months since he recorded this, and McFay seems to have dropped out of sight." said Alejandro. "No one knows where he is, though there are rumors he might have gone to Africa. He has some distant relatives in West Africa. I can't remember what country, but occasionally he talked about one of his ancestors being sold into slavery and how his grandfather always wanted to return to the land of his family."

Briefly Brendan wondered what country that was. Then he turned his attention back to the lab. "Show me what you've been working on," Brendan said. And for the next several hours, Alejandro reviewed his data with Brendan, glad to have someone to share it with. For his part, Brendan enjoyed it and found focusing on the physics helped him to process all he had learned since arriving home.

Over the next few days Brendan gradually quelled his fear of the grocery store and enjoyed several visits with his old friends. The bulk of his time, however, was spent in the basement lab, as he became convinced that Sophia and Alejandro knew what they were talking about. From their extensive calculations, it certainly looked like barring a "cataclysmic event," the natural migration of the magnetic field would continue to accelerate over the next few decades, at which time there would be a "tipping point" with no turning back. By cataclysmic event, they meant an unusual disruption of the magnetic field, perhaps from a major solar flare disturbing the energy flow around the Earth.

As the migration of the poles continued, one of their biggest concerns was that portions of Earth might experience a much-weakened magnetic field, requiring people to exercise caution when outside. They feared there might be significant large population areas in the northern and southern hemispheres where it would be dangerous to travel outside, requiring people to live in underground bunkers for at least a few years. Their current best guess was that those areas would become essentially uninhabitable, leaving only a small band around the equator unaffected.

"Loscoaya might be one of the safer places to live," Alejandro told Brendan as he was leaving the house one day. "It's hard to predict, but the area around the equator might not lose its magnetic field protection as much as other parts of the globe, at least for a number of years. When you return there, I want you to take this instrument back with you and monitor that. This will be a fun project for your students as well." He gave Brendan a small hand-held magnetometer, designed to monitor the strength of the magnetic field at any given location.

Diego watched from his chair on the porch as Alejandro gave Brendan the instrument. "That doesn't sound like a fun project to me," he blurted out. Brendan and Alejandro looked at him in surprise. They hadn't even been aware of his presence.

"What do you mean?" asked Alejandro.

"It just seems boring and lame. Who really cares?" Diego shrugged as he sat engrossed in an electronic game on his phone. He didn't look up.

Brendan thought back to his high school years, and how his friends used the word "lame" a lot. Whenever they wanted to make something sound old-fashioned, they would call it lame. It was a catch-all term for anything that didn't excite them.

"If it wasn't for the magnetic field, you wouldn't be able to use your phone," he pointed out.

"Ya, right. As if you know. I don't believe you. You're just saying that 'cause you're a teacher and you think you know everything."

"Diego, that's no way to speak! That's rude!" exclaimed Sophia, coming out from the kitchen.

Brendan shrugged. "I don't think I know everything, but I do know a little about phones and magnetic fields. So does your dad. You may want to ask him sometime about how it works."

Diego looked up momentarily. Then with a loud sigh, he stood up and stomped off.

"I'm sorry," said Sophia. "We simply can't seem to control his screen time these days. He's only allowed to use the phone in his room and outside, but it still doesn't seem to stop him."

Brendan remembered being hypnotized by a Gameboy, yet he still found it troubling. It was in stark contrast to his village in Loscoaya where none of the children had access to electronic devices, and as a result they were much more personable around adults. His students in Loscoaya could barely imagine a device like the one that Diego was playing with. Technology certainly had its place in the world, but watching Diego, Brendan wondered if here in his home country, society had swung too far in the other direction. He left the house, glad he didn't have to deal with Diego on a daily basis.

Laurie

Laurie watched Brendan spend time with the neighbors, relieved to see he was through the initial panic he had felt during his first few days back home. She wasn't surprised he experienced some reverse culture shock, but she was thrown by the intensity of his feelings, especially after his initial trip to the grocery store. She also had to admit she was troubled by his comments about how hoarding wouldn't work, as she couldn't imagine what else they could do.

During the past few months there had been several small power outages which were not well explained by the local power company or the news. However, as many neighbors shrugged it off as normal, Laurie and Stan began to embrace survivalist thinking more and more. In addition to the backyard additions, they removed many extraneous devices from their house under the guise of getting ready to move, as they didn't want to raise suspicion among more skeptical neighbors. A rift was appearing in the neighborhood between those who believed they were on the verge of catastrophe and those who debunked the idea completely.

Some of Laurie's neighbors had noticed the activity in their backyard, and she had fielded more than her share of nasty comments on Facebook. Just this morning, one of her neighbors posted a picture of their backyard well with the caption "Apocalypse now?" making her wonder if she should stop using those sites all-together. Maybe she would do that, she thought now with a smile as she made her way to George's house. She much preferred the one-on-one interactions she had with George, Alejandro, Sophia, and some of her other neighbors. The group that had been at the original showing of McFay's speech three months ago had banded together, and Laurie found herself enjoying this new-found camaraderie.

Since the initial meeting with Alejandro and Sophia, Laurie was visiting George more regularly. After his wife died ten years ago, he had become somewhat of a recluse. Many of the newer neighbors found him hard to get to know, yet Laurie recalled what a great mentor and friend he had been to Josh all through his high school years. The summer Josh was first introduced to ham radios, he spent most of his time at George's house, and they remained close for several years. Once Josh left for college though, George became increasingly isolated, rarely socializing with neighbors. Unlike Laurie and Stan, he had resisted the explosion of technology in general, and kept his house free of most devices.

Today, she told him of the nasty comments she was getting on Facebook. "I don't do any of that social media stuff," he told her. "And the whole internet could disappear as far as I'm concerned. Mark my words. For all the good we think it's done, technology is ruining the young kids in this country."

Laurie thought about this. Was George right in some ways? Maybe they were all in way over their heads with their dependence on technology. Was it possible something so wonderful and fantastical could also be dangerous?

"What about your ham radio?" she asked him. You were certainly deeply involved in that."

"Yeah, well, when cell phones came along, ham radios kind of dried up. We used to have a highly active club in the area, but no one really does much with it anymore."

George had a large ham radio setup in his basement but had not used it for a long time. In the immediate aftermath of Josh's disappearance, he had tried desperately to network with as many fellow operators as possible to locate the boy, to no avail. At the time, he thought ham radios were capable of doing just about anything, especially since he knew so many other operators all over the country. If Josh had picked up his radio at all, George would have been able to track him, but apparently, Josh didn't want to be found.

Teaching Josh had been so energizing for him—so much so that when Josh left without a trace, he felt completely bereft. Eventually, as it became clear Josh wasn't going to return any time soon, he stopped using the equipment, leaving it to gather dust.

"Tell you what, though. Maybe if this whole shifting magnetic field thing actually happens, ham radios might come in handy. I've been thinking about getting my equipment up and running again and I might try to resurrect the local ham radio club. I've actually put out some feelers and there are a few people out there still committed to ham radio technology."

Laurie was glad to hear that, and after spending time with George, she decided to pay a visit to Sophia. She and Sophia had become good friends during the past few months, especially after Laurie opened up to her about Josh. She found Sophia to be a compassionate listener. Recently, though, Laurie noticed Sophia was becoming increasingly concerned about her pregnancy and seemed more depressed. Perhaps she could use some cheering up.

"I used to think this country was safe and my children would have a better life if they were born here. But now, I'm not so sure," Sofia confided in Laurie that afternoon. "What will it be like for a new child to grow up in this crazy and chaotic world? And look at Diego! Sometimes I feel like he has been taken over by the devil. He can't survive without his device nearby. I never knew being a parent would be this hard!"

"It's the hardest job in the world," said Laurie, recalling conversations with her neighbor Jenny (in this very house) years ago when Brendan and Josh were teenagers.

While her concerns then were mild compared to what Sophia was currently grappling with, she thought of Jenny's words to her. "Many years ago, when I was feeling stressed about Brendan and Josh, my best friend said to me, 'They do grow up eventually, and then you'll really miss them.' And she was so right."

Sophia looked at her. "How do you do it? How do you get by day after day without knowing what happened to Josh?"

"Honestly, I don't know." Laurie replied. "Somehow, I keep thinking he is alive somewhere, and it will all work out. Because I can't even contemplate any other scenario."

Sophia was quiet. For a moment, both women were lost in their own thoughts. Then Laurie broke the silence. "I guess I hold on to that thought, and I am grateful that Brendan is home now for a few weeks. And you can hold on to the thought that Diego will find his way and you will soon have a beautiful new child to hug and treasure."

Josh

It had been a whirlwind couple of months, and Josh now found himself in charge of the city's emergency communications network. His expertise with ham radios was a godsend to the fire and police chiefs, both of whom worried about communications in the event of a breakdown in cell phone service. Several years ago, the local radio club had fallen apart due to lack of leadership and the group had simply stopped meeting. In a few short months, Josh revived the club and re-energized some older members as well. Many of them had been sidelined years ago, and they appreciated the opportunity to step up and help. In his quiet way, Josh took on a huge leadership role.

The countless hours of getting equipment, setting it up, and training were finally beginning to pay off. He had a skilled network of people and felt like the city was far more prepared for an emergency than it had been just three months earlier, at least in the realm of communications.

As the weekly meeting of the local radio club wrapped up, Josh felt energized in a way he hadn't experienced for a long time. Attendance was way up, and each week brought in new members.

"Great meeting, Josh! See you next week, and don't stay up all night!" said Ralph, one of the old-timers, as he exited the building. With his bushy gray hair and large wire-rimmed glasses, he reminded Josh of his mentor, George.

"I won't Ralph! I just want to test one thing on this new radio. It shouldn't take long. I'll lock up when I leave."

Josh thought of George as he tinkered with the ham radio setup in the basement of the old firehouse. He remembered how George helped him build his own two-way radio. His parents had given him a kit for his 14th birthday, and he spent hours putting it together. It was primitive, but at least worked over a short range. Then Brendan had some friends over, and they made fun of it, while showing off all the things they could do with their cell phones. At the time, he felt embarrassed, but as he thought about it now, he realized how stupid that was. Why did it even matter to him what Brendan's friends thought?

He shook his head, thinking of his family. The more he thought of them, the more he missed them. Even Brendan. He felt almost ready to take some steps to reconnect with them, though the idea terrified him. He still had some healing to do before he could face those demons and fully explain what happened. Perhaps he could contact George first and ask him to be an intermediary. Yet he wasn't sure he could face him, either. Even now, he clearly remembered that last night at George's house, and the man he saw there. Thinking about it now, though, he wondered if they really were friends. After all, he had never seen them together prior to that night. At any rate, he knew George's call sign, and over the past few weeks, he had made a few discreet inquiries over the radio. He could see his mentor was once again active on the ham radio network. Knowing that made the possibility of communicating with him even more real, though he wasn't quite ready yet.

Josh's friendship with Steve had grown in the last few months as well. Steve lived in a small bungalow outside of town with his wife and two young boys, and Josh visited them often. It was the first real friendship Josh had allowed himself in a long time.

Steve's wife was away for a few days, and Steve invited Josh over for dinner. Upon arriving, Josh could see how harried Steve was.

"Thank goodness you're here!" exclaimed Steve. "My boys have been fighting nonstop all day."

Josh smiled, looking down at six-year-old Hale and four-year-old Joey. Memories of his younger years suddenly came crashing back. The boys ran up to him, thrilled to see him and even more thrilled to see Amigo, who patiently allowed the boys to climb all over him.

"I'm hiring that dog as my permanent babysitter," said Steve. "I think my wife went away to force me to see what she deals with day in and day out."

"Reminds me a lot of myself and my brother," said Josh as they watched the boys bicker over who should throw the stick for Amigo first.

"I didn't know you had a brother," Steve said. "In fact, you've never mentioned your family. I don't even know where you're from."

Josh didn't answer. He still wasn't ready to look too closely at his past. At the moment, he was content to sit and watch the boys fight, and then enjoy a sumptuous barbecue meal with them. Steve was an expert cook who loved to show off his skills on the grill. He got the boys involved in the cooking as well, which kept them occupied almost as much as Amigo. Josh reveled in the feelings of companionship, friendship, and family.

Once Steve put the boys to bed, they sat on the porch overlooking the desert. Josh surveyed the surrounding landscape. It was all desert—a mixture of browns and tans. There was so little green. Suddenly, he felt nostalgic for home.

"I grew up in Connecticut," he offered. "Much, much greener than around here. Lots of trees and lawns. Everyone had a perfectly manicured green lawn. The grass grew so fast there in the spring we'd have to mow our lawn twice a week. That was one of the things my brother and I would fight about—whose turn was it to mow the lawn. The one thing that saved me from that chore was my friendship with George. I spent 90% of my free time at George's house all through high school."

"What happened, Josh?" Steve asked. "Why don't you ever talk about home? And who's this guy, George?"

"George was my ham radio mentor," Josh responded slowly. "He lived in my neighborhood, and that first summer after I learned about hams, I practically lived at his house. I just couldn't get enough of it. He ran the ham radio club at school, and I got deeply involved. Unfortunately, I also got involved with Boy Scouts as well."

Josh stared down at the ground in front of him, shredding a dead leaf with his hands. Steve started to say something but held back. He had a sense Josh simply needed to talk without being interrupted.

"I joined Boy Scouts when I started high school, after that summer learning about ham radios. I was a little old for the program but thought it would be fun. And my older brother seemed to enjoy it." He paused, trying to get his thoughts in order. "For a while it was fun. We learned a lot about camping and even learned how to make a compass from materials we could find in the wild if we were completely lost. We did all that to get ready for a weeklong retreat. I think you can probably guess what happened during that…" Josh trailed off, still staring at the ground, little pieces of leaf dust now littering the porch around his feet.

For a moment, they sat in silence. Steve looked at his friend, debating whether to say something and what that something should be. Given what

Josh had just shared, he had an inkling as to what had happened, but he didn't want to put words in Josh's mouth. Finally, he decided the best path forward was to keep Josh talking.

"What happened during that retreat, Josh?"

Josh raised his head, tears forming in his eyes. He wiped them away, then looked down again, unsure if he could continue. Yet he had gotten this far and was desperate now to get this off his chest.

"I was… The Scout leader, Reggie, had a thing for me, and there was nothing I could do to stop it. He did some horrible things to me, more than once on that trip. I remember he carried a walking stick with him all the time, and he used it to threaten me." He was openly sobbing now. "I was f-ing 14 years old, and I couldn't do a damn thing to stop him."

The words came faster now. "When I got home from that trip, I dove into school and told no one. I buried it. I kept up the ham radio stuff with George, but that was the only thing I did outside of school. It changed me, but I couldn't see it at the time. I hid out, and while I did go drinking a bit with friends, mostly I wanted to be alone. I didn't have a great relationship with my brother then—we were pretty competitive—so I didn't feel comfortable talking to him. It was much easier to try to forget about it. And that worked, at least for a while."

He looked up now, wiping the tears from his face with his sleeve. "Eventually, it came time to go to college, and I wanted to go far, far away. Deep down I hoped I could start my life fresh and put everything behind me. I had a great first semester at school. I made some new friends and started to be more comfortable around other people. Then I came home for Christmas."

He paused again as the memories assaulted him. "Christmas break was good, up until the very last day. That evening, I visited George, and who do you think was there? Turns out 'Reggie-Wedgie' was a friend of his, and I never knew that. I walked into the house—a house that had been a haven for me all through high school—and I saw that monster standing in the kitchen with his walking stick, like he belonged there. Something inside of me snapped. All the memories of that Boy Scout week came crashing down on me, and I swear, it was the worst panic attack ever. I couldn't wait to get out of there, to get out of the neighborhood, to get as far away from home as possible. I thought when I returned to school, everything would go back to normal, but once the floodgates opened, I couldn't concentrate on anything. I stopped going to classes and partied my way through the semester. When it came time to go home again for spring break, I couldn't face the idea. I was terrified and ashamed and needed to stay away. I didn't want to face my family, to have to explain anything. So... I disappeared."

"You what?" asked Steve incredulously. He thought he could understand most of what Josh had gone through. The shame must have been unbearable, and he could certainly see how Josh would want to disappear, but the fact he had actually done so seemed outrageous. For a moment he thought of his two boys. As a parent, how would he feel if either of them vanished without a trace?

"I disappeared from my family. A group of guys at school were going on a trip to Colorado and I asked my parents if I could go. They had no idea I was failing at the time, so they agreed. Once there, I slipped out one night, got on a bus, and ended up in California. I've been here ever since, doing menial jobs and trying to fly low enough under the radar so no one from my past could find me.

"For four years, I drank and partied, and did everything I could to forget. I'm not sure you can even call what I was doing living. I existed. That was all. Then one morning, about nine months ago, I woke up on the beach unable to remember anything of the previous night, and I decided it was time to rejoin the human race again. That was the day I met you in the café, by the way."

Steve nodded, glad his friend had finally opened up to him. Yet he still wondered about Josh's parents. "Do you ever think about your family—about letting them know what happened?"

"All the time," replied Josh. "But I have no idea how. And the more time goes by, the harder it gets. What would I say? *'Hi Mom! It's me, Josh! I just wanted to say hello...'"*

"What about contacting your friend George?" asked Steve.

"I've thought about that as well, but in my mind, George betrayed me. How could he possibly have been friends with that beast?"

"Maybe he didn't know he was a molester," Steve offered. "It's likely he had no idea what happened to you."

"I know," said Josh, "But still, I can't get the image out of my head of that guy at George's house. And what would I say to George as well? *'Hi George! Your friend is a pedophile... just thought you'd want to know....'"*

"Well, I'm glad you at least trusted me enough to tell me. I'm sure none of this has been easy for you. If you ever do decide you want to try to make some contact, I'll help you in any way I can. I hope I'm not overstepping my bounds here, but as a parent of young kids, I can tell you nothing would devastate me more than one of my boys disappearing. Your parents were innocent, and you may want to consider that as well. You have nothing to be ashamed of. Shame was the response of a helpless 14-year-old boy, but you're a lot older now and a lot more mature. Just think about it, okay?"

"Okay," replied Josh. "I already told you I think about it all the time, so who knows? But the time needs to be right. At any rate, I appreciate you listening. It feels good to know I can talk about this. I've kept it in for so long I wasn't sure I could find the words."

"I'd say you did pretty well," said Steve, rising. "Wait here and I'll get you another beer." Steve retreated into the kitchen, while Josh looked out over the landscape. The spaciousness of the desert seemed to mirror the lightness he felt inside. He felt like a huge weight had been lifted off his shoulders.

As Steve returned, Josh asked, "Have you gotten any more updates from the Environmental Police group?"

"Nothing substantial," Steve answered. "It seems Leonard McFay has fallen off the radar. I've heard rumors he has returned to his family's ancestral homeland in Africa, but none of that is confirmed. They're still saying we should expect more power outages and be prepared for the worst. And if McFay's predictions do come true, we may face a vastly different crisis here at the border if everyone decides to move south. I hope the border wall isn't completed before that happens because, according to McFay, we may all need to head in that direction."

Josh pondered that. Construction of the wall had sped up in the past few months, and it was only a matter of time before the border would be completely sealed off.

"Just in case, I've decided to stockpile more supplies in the desert," Steve continued. "That may seem a little absurd, but with all the craziness going on in the world, you never know what might come in handy for people. Right now, we have migrants coming north from Mexico, but it's possible that may be reversed sometime in the future."

Brendan

The weeks flew by and suddenly it was time for Brendan to return to Africa. He was excited to reunite with his community and felt energized for the coming school year. Even as he had immersed himself in the research project across the street, it felt like they were studying something that wouldn't happen for at least another 30 years, so why worry? He still thought his parents and other neighbors were silly to be stockpiling so many provisions (though he had to admit that he enjoyed the fresh eggs). But he couldn't be concerned with their hoarding right now. That was their life and their choice, not his. He had a year ahead of him trying to change the world by giving his students an education which would hopefully help them move up in their world.

As he packed his things for his long cross-Atlantic day of travel, he opened the box Alejandro had given him. Inside was the magnetometer, along with fifteen small compasses for his students. They could compare these compasses to the homemade one they had made a few months ago using a needle and leaf. He thought it would be fun for his students to continue to track the movement of magnetic north over the course of the year. He doubted they would see much change in that time, yet still he thought it would be an interesting project.

The trip to Troeburg was a long one, and after a lengthy layover in Casablanca, Brendan boarded the plane for the last leg of the journey. Settling into his seat, he glanced at the man sitting next to him, thinking he looked vaguely familiar though he couldn't quite place him. However, when the man spoke to the flight attendant in a slight West African accent, Brendan realized he was probably Leonard McFay. He remembered Alejandro telling him McFay had family in West Africa. But was it really McFay? Brendan thought it would be rude to ask. Maybe if he started a casual conversation with the man, he could find out for sure.

"Do you live in Loscoaya?" he asked tentatively.

"No, but I have some distant relatives there. I actually have never been to the country." The man glanced briefly at Brendan, then stared out the window, seemingly uninterested in talking.

Brendan persisted. "I've lived there for the past two years. It's a beautiful place," he offered.

The man turned to him now. "Two years is a long time. What have you been doing there?"

"I'm a high school physics teacher. I work for TeachAfrica in a tiny village," Brendan replied.

The man nodded. "That's good. I'm glad some of those children are getting an education in science. They will need it to survive in the world."

"That's what I think, though in my village, I often feel like I'm swimming against the tide. Most adults there don't value education much, especially in science. Still, I have three 12th grade students who are doing well and hope to study at the University in Troeburg next year. I don't know if they can do it, but maybe if they study hard, they can. I want them to graduate high school and I want them to have a chance to go on from there."

His seatmate seemed intrigued. "I will be working at the University for a while. I'm trying to set up a research facility there."

"Wait a minute!" exclaimed Brendan, now sure of who his seatmate was. "By any chance, are you Leonard McFay?"

The man looked at him with complete surprise. "How do you know me?"

"I saw your recording," explained Brendan. "My neighbors are physicists and showed it to people in our neighborhood to try to warn them."

McFay nodded slowly. "I'm trying not to draw attention to myself, but I guess that's more difficult than I thought it would be. What did you think of the video? Did it motivate people? Or have they buried their heads in the sand and gone back to their usual ways?"

"Well, it certainly worked for some people," Brendan replied. "My parents for sure. They're definitely doing things differently. But it's still a little hard for people to worry about something that may be 30 to 50 years in the future. And of course, there are always the deniers out there. My parents have a few neighbors who think they are totally crazy. In fact, there are several people who take great pleasure in ridiculing them."

"I know," said McFay ruefully. "I had to leave for that reason. It was not safe for me to stay in the country. But truthfully, if things change rapidly, I'd rather be in Troeburg than anywhere else. The more I've learned, the more I am convinced the safest part of Earth will be at the equator."

"Why would it be safest there?" Brendan asked.

"Truthfully, we know so little about the behavior of our magnetic Earth" McFay replied slowly. "While we know the magnetic field of the Earth is weakest at the poles, the movement of the poles has disrupted things so much and been so erratic that it is impossible to make predictions. The changes we see on the surface reflect changes happening deep in the Earth's core, and our best guess right now is that as the poles move toward the equator, their movement may speed up. In fact, several prominent scientists think an actual north-south flip might be instantaneous at some point if the poles get close enough to the equator. If that happens, the area around the equator may possibly keep its protective magnetic field."

Brendan thought about this for a moment. "Do you really think things will change that rapidly, like in my lifetime?"

"I am almost certain of it," he said. "I think we have been lucky so far, but things are already changing and soon it will be too late to do anything about it. I guess I am hoping we can ride out the storm by trying to stay ahead of it, and Loscoaya seems like a good place to do that.

"I have some distant relatives there," he continued. "My grandfather used to tell me stories about how his great, great grandfather was sold into slavery. He dreamed of traveling to Loscoaya someday, but that wasn't meant to be. After his passing, I found some cousins still living in Troeburg, and they are excited I'm coming. They have friends at the University and have arranged for me to work there for a while. Resources are limited there, but we'll see what we can do. I want to continue to monitor the movement of the poles. If I can set up a research facility, I will. And who knows, maybe a year from now I'll still be there and can give your students some guidance if they go to the University."

As they parted ways at the end of the flight, Brendan felt at once scared and uplifted. On one hand, his conversation with McFay was quite sobering. Any doubts he had about an impending crisis were gone. Maybe it wasn't imminent, but it was going to happen. On the more positive side, he liked McFay and enjoyed talking with someone who recognized the importance of the work he was doing. The research facility in Troeburg also sounded promising and at the very least, Brendan thought, McFay could be a great role model for his students if they could make it to the University the following year.

Chapter 5
Three Days Before

Brendan's physics students loved their shiny new compasses. In a class where only one or two students had a calculator, the fact that everyone could have their own tool caused quite a stir. After Brendan returned from his vacation, they monitored the location of the magnetic north pole daily, making charts and graphs to track its movement.

At first, they were extremely excited. Brendan explained how the changing magnetic field would affect the power grid all over the world. But there was little change in the location of magnetic north for two months and once the students realized that "all over the world" didn't really include their village, they began to lose interest. They would still be able to get water from their wells. They would still have solar-powered lights in the buildings that had them, including the schoolhouse as well as a few other prominent buildings in town. Those families who had generators would still have generator power, though Brendan warned them they eventually might not be able to get gas to power those generators. But Brendan also told them this was years away, and many more houses would have solar-powered panels by then.

Suddenly though, after two months of no movement, there was a shift. It was a small shift, but it showed up on every compass in the room, so it couldn't possibly be a fluke. The students were all atwitter with ideas about how fast it might move and what it might mean. In truth they knew very little about this whole subject, but it caught the attention of the entire class. Here was something they could measure and see in real time and Brendan had a hard time re-focusing their attention on the lesson he had planned for the day. One thing he had learned during his two years teaching here was that once his students got interested in a topic, it was useless to try to stop them. It was much better to let them ponder what it meant if magnetic north and magnetic south switched sides.

"I think the whole world would turn upside down" quipped Janice.

"Nah, it jus' means the North Star will have to be re-named the South Star," responded Cyrus.

"My dog will be really confused," said Ian.

"Your dog would be confused?" laughed Brendan. "Why?"

"I'm serious. Ever since we made that compass last year, I been watching him closely. When he pees, he always, always lines himself up facing north. Every time."

Only in Africa, Brendan thought. Where else would a teenage boy take the time to notice which way his dog stood when peeing? Every time?

"Would cars still be able to drive?" someone wondered. "Would we be able to get to Troeburg?"

"If you had enough gas, maybe," said another. "But gas might run out and then we would be stuck here for always."

Brendan felt a little chill when he heard that. Based on everything he had seen when he was working with Sophia and Alejandro a few months ago, he hadn't believed this would happen so quickly, but then he remembered his conversation with Leonard McFay on the airplane. He shivered as he thought of his home and family back in the U.S. As much as he felt at ease here, he couldn't imagine this as his permanent home. With shaking hands, he put away his papers and dismissed the class. Somehow, he could endure all sorts of hardships as long as he knew it was temporary, even if temporary meant one more year. But what if this student was right? What if he was stuck here for always?

Laurie

Posted on Laurie and Stan's refrigerator were all the tasks they decided should be attended to every day. "Preparation tasks," she called them. Things that needed to be checked and rechecked just in case.

- Make sure car is filled with gas
- Check charge on solar batteries. Rotate batteries on the solar charger
- Check all ten refrigerators and freezers in the bunker
- Check water filter in basement and make sure well is in working order
- Check disaster kit: Flashlight still working?
- Test radios

This was all so routine now that Laurie could do it in her sleep, though she slept fitfully these days. Alejandro and Sophia reassured her disaster was not imminent, yet more frequent power outages in the last few months made her increasingly worried and fearful, and performing these tasks eased her angst. While she understood Brendan's arguments against hoarding, she still felt this would provide them with a buffer to keep them going for a short time until they figured out how to adapt to a new lifestyle. And assuming these short-term outages remained just that—short term—did they really need to alter their entire lives? Maybe collecting things "just in case" would be the thing to see them through this craziness.

For Laurie, anxiety had really kicked in about a month ago when the power grid shut down for a full week, the result of some unusual sunspot activity that impacted the central power lines on the entire east coast of the United States. Communications networks weren't disrupted, but it was a good wake-up call and dry run, and spurred Laurie and Stan to do more extensive preparation. It was a test of systems already put in place and prompted the neighborhood and the entire town to act on some other initiatives. The town purchased new generators and was in the process of adding solar panels to many civic buildings. That would take a while, but at least it was starting to happen.

Though problems with communication were not an issue in this latest outage, the police and fire departments realized they needed a better emergency communications plan, so the town management reached out to local ham radio operators. Spearheaded by their neighbor, George, who updated and tested all his old equipment and became active again in the local ham radio club, the town reestablished neighborhood watch groups. Every neighborhood in town chose several people who could go door-to-door to deliver information in an emergency. All this activity helped Laurie deal with her sense of unease, though she still felt nervous when she thought about the longer-term consequences of no power grid and how they would adapt. How would they buy food if grocery stores were closed? How would they buy anything, for that matter? Could they access their money if banks were closed? She had the nagging feeling these questions weren't being addressed by all the emergency preparation teams.

The short power outage also sparked a heated discussion between Laurie and Sophia about the imminent arrival of Sophia's baby.

"I'm not sure I want to go to the hospital when this baby comes," Sophia told her. "I've been going there for checkups and so far, they have accepted me, but our insurance just ran out. What if they turn me away?"

"I don't think they can, legally," said Laurie. She couldn't imagine the hospital would deny service to a woman in active labor.

"But what if I'm there and the power goes out? It would be chaos. I'll just be one of hundreds of patients stuck there in the dark. How could they possibly take care of everyone?"

"Sophia, you're being paranoid! I'm sure the hospital has emergency generators. You need to deliver this baby in the hospital. We have hospitals for this exact purpose!"

But try as she might, Laurie felt the more they debated, the more Sophia wasn't persuaded. It was one of the few things they disagreed about, and they finally agreed to disagree. After all, it was Sophia's decision to make. If she wanted to hire a midwife and have her baby at home, who was Laurie to question her choice?

Josh

For weeks, Josh mulled over his conversation with Steve. The urge to reconnect with his family was getting stronger, and every day he contemplated the best way to do that. Finally, he decided he should enlist the help of George, and he thought an email would be best. He had George's ham radio call sign but didn't want to contact him directly via radio. For one thing, communication over the ham radio network was not always private. Also, he knew George would be completely shocked to hear from him after all this time, and he preferred to send a written message to allow George time to think about a response. After agonizing over what to write, he settled on something simple:

"Hi George, it's me, Josh. I want to talk to you. I know you may be pissed at me for leaving the way I did, but I can explain, if you are willing to listen. Can we talk? Please write back so we can set up a time."

He added his cell phone number, signed his name, and hit send. The ball was now in George's court. A few hours later, he checked his email and was disappointed to see the email had bounced back with no forwarding address. As he considered how else to get in touch with his mentor, he remembered George once showing him how ham radios could be used to relay messages to people when other methods of communication weren't available. The technique involved sending a message digitally to a nearby relay station, then having that station relay it on to another station until the message eventually reached a place where it could be delivered directly. The system was set up to deliver messages by email, phone, or snail mail. At the time, Josh wondered why anyone would want to deliver a message to a street address. It seemed so archaic. Yet, now, since he didn't have George's email or cell phone number (he had lost all his contacts years ago when he ditched his old cell phone), he realized this was probably his best option. It might take a few days, but Josh figured that given he had waited this long, a couple more days wouldn't really matter. He reworked the message, asking George to call him. Taking a deep breath, he once again sent it off.

After hearing nothing for a week, he wondered if George still lived at the same address and if the relay system had worked. Maybe his message never got through. Suddenly, his phone rang. He glanced at it, realizing it must be George. Gingerly, he accepted the call and put the phone to his ear.

"Hello," he said tentatively.

"Well, I'll be!" exclaimed George. "Where the hell have you been all these years? Your family thinks you're dead! We all figured that."

"I can explain," Josh began. "I know it sounds crazy, and I know I hurt a lot of people, but I had to get away."

"I'm all ears," George replied. "Talk to me!"

For a moment, Josh was silent. Could he really do this? He wasn't even sure he could find his voice. He took a deep breath, remembering how good he had felt after finally confiding in Steve. "I need you to just listen to me for a few minutes," he began. Then slowly, deliberately, he told George his story, ending with the night at George's house when he completely snapped.

George remained silent throughout, interrupting occasionally with a few well-placed grunts. Once Josh finished, though, he exploded into a tirade. "That murderous son-of-a-... I'd kill him myself if he weren't already dead."

Josh's ears perked up. "When did he die?"

"Almost a year ago, now. In fact, I think it'll be just about a year next week. Major car accident, though the family didn't release much in the way of details. I remember an article in the paper saying he was driving drunk. Honestly, Josh, I didn't know him well. I wouldn't have called him a friend of mine."

Relief flooded through Josh upon learning George wasn't this man's friend. And Reggie was *dead*! He felt both freedom and regret on hearing this. He was relieved he would never have to face the man again yet disappointed he didn't get to confront him. Not that he ever would have, but still, occasionally he had fantasized about it. Did Reggie feel any remorse? Did he hurt others? These were questions Josh would never be able to answer.

He paused for a moment. One year ago next week would have been around the time he decided had to turn over a new leaf—the day when he woke up alone on the beach and then met Steve at the café. Was that a coincidence? It didn't matter now, he thought. What mattered was for him to set things right with his family.

"George, I need you to help me tell my parents. I've been thinking about this for months, and I don't know how to approach them."

"Well," said George slowly, "I agree you need to talk to them and calling them out of the blue is probably not the best plan." He mulled this over for a moment. Simply learning Josh was alive was going to be a complete shock to Laurie and Stan, and he had no idea how to approach them either. For Josh's sake, though, he knew he had to do something. "I can try to prepare them, soften the impact a bit," he continued. "How about this? I'll go over and talk to your mom now and see if they can call you a bit later. That way, they'll have time to think about what they want to say and won't be completely blindsided. With all the crazy technology these days, maybe you can video chat or whatever so they can see you. Let's set up a time now for you to talk with them and I'll do my best to make it happen."

Josh hesitated. "I'm not sure I want to video chat with them. It might be easier to start with a phone call. Just give them my number and tell them to call me." He stood now and paced back and forth in his kitchen. "And thanks! I feel better already having talked to you. I'm sorry I put you through all this. I just couldn't face it for a long time." He found it hard to believe but talking to George had not been nearly as difficult as the conversation with Steve a few months ago, and the lightness he had felt then paled in comparison to how he felt now. The die was cast and there was no turning back. He only hoped his parents would be as understanding as George.

"I understand," said George. "And I think your parents will too once they know the full story. But you need to be the one to tell them. I'm not going to say anything more to them other than you and I spoke, and you want to talk to them to explain what happened, okay?"

"Yep, got it. You're a true friend, George."

"Yeah, well, glad to help," George mumbled. "That SOB! Still can't get him out of my mind…."

Laurie

As Laurie finished up her checklist, there was a knock at the door. She smiled, remembering how just a few short months ago she rarely had visitors at her house. Lately, it seemed, her neighbors showed up unexpectedly to visit for no other reason than to check in. *Who would be visiting now?* she wondered.

Opening the door, she was surprised to see George looking completely disheveled and out of sorts. His bushy white hair stood on end, and his face was drained of color. He flashed her a quick, forced smile, as he stood fidgeting in the doorway. Clearly, he had something important to tell her.

"Come on in," she exclaimed, quickly ushering him in as she wondered what had spooked him so much. "What brings you here today? You look pale. I hope it's not bad news! I'll get you some coffee."

George hesitated. Much as he had tried to compose himself on the walk over, he still hadn't figured out the best approach. His natural inclination was usually to speak first and think later. Impulsive, his wife used to call him. But as he looked at Laurie now, impulse failed him, and he was temporarily at a loss for words.

Laurie handed him a cup of coffee. She wanted to talk with him about an idea she had for hydroponic gardening but could see he had something important to say first. She stood expectantly for a moment, waiting for him to speak. His hands were shaking as he set the cup of coffee down. Finally, he found his voice.

"Sit down a minute, Laurie," he began. "I have news for you, and it's not bad news, so don't worry."

Laurie sat, looking at him anxiously. "Is it about Josh?" she asked. Somehow, she knew. They hadn't spoken of him in weeks, but Josh was always there, underscoring all their interactions. In her mind, Josh was still alive. No matter how much time went by, she refused to believe anything else.

George nodded slowly, deciding it was best to be direct. "I spoke with him this morning."

Stunned, Laurie sat with the coffee cup halfway to her lips. "You *what?*"

"I spoke to him this morning. I got a message from him completely out of the blue asking me to call him, so I did, and we talked."

"How…? Why…? Where is he?" Laurie finally blurted out. She was flooded with emotions from relief to raw anger and everything in between. "Is he okay? Has he been hurt?" For a moment she couldn't believe what she was hearing.

"He's okay. He's good, actually. But from what I gathered he wasn't for a long time. He told me a lot of things this morning, and I think it's best if you hear it all from him and not from me. In fact, I promised I wouldn't say much beyond that he's okay and wants to talk to you. We thought it'd be good if you and Stan had some time to digest all this, and then you can maybe call him later today? I asked him if he wanted to do one of those fancy video chats or whatever, but he said he would prefer a plain phone call first. He thinks that would be easier."

Laurie remained still. *Josh, alive!* He wanted to talk to them. Today. She looked at George with tears in her eyes. "I knew it! I knew it all along. Call it a mother's intuition, or whatever, but I was sure he had to be out there somewhere. Can you at least tell me where he is?"

"Southern California," replied George. "Right at the U.S./Mexican border. Right where they're now building that huge wall."

"Has he been there this whole time?" she asked.

"More or less, sounds like," replied George. "We didn't talk too much about that."

Laurie stared out the window of her living room, engrossed in thought. Why had he been out of touch for so long? More tears sprang to her eyes as her emotions again ran from relief to anger to elation all in the space of a few moments. She needed to call Stan but felt too paralyzed to do anything besides sit. She was still having difficulty absorbing it. Finally, George cleared his throat, startling her out of her reverie. "Well, I'll be heading out now… here's the number he wants you to call and he will be there at 7:00 pm tonight our time. I'll leave you to get in touch with Stan, and then talk to you tomorrow, okay?"

"Okay, thanks George," Laurie mumbled. She tried to stand, but George gently pushed her back down. "I can see myself out. You just sit there for a bit and take it all in." And with that, he left.

Josh

Nervously, Josh sat with his phone in hand. He had planned what he would say, had even written it down. But now, as he waited for the call, he wondered if this really was a good idea. Idly, he petted Amigo who had strategically placed his head in Josh's lap and nudged the phone aside. The blaring phone caused him to jump. For a moment, he thought of not answering. He stared at the incoming call number—his dad's. Closing his eyes, he took a deep breath and clicked on "accept." Somehow, he managed to get out a brief, "Hi…."

He could hear both of his parents on the other end breathing heavily. They must have it on speaker phone, he thought. "Josh…" his mother began, her voice failing as well.

"Hi Mom," he said. "It's good to hear your voice."

"Same here, Son," his dad piped in.

"I'm so sorry!" Suddenly the floodgates opened and Josh burst into tears, glad they weren't doing a video chat. He poured out his story, grateful his parents simply let him go on without interrupting. In truth, Laurie and Stan were too stunned to say much of anything.

As Josh finally finished, Laurie found her voice. "We had no idea of any of this."

"I know," replied Josh. "Remember when I called the guy 'Wedgie' and you yelled at me? That was when I knew I could never say anything. I felt like you wouldn't believe me, that you'd always take his side if he denied it. So, I thought it better to bury it."

Stan cleared his throat and looked at Laurie questioningly. "You never told me about that."

Laurie winced. "Now it's my turn to say I'm sorry," she said slowly. Tears were freely flowing down her cheeks, though she tried to keep her voice even. "We should have been more attentive." She felt such sorrow for her son, for all the pain and suffering he had been through, and so much guilt for not seeing it at the time.

"Well, just so you know, Reginald Lamprey died about a year ago. It was all over the local paper. I think he was driving drunk," said Stan.

"I know. George told me. I suppose I should be relieved, but I just feel kind of empty inside."

"Well, I can understand that, but what's important now is that you know we love you no matter what. You did nothing wrong," said Laurie.

"I'll echo that," added Stan. "We both love you so much."

"What do you think about a quick visit home?" Laurie asked tentatively. It was almost more than she could hope for. "Maybe it would help you to put all this behind you, and besides, I want to see and hug you!"

Josh paused. "I think I'd like that," he said slowly. It wasn't what he had planned, though perhaps it would be beneficial for all of them. At the moment, however, he felt so drained it was hard for him to think about much of anything. Yet at the same time he also felt surprisingly light and unburdened, and the thought of a trip home *was* appealing.

Glancing at the clock in his kitchen, he suddenly realized they had been talking for over an hour, or rather that he had been talking while his parents listened. No wonder he felt drained. He didn't think he could take much more. "I have to go now," he said hoarsely. "I'll see if I can arrange something in the next few days and I'll call you tomorrow. I love you both and really am sorry I put you through all this."

"Can we do a video chat tomorrow?" asked Laurie. "I want to see your face!"

Josh smiled. "Sure, that would work. It would be good to see you both as well. But I do need to go now."

He was starting to feel tears forming again, and not wanting to prolong the goodbye, he quickly ended the call and stared out his window, barely breathing. He had done it. A new chapter was beginning in his life. It felt like a fresh start. He couldn't turn back the clock, but he could try to make it up to his family and George, and in doing so, maybe he would feel more fulfilled. In many ways, that process had already started through his friendship with Steve and the work he had done in the past year. He'd accomplished a lot, he reflected. Maybe he wasn't such a loser, after all.

When North Becomes South

For a few moments more, he sat quietly then took a deep breath and shook his head, ready to refocus his mind on the upcoming evening. He had little time to prepare. Steve's sister, Marguerite, was visiting from Colorado and had agreed to a date with him. Since her arrival four days ago, he had been quite captivated by her. She was only in town for a few more days, and he planned to take her out for what he hoped would be a memorable evening. Quickly he fed Amigo, who looked at him with soulful eyes. "Sorry, bud. You're on your own for a little while tonight. But I'll try to bring you something back from dinner. And listen, I expect you to be on your best behavior if I bring a guest home."

Chapter 6
One Day Before

Laurie and Stan awoke to a crisp, clear Saturday morning, made even more beautiful by the prospect they would see Josh the next morning. Yesterday, they had connected with him via a video chat and couldn't get over how he looked While his face had filled out and he had a slight stubble on his chin, he still had that boyish look, with his straight blond hair falling over his eyes. He managed to get a plane ticket on a red-eye flight home within a few days, and Laurie had been on cloud nine ever since. The only snag was a brief call to Brendan to tell him Josh had resurfaced, and Laurie could tell Brendan hadn't taken it very well. She and Stan expected Brendan to be as happy and ecstatic as they were, but his reaction was more guarded. He had all sorts of questions they refused to answer because they wanted him to hear the story directly from Josh.

"Josh is coming home in two days and you can talk once he's here," Laurie told him.

"Can't you at least tell me why he waited five years to get in touch?" Brendan asked again.

"No, it's his story. I'm not going to be the middleman."

Brendan was understandably put off by this, but Laurie held her ground. She was certain once Brendan heard what Josh had endured, he would be more sympathetic.

Today, however, Laurie and Stan were taking advantage of the gorgeous autumn weather with other plans. For years, they had enjoyed the sport of orienteering. They belonged to a club that ran competitive events most weekends in the spring and fall, and today was one of the biggest meets of the season. Orienteering involved hiking in the woods with a map and compass, looking for "controls" which were hidden along a specified course. At most meets, there were several course options to choose from ranging in difficulty from quite easy (all controls on well-marked trails) to extremely difficult (bushwhacking with all controls hidden in the woods). It was a timed activity, but Laurie and Stan usually enjoyed it simply as a chance to be outdoors exploring different park areas, and they generally chose courses of moderate difficulty. On this particular day, however, because it was an elite competition, Stan wanted to tackle a more difficult course than Laurie, so they decided to split up and do separate courses. With map and compass in hand, Laurie set off on her way.

Stan had competed in orienteering meets for years and had taught Laurie the basics, though she was not nearly as experienced as he was. However, she was confident that if she stayed on the marked trails, she would be able to complete the course in about an hour and expected Stan would take about a half-hour longer. He had trained her to orient using the sun and her shadow first, employing the compass as a backup. But by the time the meet started, what had been a beautiful sunny day had turned gray and overcast. With no shadow, Laurie was forced to rely completely on her compass. She managed to find the first few controls with no problem before coming to a three-way fork in the trail. Glancing at her compass, she determined the path to take and set off at a good clip. After walking for a while, though, she became confused. Suddenly she realized the trail she was on didn't match what she was seeing on the map. Added to that, a brisk breeze had picked up and she was starting to get cold. Damn! Why didn't I bring a sweatshirt? she thought.

She walked a bit further, still hoping she was on the right path, but then another fork appeared. She sat down and stared at the map, realizing she was completely lost. Her eyes started to tear up, and as she reached up to wipe them, she dislodged and ripped a contact lens. *Great!* she thought, looking at the torn lens in her hand. *Not only am I lost, but I can't see and can't read the map. Why did I ever agree to do this alone?*

Cursing Stan for wanting to go separately and cursing herself for agreeing to it, she sat on a log and stared at the map and compass, trying to make sense of what she was seeing, but with only one contact lens, she couldn't see the map clearly. Surely, someone else from the meet would come through this way she thought, deciding to stay put rather than wander through the woods in circles. As she sat though, the wind picked up and there was a distant rumble of thunder. Hugging her knees, she shivered as the first drops of rain began to fall.

A small rustling in the woods caught her attention and she looked up, feeling her heart skip a beat. Standing about 20 feet in front of her, beady little eyes staring directly at her, was a small fox. For a moment, she locked eyes with the animal, then leapt to her feet and scrambled up the small cliff behind her. *"Can foxes climb?"* she wondered. Glancing upward, she noticed a branch overhanging the rock she was on, and gathering all her strength, she grabbed it and swung herself up. Luckily, she was light enough and the branch was sturdy enough to hold her and she sat on her perch, looking down as the fox circled the rock below glaring up at her. *Mean eyes*, she thought. Finally, the fox got bored and ambled off with barely a glance back. Too terrified to move, Laurie remained glued to the branch.

After sitting and shivering for what felt like hours, she finally decided to move. The rain was pouring down in sheets, and it was apparent no one else was coming this way. All she could do was try to retrace her steps as best as possible and look for some of the orienteering controls, where she would have a better chance of spotting other people from the meet. Slowly she lowered herself off the branch and slid down the side of the rock. It was far more slippery than when she had climbed up.

She stood up, clutching at her belly as she felt fear roiling in her gut. *Breathe*, she reminded herself. She had never been one to have panic attacks, but at this moment, she was wondering if she might be in the throes of one. She was cold, wet, alone, and lost in the woods. By the moment, it got darker and windier. How had this beautiful day turned horrible so quickly? How had she gotten so disoriented? Still, she knew she had to move. Sobbing, she looked up and saw some movement in the distance. Peering at it out of her one good eye, she thought she saw a cluster of people and ran toward them. She stumbled on a root, pulled herself up, and kept running. With her head down, she ran smack into another hiker, knocking them both over.

"Are you okay?" asked the man as he picked himself up. Gently helping her up as well, he continued, "Are you here for the orienteering meet?"

Laurie nodded, momentarily unable to find her voice. Thankfully, he was one of the meet volunteers.

"Am I ever glad to see you! I lost a contact lens and couldn't read the map and got completely turned around," she said, fighting back tears.

"Come on, we're close to the finish area. I'll help you out of here." He took her arm and guided her along the path. When they came into a clearing and saw some tents and a crowd of people gathered around, Laurie had never felt more relieved in her life. One of the men placed a blanket around her and brought her to a bench. As he read through a long list of people, she told him her name through chattering teeth. Apparently, she wasn't the only one who had gotten lost. There were at least 20 people still out there, and Stan was one of them. A team of volunteers was looking for stragglers, but the search was hampered by the wind and rain. They were hoping all the missing people were together in one group.

"The bloody compasses all malfunctioned" the meet leader was saying. "All of them. Not a single person was able to find their way. I don't understand it."

Stan was indeed with a group of several other hikers. At first wary of one another because this was an individual competition, they finally realized they were all lost and none of their compasses were working correctly. Eventually, they joined forces, trying to make sense of the map. After wandering aimlessly for about an hour, picking up more and more hikers along the way, the group finally found a landmark they all remembered. From there they were able to navigate their way back, arriving at the finish well over five hours after the start of the meet.

Someone had built a small campfire. Wrapped tightly in a blanket, Laurie was warming herself when Stan emerged from the woods with a gang of others. Relief flooded through her as she saw him run towards her.

They were both quiet as they drove home, exhausted and lost in their thoughts about what had happened. As Laurie recalled what the meet leader said about all the compasses malfunctioning, she wondered if things might be changing far more rapidly than predicted. Up to this point, the idea that magnetic north might move had been theoretical, something in the distant future. But what happened to the compasses today made it suddenly more real. Was this the beginning of the end?

Pondering this, she barely heard Stan's question. "I wonder if compasses are messed up all over?" Stan mused. "This might affect Josh's flight. He's supposed to leave from California later tonight." Because it was a last-minute reservation, Josh had to make several connections. He would be leaving San Diego at midnight and was due in Boston about 2:00 pm tomorrow.

Laurie looked at him with tears in her eyes. "Don't even think that!" she snapped, as if her voice could drive away those bad thoughts. "There's no way he isn't coming home tomorrow."

But even as she spoke the words, she wondered if Stan might be right. Fervently, she prayed this whole thing with the compasses was just a local anomaly, but deep down, she had a foreboding that went beyond anything she had ever felt in her life. What if this was a more widespread problem and what if the airplane's navigation systems didn't work?

Upon arriving home, Laurie took a hot shower, trying to banish the chills. Thoroughly exhausted, she fell into bed hoping the next day would bring a semblance of calm.

Brendan

Lying in bed, Brendan desperately tried to process what he had heard. How could his brother have turned up out of the blue after no contact for five years? Was he even aware of how much pain he had caused them all? They all thought he was dead! And how could his parents be so accepting? It made no sense to him.

A knock on his door got him up. Neighbors were always stopping in, and it had taken a long time for them to understand he preferred they knock before barging into his house. The concept of privacy differed here. It was far less important than he was used to back home. He opened the door to see his neighbor Anna.

"You comin' for dinner?" she asked. "My ma sent me over to fetch you. She says it's not like you to be late." Teasingly she added, "See, I remembered to knock on your door this time. Ma reminded me of that when I left the house. She said we need to respect your need to be alone more."

Brendan glanced outside at the setting sun, surprised at how late it was. He had been so lost in thoughts of his family that he didn't realize how long he had been lying there. He considered passing on dinner but decided his neighbors might be insulted. After all, they had taken the time to cook for him, and he didn't want them to think him rude. Anna's comment about respecting his need for privacy might be just the tip of the iceberg. As they walked back to Anna's house, he tried to explain. "It's not really a need to be alone, as much as it is a need to have my own space or at least to control my own space. You live in a house with lots of people in it all the time. But where I grew up, we were only four people in a much bigger house, and I had my own bedroom. I had a place I could go to that I could call mine, and people knew not to disturb me when I was there." He was afraid he wasn't making much sense, but Anna tried to follow him.

"How can you own space?" she asked. "I mean, you can own things, like a house, or a bed, or maybe some clothes, but you can't own space. That just don' make sense. Space belongs to everybody.

Brendan laughed. He had to admit she had a point. "You're probably right. But all the same, it's how I grew up, and I sure appreciate you understanding that."

"Well, we're about to add another person to our space. Anjali's baby is due any day, now," Anna told him. "I think it may even come tonight. She been talkin' 'bout labor pains startin' up this mornin.' The midwife is on her way over now." Brendan glanced at Anna. In some ways, he envied her relationship with her sister. They always seemed so close, even though Anjali was eight years older. Once again, he thought of Josh.

As they approached the house, Talah, his adopted mom looked at him. "You okay? You look like a ghost or something. I didn't know white people could get any whiter, but you sure look whiter than white now."

"I'm okay," Brendan replied slowly. "I just had a weird conversation with my parents."

"What you mean, weird?" Talah asked.

Brendan sighed. "Apparently my brother has reappeared after being missing for the past five years." Everyone chimed in at once.

"You have a *brother*?"

"What you mean, missin' for five years?"

"Why you never tol' us about him?"

Talah finally spoke up. "Quiet everyone and let the boy speak. He can't get a word in edge-wise with y'all talking so much. But first, let's sit down for dinner. There's chairs for everyone."

The family gathered around the table, except for Anjali who had been complaining of pains all day. Everyone filled their bowls with the usual rice and beans. "Go ahead, Brendan, we all listenin', now," Talah said, once they had all settled down.

"I have a younger brother. Josh. Two years younger than me. About five years ago, he was in college and went on a trip for his spring break." Brendan took a deep breath. Although he'd thought about this constantly, he had never talked about it with anyone. He brushed away the tears that were forming in his eyes. "During that trip, he... disappeared."

He could barely get the word out. Finding his voice, he continued. "We haven't seen or heard from him since. We all thought—at least I thought—he was probably dead. We had no way of knowing. My mom, though, she just hung in there, refusing to believe anything until she knew for sure. And then, yesterday, he contacted them. Seems he's been living in California all these years."

For a moment everyone at the table was silent. Then Talah said gently, "I can' even imagine that. What your mamma must have been going through. Not knowin' anything. So, he's back now. What more do you know?"

"I don't know anything more! That's the problem." Brendan felt the tears forming again. "He's not back home yet. Supposedly he's flying home tomorrow, and my mom said the two of us can talk and he'll explain everything. But I'm so mad at him right now I don't think I even *want* to talk to him! Unless he was kidnapped or something, I can't imagine why he would not have communicated with his family. I watched as my parents went through such anguish and there was nothing I could do to help. How could he have done this to them—to *all* of us?"

"Maybe he was kidnapped," piped up ten-year-old Willie. He shrugged as Brendan looked at him. "Maybe he was tortured and beaten and all sorts of bad things."

"I hope not," said Talah, "but Willie does have a point. Maybe there is a reason your brother couldn't contact y'all. You need to at least hear him out, Brendan."

"I suppose," said Brendan slowly. "I just wish my mom had given me more information. She seemed happy, but then again, she always was so quick to forgive anyone and everyone. I am just so angry at him right now. I don't even know if I can talk to him! I wouldn't know where to start."

"Listenin' is always a good place to start," said Talah quietly. "Let him talk and then decide whether to stay angry or not."

"Maybe," though Brendan didn't sound convinced. "He has a *lot* of explaining to do."

He trudged home after dinner through the darkness, alone in his thoughts. Perhaps Talah was right, but for now, all he wanted to do was sleep. He crawled into bed under his mosquito netting, grateful that at least tomorrow was Sunday, and he could sleep in a little.

Chapter 7
The Day of the Superstorm

Laurie jolted out of a deep sleep awakened by a loud rap followed by a deathly silence. All the normal household noises—the quiet hum of the refrigerator in the kitchen, the fan in the computer, and the furnace for the hot water heater cycling on and off—had ceased, and the room was pitch dark. Something was making her skin crawl. Sitting up in bed, she realized what it was… once again, power had gone out. She contemplated pulling the covers over her head and going back to sleep, then heard a distinct knock on her door. A moment later, it became more of a pounding than a knock.

She chided herself as she glanced at her bedside clock. *Duh, no power!* At least her phone was charged, and a quick peek told her it was 3 a.m. Josh's flight should be taking off right now, she thought as she shook Stan awake. Grabbing a flashlight, they crept down the darkened stairs together, unsure of what awaited them. The knocking became more insistent. "Laurie, Stan, wake up! We need your help!" The muffled voice of Alejandro came through the door. "It's Sophia. The baby is coming, and power went out. She's so scared! Can you come?"

Great! thought Laurie. *Now, of all times.* After all their discussions during the past few weeks, she had hoped Sophia would be willing to go to the hospital, but with the power out now, Sofia might be even more fearful. Recently Sofia and Alejandro had contacted a midwife, and Laurie offered to be backup support, though she had absolutely no confidence in her ability to do anything useful. Sure, she had two boys and had gone through childbirth, but that was years ago, and she recalled little of the experience. To this end, Sophia had forced her to watch a video on home childbirth, so she at least knew the basics, and she figured she knew enough to support the midwife. Her neighbors, Lisa and Sally had watched the video as well. Sophia and Alejandro had an appointment scheduled with the midwife later today and had asked them all to be at that meeting, but now it looked like Mother Nature had other ideas.

Laurie and Stan raced across the darkened street and entered the house. Scattered around the foyer, living room, and bedroom were about 50 small battery-operated candles. They flickered now, casting an eerie glow. Diego sat upright on the sofa in the living room, looking wide-eyed and scared, as Sophia reclined in her bed, pale as a ghost.

"Did you call the midwife?" Laurie asked Alejandro. He shook his head and pointed to his phone. "The phone doesn't work."

This is new, Laurie thought. During the outages of the past few months, phones had always worked. Why would they fail now?

"She lives far," said Alejandro. "Probably at least a half hour away. I could get her, but it would probably be about two hours before I would be back here, assuming she can come right away, and I can find the house without GPS. Can you stay here with Sophia?"

Laurie nodded slowly, fear boiling up in her belly. *Breathe!* she commanded herself. And then to Sophia out loud "Breathe!"

Sophia looked at her beseechingly. "I know you didn't want to be put in this position, but if you can stay until the midwife comes, that will be enough."

Two hours thought Laurie. *I can do this*. "Okay," she said aloud, turning to Alejandro. "You and Stan go together. He knows the area better than you. Can you wake up some other neighbors and send them here as well? I can't do this alone. And take Diego! I don't want to worry about him while we're busy here."

As an afterthought, she grabbed Stan. "Go down the street and wake up George. Ask him to contact the police station and send help." George had told her over and over that no matter what happened with the grid, he would always have a direct line to police and fire dispatch with his ham radio. At the very least, the EMTs would have more experience in emergency childbirth than she had. Perhaps Sophia would let them take her to the hospital.

Alejandro and Stan left just as Sophia began another contraction. "Squeeze my hand and breathe!" Laurie commanded. Never in her life had she been more terrified. She looked around the room at the flickering lights, praying they would all maintain battery power for the next few hours. The light was dim, but it was enough to work in. And the baby wasn't coming immediately, she reminded herself. The EMTs would come, the midwife would come, and everything would go smoothly. She was only there temporarily. "Breathe!" she commanded again aloud, both to herself and to Sophia.

For a short while, Laurie and Sophia sat quietly in the room, until Lisa and Sally showed up. Relief flooded over Laurie for a few minutes, until suddenly, Sophia's whole body contracted, and her water broke. "Shit!" said Laurie under her breath. Sophia was going into active labor, and the only expertise her attendant neighbors had was from a video they had watched a week ago. Yet here they were, and the baby was coming, with or without their help.

Where were the EMTs? she wondered just as there was a knock on the door. George's bushy hair could be seen in the crack of the doorway. He poked his head in, clearly distraught. "There's a problem!" he cried. "I reached dispatch, but they can't do much. There was a big explosion at a power substation, and all available emergency personnel are there now. A bunch of workers are injured and they're trying to contain the fire. The dispatcher said he would try to get someone over here, but it may be awhile. I'll stay on it but wanted to warn you."

With that, he departed, leaving the women to themselves. They looked at each other, fear clearly etched into each of their faces. Following the guidelines in the video, they had gathered pillows and towels and wet cloths and were trying their best to keep Sophia as comfortable as possible. For a while, everything seemed under control, and Sophia was clearly grateful for their presence. Between contractions, she chatted softly with them, telling them she and Alejandro knew they were having a girl and had decided to name her Dawn.

"What a beautiful name!" exclaimed Lisa. Laurie and Sally nodded in agreement. Sophia smiled weakly, then suddenly her body contracted again. "Breathe through it!" commanded Laurie, as Sophia looked at her with wild eyes. "You can do this, Sophia. I know you can."

Sophia tensed up, then fell back against her pillows sobbing. "It's too much! It wasn't like this with Diego. I don't remember it being this hard!" The contractions were more frequent now, and she was becoming increasingly agitated. Wiping the sweat from Sophia's brow between contractions, Laurie tried desperately to focus on something positive. A new baby was coming into the world, and she was there to witness it. This was truly a miraculous thing.

For two turbulent hours, the women took turns holding Sophia's hand and mopped sweat off her face as she pitched and rolled like a boat tossed in a hurricane, moaning with each contraction. Suddenly, she vomited. Laurie cast about in her mind, trying to recall anything that would help them in this situation. How was it all the women in the room had gone through childbirth, yet it had never seemed quite this raw? This was far different from the sterile hospital delivery room that she vaguely remembered.

Was this normal? Laurie, Lisa and Sally had no idea. And then, just as the sun was rising, Sophia let out gut-wrenching scream and baby Dawn entered the world. She was a slippery bundle, and the three women wrapped her in a towel, collectively holding their breath while waiting a beat for her to inhale. She emitted a small cough, then took in a gulp of air. But they weren't out of the woods yet. Dawn was breathing, but Sophia continued to bleed. *So much blood,* thought Laurie. *Was this right?*

Stunned and shaken, they gently placed the child on Sophia's chest. "You have a beautiful baby girl!" exclaimed Laurie. "True to her name, she arrived exactly at sunrise." For a brief moment, Sophia opened her eyes and gratefully smiled at them. "Hello, my dear Dawn," she whispered. Then she drifted off. Blood was still pouring out, and they were helpless to stop it.

Suddenly the mood was broken as the midwife rushed in. Surveying the scene, she quickly focused her full attention on Sophia. The women backed away, unsure what to do as the midwife checked Sophia while asking all sorts of questions: Exactly what time was the baby born? How much blood did Sophia lose? Had they done anything at all to try to stop the bleeding? What were they doing to keep things clean and sterile? Had they worn gloves the entire time? Did the baby breathe right away? Had they done any other assessments on it? On and on she went as she cut the umbilical cord and continued her assessment of Sophia.

"She needs to get to a hospital!" the midwife cried frantically. "She is bleeding out."

At that moment, the EMTs burst in. Quickly they took control and within minutes were wheeling Sophia into a waiting ambulance. A stunned Alejandro went with them, carrying the new baby. "Stay here with Diego," he cried out, leaving the three women staring after him.

Brendan

"Brendan, come quickly!" Anna was calling from right outside his bedroom window. Brendan grumbled as he once again bemoaned his lack of privacy. So much for sleeping in this morning. He rolled over, pulling the bedsheet over his head, but Anna was insistent. "You don't want to miss this," she cried. With a herculean effort, he sat up, swung his legs over the edge of the bed, and grabbed a t-shirt and shorts. He trusted Anna. If she said this was something he didn't want to miss, then he figured he'd better not miss it.

Still rubbing the sleep from his eyes, he opened his door slowly and stepped outside—and stood in awe. Directly in front of his house was the most extraordinary sunrise he had ever seen. The sun hung like a huge orange fireball on the horizon with streaks of blood-red flames emanating out in all directions. He was reminded of the sailors' rhyme he used to hear when they were at the beach:

"Red sky at night, sailors delight;
Red sky in the morn, sailors be warned."

It seemed the entire village was gathered at the well, witnessing this fluke of nature. Anna came up beside him. "Aren' ya glad I gotcha up? You would've slept through this." Brendan nodded, staring at the blood-red sunrise. It was truly awe-inspiring, and he was grateful Anna had awoken him. This was one spectacle he wouldn't have wanted to miss, especially since he knew everyone would be talking about it for days.

"Come with me now. This wasn't even the reason I got you up. There's something else even more important you need to see." They walked down the path to Anna's house a few hundred yards away, where several village women were gathered.

"Look what Anjali brought into the world!" she said proudly. Brendan looked. And, for the second time that day, he was awestruck. A tiny human being stared back at him with wide-open eyes. Anjali had gone into labor late at night, and the family had summoned the midwife, along with a collection of other neighbors, to help with the delivery. Home delivery of babies was routine in the village, as the nearest hospital was too far away for a woman in labor to reach. They were lucky to have some highly trained midwives in town. Occasionally things happened that the midwives couldn't handle, yet births were considered a natural part of life and it was a special blessing when a child was born healthy.

There was still a lot of commotion in the house as the midwife attended to Anjali, but outside, Brendan watched as neighbors passed around this new baby boy, just hours old and wrapped tightly in a blanket, so everyone could admire him—quite different from the way a newborn would be treated back home. No hospitals here meant no nurseries either, so babies were immediately handled by many. No wonder babies here grew up so much more quickly, he thought. He imagined the newborn would be walking within six months.

"They are naming him 'Debrak' for the morning sunrise," Anna told him. She was Brendan's go-to person for all things Loscoayan, especially when it came to language. She knew he had difficulty with the language at times and liked to show off her English skills.

Beaming, she continued, "In English I think you would spell it: D-a-y-b-r-e-a-k. It's a good name, don't you think?"

Brendan nodded, trying to absorb all the happenings. It was barely 6:00 a.m., and here he was, greeting a new baby boy after witnessing the most spectacular and awe-inspiring sunrise of his life. What else would this new day bring?

Back at his house, he once again looked at the sun. It still blazed red, though it was a bit less dramatic than it had been a half hour ago. He thought again of that childhood rhyme and realized there was only one thing that would cause this. *Sunspots,* he thought with a chill. *Could this be what caused the compasses to go whacky three days ago?* From his studies of physics, he knew it could take anywhere from eight minutes to three days for a solar flare to be visible from Earth. If there was a major flare three days ago when the compass readings shifted, they could be seeing the remnants of that now.

Quickly, he went inside and pulled out the magnetometer Alejandro had given him. He had been checking it weekly and noticed some small spikes in the last three months, but nothing major. Alejandro had told him that was to be expected. Today however, there was a huge spike *up*. He checked the reading again. Could that be right? Alejandro had said sunspot activity could disrupt the magnetic field of the Earth substantially, but he had predicted a weakening. Or was that in certain areas, while other areas would be strengthened? Brendan made a mental note to investigate that the next time he could get good enough Wi-Fi reception to access the internet. Reception here tended to be spotty at best, but usually late at night he could log on long enough to get answers to some of his basic questions. He needed those answers and wished there were a way to get them faster.

Suddenly he felt scared and isolated, once again haunted by the question raised by one of his students a few days ago when they talked about how a disruption in Earth's magnetic field would affect them: *What if he was stuck here for always?*

Laurie

Exhausted, Laurie and Stan returned home, taking Diego with them. Stan fiddled with the radio as Laurie settled Diego into Brendan's room to rest. When she returned downstairs, the sound of static filled the room. "There's so much background noise. It's impossible to hear anyone clearly." Laurie shivered. Communication of some sort was one of the many things they had taken for granted. A few weeks ago, during the brief outage, the communication network had not been affected. While they realized it could have been, they did not put much thought into the potential ramifications if it were. It was one of those things they were planning to get to but didn't seem urgent at the time. And now they were paying the price. A defunct communication network threw a huge monkey wrench into all the planning they had done over the past few months. At least George had his ham radio. Though it hadn't done them much good last night, she reflected glumly.

When North Becomes South

Laurie thought of Josh and remembered Stan's comment the night before in the car. At the time, he was talking about the compasses, but this event was something else altogether. Or was it? How widespread was this outage? Had Josh's plane taken off as scheduled? She had all his flight information online and hadn't paid much attention to the details. Right now, she wished she had printed it. She had to talk to George and get more information.

"As we were driving early this morning, there were already long lines at the gas stations. Seems like everyone is going into panic mode. That weeklong outage a month ago must have really spooked people," Stan commented. "At least we have our solar panels and can convert the house over from the grid, so we can have power during the daytime. But this lack of news bothers me. We need to know what's happening outside of our neighborhood."

Why? thought Laurie silently. *Who cares about outside this neighborhood?* Aside from knowing that Brendan and Josh were okay, she didn't feel the need to know about anywhere else. Maybe she simply felt jaded and numb, but one thing Laurie appreciated was the more she focused on preparing for the worst here, the less she worried about the larger world. It had been several weeks since she had watched or listened to a national news broadcast, and she now realized she felt a bit unburdened as a result.

North Korea be damned, she thought. They had enough to worry about right here without adding the threat of nuclear war to the mix. Though as she considered that, she realized Brendan and Josh were part of the global world. What was happening to them?

She didn't want to voice her fears aloud. At the moment, she was too exhausted to worry about much other than crawling into bed for a few hours' sleep before heading to the airport to pick up Josh. Between yesterday's scare with the compasses malfunctioning, the birth of a new baby, the sight of a ghostly pale Sophia being wheeled out of her house, and the power outage today, she felt completely overwhelmed. Maybe if she slept long enough, she would awaken to realize it was all a dream—or the worst nightmare she had ever experienced. She collapsed into bed, thinking of Brendan's words to her as they talked about preparing for the worst:

"How much can you possibly save up? For how long? This could go on for years. You need to look at strategies to live with less, not hoard more! The idea that you can save up all this stuff for when you lose power for several years is crazy. It won't work."

Several years? What if this was the start of that? What if he was right?

Josh

As he buckled himself into his seat, Josh wondered if he was crazy to be going home now. Since talking to George a few short days ago, he felt like he had gone on autopilot. He wasn't sure if he was ready for this quick visit. Yet he also knew if he hadn't impulsively leapt at the opportunity when his parents suggested it, he probably would have dragged his feet for weeks, maybe even months. Momentum was on his side now, and it was better to go with the flow.

Briefly, he thought of his date with Marguerite two nights ago. It had indeed been a memorable evening. The sound of her laughter and the way her whole face lit up when she spoke still remained with him. She was the first woman he had been with after many months of celibacy. Smiling to himself, he allowed for a few moments of fantasy. Maybe this could turn into a full-fledged relationship. This was a new feeling given the way he had behaved for years, but he was willing to entertain the thought.

As the plane prepared for take-off, Josh put on his headphones and tuned into the flight deck. He loved listening to the pilots talk with air traffic control. The plane rose into the air and Josh gazed down at the city that had been his home for the past five years. He briefly thought of Amigo, grateful that Steve was willing to take the dog for a couple of days. Below him, the lights of the city twinkled. It looked pretty at night. On the headset, he heard air traffic control. "Flight 432 turn -" He looked out the window again and his heart skipped a beat as the lights below him winked out. The plane jolted slightly, and there was static on the radio.

"Damn! We lost radio contact!" said the pilot and suddenly, all Josh heard was music.

There was a collective gasp from his fellow passengers. Something unusual was happening. One moment, they were looking at the glittering lights of the city, and the next moment it was plunged into darkness.

Great, thought Josh. He looked around the plane. Everyone was sitting bolt upright, as if by making themselves taller in their seats they could somehow have more control over the situation. He slouched further down in his seat hoping the pilot knew what he was doing.

For a while, the plane continued on as if nothing was wrong. And nothing *was* wrong, except for the almost complete darkness below. It was clear to Josh there must have been a massive power outage. People were edgy; but thus far, no information was forthcoming from the flight deck. In the distance, Josh could see a few lights on the ground beneath them, probably powered by emergency generators. He wished the pilot would tell them what was going on.

On the flight deck, the pilot and copilot were arguing. "I'm telling you, that's the El Paso airport," the copilot said. They had set the directional gyro before they left San Diego, and she was certain they had been heading due east since taking off. The sky above them was clear enough that she could easily locate the North Star, and once they had a break in the clouds, it was easy to see the ground. "It has to be El Paso. You can see the runway lights. They must be on generator power. And look, there's the tower with a green light showing. I say we go for it and land there, given there aren't any other major airports around for miles."

"I'm not so sure," the pilot countered. "I agree it's El Paso, but without radio communication, I'm still a little nervous about descending. What if there are other planes in the area?" At least the plane was mechanically functional, and the altimeter seemed to be working. They were at high altitude now, but he worried that as they descended, they would encounter more traffic.

His best guess was that power probably went out on the ground from a solar flare which caused a massive electromagnetic pulse (known to pilots as an EMP). He thanked his lucky stars this was an older model plane, due to be retired within the next month. The newer planes had far more sophisticated electronics which would be much more susceptible to damage by an EMP. He wished they had more information though.

"We can't stay up here forever," the copilot said. "There's still about three hours of darkness left before we'll have more landmarks on the ground. As it gets toward morning, we run the risk of even more air traffic. I say we put down here."

Back in the main cabin, Josh sat up in his seat and looked around. It seemed eerily calm. After that initial small jolt, the plane kept going, yet music was still coming from his headset. He wondered why they couldn't listen in on the conversations of the pilots as they checked in with air traffic control along the route. Every other time he had flown, that had been a normal thing. He peered out the window at the darkness below. Faintly up ahead, he could see a few lights on the ground and a green light coming from a tower. He wondered if that might be an airport.

Others on the plane saw that as well and were pointing to it. People were agitated and more than one passenger asked the flight attendants what was going on. The crew simply smiled and assured people everything was under control, but tension in the cabin was building. Something was clearly out of the ordinary on the ground. Finally, the senior flight attendant spoke to the pilot. "Captain, we need to do something soon to calm the passengers. They all see the darkness below and they're starting to panic."

Glancing at his colleague, the pilot decided to trust the stars and their ability to do a visual and manual landing. His copilot was right, they couldn't stay up there forever. Taking a deep breath, he signaled his flight crew to prepare the plane for landing.

Laurie

After a few hours of sleep, Laurie woke to bright sunlight outside and voices coming from downstairs. Glancing at her bedside clock, she again chided herself for forgetting the power was out. "Guess that part wasn't a dream," she mumbled under her breath as she got out of bed and made her way downstairs where George and Stan were talking.

"I'm telling you, Stan, no airplanes are flying today. With communications as screwed up as they are, there is no way a plane would be landing here. If Josh did take off last night, his plane would have either returned to San Diego or landed somewhere along the way."

"So, you're saying we should not pick him up at the airport?" Laurie asked as she entered the room.

"That's exactly what I'm saying. Wait until things settle down, and then you'll be able to get more information. If you head to the airport now, all you'll be greeted with is confusion, and your presence will simply add to the mess."

"But how will Josh get in touch with us if he needs a ride?" asked Laurie.

"He's a smart, resourceful young man," said George. "He'll get here soon enough. Trust him, Laurie."

Laurie and Stan glanced at each other. Stan shrugged, "I guess George is right. No sense in adding to the craziness in the city today."

"Truth be told, I've never seen anything quite like this," George said. "Losing cell phone service is one thing but having the ham radio signals disrupted is something completely different. It seems to work okay for short distances, like my call to the police dispatch last night. But anything farther is all scrambled. We're still sorting it out. All the major frequencies seem to be jammed."

Laurie nodded, the events of the previous night crashing back. "Is there any word from Alejandro?" she asked.

"No, though I don't know how he'd get word to us if he wanted to," George said. "No communication, remember?"

Vaguely, Laurie remembered Alejandro getting into the ambulance with Sophia. "If we're not going to the airport, maybe we should go to the hospital to see if he needs help."

"How about I go with Diego?" suggested Stan. "I checked on him a few minutes ago and he was sleeping. As soon as he wakes up, we'll head over there. You can stay here and rest up a bit more."

Laurie was grateful for that. Stan was so level-headed, and he would be able to help Alejandro and Sophia navigate the hospital paperwork and other administrative matters if needed. And the rest would certainly do her some good.

Chapter 8
The Day After

Usually, Brendan woke early with the sunrise, but this morning, he labored to rouse himself. The events of the previous day had completely turned him upside down. What had started as an incredible day, with the birth of Debrak and the awe-inspiring sunrise, had quickly turned bleak. Shortly after Brendan returned to his house, as he was studying the magnetometer and wondering about being stuck here 'for always,' Anna came running over in tears.

"It's Anjali!" she wailed. "We thought she was okay, but she kept bleeding. The midwife couldn't save her!"

Brendan was stunned. How was that possible? Back home, delivering a baby was such a routine thing, at least from his perspective. The woman went to the hospital and came home the next day with a newborn. Yet here, with no hospital access, complications from childbirth were apparently far more common.

For the remainder of the day Brendan stayed with Anjali's family, who he now thought of as his own family. He sat with them as countless neighbors came by to offer condolences and support in the care of the new baby. He quickly realized Debrak would be considered a child of the entire village and raised by many mothers, one of whom was already nursing him.

After an exhausting day at his neighbors' house, he had returned to his own house and collapsed into bed, all thoughts of the morning sunrise erased from his mind. He knew he needed to get up and teach the next day. As he struggled to wake up this morning, the events of the previous day weighed heavily on his mind. He wondered how life could go on normally.

He was a bit late to his class, and as he entered the classroom, he couldn't believe his eyes. His students had assembled all the compasses in the center of the room and were talking excitedly over one another. Sensing his presence, the entire group looked up and quieted when they saw him.

"It's happening!" exclaimed Janice. "All the compasses agree. Magnetic north has migrated ten degrees since Friday."

Ten degrees? he thought. "That's not possible," he said aloud.

"Take a look," said Cyrus. He was by far the best student in the class and the one who had taken the most interest in this project. It had been his idea to create a chart with all the data they had collected over the last few weeks, and he regularly checked to make sure everyone entered their information correctly.

Brendan looked at the compasses, neatly lined up with their needles all pointing in the same direction. Then, Cyrus showed him the chart. They had been tracking this for about two months now and Cyrus had carefully plotted out a graph showing the location of magnetic north each day. While there had been extremely slight movement earlier in the month, the graph clearly showed a huge jump in the movement since Friday.

For the past 24 hours, Brendan had been replaying his conversation with Leonard McFay in his head, trying to remember all the physicist had said about the timing of this shift. Like Alejandro, McFay did not think a disaster was imminent. But one thing he said had Brendan worried, and it had jiggled around in his brain since yesterday morning.

"I truly don't think we need to worry right now unless something happens to disrupt the magnetic field in a really big way."

"Like what?" Brendan had asked.

McFay shrugged, "I don't know. Maybe a huge meteor or comet hitting Earth's atmosphere. But it would have to be massive. Or maybe a series of solar flares. I'm sure you know about the Carrington event of 1859. That solar eruption knocked out global telegraph lines and sparked fires all over the Earth. Then, there was an enormous solar flare outburst recently in 2012, a 'solar superstorm.' Something like that could have done all sorts of damage, but it was on the side of the sun facing away from Earth at the time, and all the damaging rays went out into the universe. If Earth had been on the other side of the sun at that time, it would have disrupted the magnetic field and wreaked all sorts of havoc on our planet. Something like that might be enough to trigger this shift to happen faster. We simply have no way of predicting that right now."

Recalling how the sun looked yesterday, Brendan wondered if this was all connected. He wanted to do more research on the internet, but the Wi-Fi connection had been down for the past several days. That in and of itself was not unusual here in the village, but it was still frustrating. At any rate, he had a class to teach and couldn't worry about all that right now. The best he could do was try to incorporate this into his lesson planning, as his students continued to have a focused interest in the topic. He took out his magnetometer and showed it to the class. "Today, we're going to talk about magnetic field strength," he said.

Laurie

Laurie woke early as usual. She thought briefly of getting up to meditate but didn't have the energy to get out of bed. She curled up against Stan, her face still wet from tears, wishing she could turn back the clock.

She couldn't get her neighbor's pleading face out of her mind and remembered the last coherent words Sophia had spoken to her, just a few moments before Dawn was born. *"Take care of our new baby. We are naming her Dawn, for the start of a new day."* How could things have gone so wrong? It seemed like the world had completely turned upside down in the space of a few short hours. How could they possibly go on?

And yet, she knew they had to, if not for themselves, then for the sake of Sophia's children. Diego needed a mother now more than ever, and baby Dawn…well, Laurie vowed she would do everything in her power to ensure this child had the life that Sophia had wished for her.

The day before, when Stan and Diego arrived at the hospital, they found a dazed Alejandro, desperately trying to get more information from the overworked medical staff. "Please, I don't understand!" he was tugging on the sleeve of an extremely harried doctor. Although he spoke English fairly well, he was having difficulty navigating all the medical terms. The stress of the day made it even more difficult for him to communicate in a foreign language. Stan quickly took charge and helped translate.

"I'm telling you—we did all we could, and it wasn't enough." The doctor tried to keep his voice calm. "When she got here, your wife had lost a large amount of blood. She needed a transfusion, and we were able to give her a little, but then we ran out of her blood type, and with the internet down, we couldn't get any more. No internet meant no access to the blood bank database. All that information is stored online."

Stan shook his head sadly. Even though a routine transfusion probably would have saved Sophia, they couldn't obtain the blood without a way to get into the database. Apparently, life or death depended on technology far more than they realized. The doctors had done their best, but it wasn't enough. He gently took Alejandro's arm as awareness of what the doctor was saying began to sink in. Alejandro stood rooted to the ground, unable to speak. Stan guided him slowly to a chair and asked Diego to watch him. The boy simply nodded through the tears in his eyes. He, too, seemed numb.

There was no way Alejandro could bring the newborn home yet, so Stan arranged for her to stay at the hospital for a few days. Suddenly, Alejandro yelled to him from across the room. "Dawn!" Alejandro exclaimed.

"What?" asked Stan.

"Dawn! Sophia and I want to name our baby Dawn for the start of a new day." Alejandro had stood again and was waving his arms frantically, as Diego tried to calm him. "Make sure you tell them! Her name is Dawn!" Stan was grateful for Diego's presence, as the boy somehow managed to settle his father down. It was difficult enough navigating all the paperwork without the internet, and he didn't need the added distraction. The nursing staff was as bewildered as he was. Finally, he hustled Alejandro away after promising they would return in the next day or two once power was restored to complete all the necessary documents. Then they peeked into the nursery to check on baby Dawn. As far as they could tell she was being well cared for.

As they exited the hospital one of the nurses ran up to them, exhaustion showing on her face. She had clearly worked the night shift. "Wait! I have an idea for you. You're the father of baby Dawn, right?" Alejandro simply nodded.

"I feel horrible for your loss. We tried so hard to save her. At least your daughter seems healthy but you're going to have to figure out how to feed her when she leaves the hospital in a few days. We're giving her formula we have here, but that might be hard to get once she's discharged, especially if the power remains out for more than a day or two and grocery stores are closed. Even if power comes back on, though, there might be a better option."

Stan and Alejandro looked at her questioningly. With all the turmoil of the past several hours, neither of them had given much thought to how they would feed baby Dawn.

"Infants can't drink cow's milk, but they *can* drink goat's milk. In fact, goat's milk is remarkably like human mother's milk. I know this because I have a cousin who owns a farm and raises goats. Here's his address. You may want to pay him a visit in the next day or so and see if you can arrange to get some goat's milk from him for the next few months, until the baby can tolerate other food." She handed Alejandro a slip of paper with an address scribbled on it.

Alejandro looked completely overwhelmed as he took the paper. "Thank you," he whispered. "You are very kind."

Stan ushered Alejandro and Diego out of the hospital and into his car. He dreaded telling Laurie the news. He knew it would devastate her, given how close she and Sophia had become during the last few months. Indeed, once they reached home and Laurie heard what had happened, she could barely breathe. *Sophia!* How was this even possible?

For Laurie, the entire rest of the day was a blur. Bad news traveled quickly through the grapevine, and countless neighbors came by to console Alejandro. Much as she wanted to help, Laurie remained locked in her room, secluded from the constant traffic of people in and out of the house across the street. Chaos engulfed their quiet little neighborhood as people congregated outside, talking and clamoring for information. Rumors abounded. Their neighbor George had his hands full explaining how even though he could communicate over a short range, longer-range communication was down everywhere. The inability to connect with the outside world made everyone wary and on edge, even more so than they had been a few weeks ago.

Added to their grief for Sophia, Laurie and Stan were desperate for information about Josh, but it was impossible to track his whereabouts. Laurie couldn't believe they had gone back to not knowing if he was alive or dead, after speaking with him a few short days ago. It simply didn't seem possible.

And of course, she was anxious to get in touch with Brendan, to tell him about the hectic happenings and tragedy of the previous day and make sure he was okay. Earlier she had scoffed at Stan's concern for the wider world, yet now she realized maybe she *was* a little worried about the larger world after all. At least where it concerned Brendan and Josh.

She also desperately needed to know more about this latest outage. Was it the start of something bigger? Just yesterday, she had hoped the outage would last a short time and life would go back to normal. Now she wondered what "normal" truly meant. Normal had become a waiting game, a time of preparing for the worst when they didn't even know what the worst would be or when it would come. It was kind of a paradoxical existence. Even if the power did come back on soon, how could life go back to normal without Sophia, especially for Alejandro and his family?

She had a lot of questions for Alejandro, though she knew he was in no way able to process this right now. *One day at a time,* she thought. She needed to focus on getting through today, helping Alejandro with the new baby, and helping Diego cope with the loss of his mother. Then, she could worry about Josh and Brendan. Somehow, they would find a way through this.

Josh

Josh looked up at the 20-foot-high wall. While he had heard about it for several years and seen picture after picture on the internet, witnessing it up close was an entirely different experience.

Since arriving in El Paso, Josh had been trying to figure out his next steps. The previous day was all muddled in his mind. From the moment the plane landed in El Paso, everything felt surreal. One by one, the shaken passengers had exited the aircraft, thanking the flight crew profusely as they ventured into the darkened airport. It was disconcertingly still in the gate area, and people talked in whispered tones. Somehow, the darkness made everyone wary. The flight crew cautioned them to stick around as they hoped to take off again once power was restored, though no one had any idea when that would be. There was nothing to do, as all shops, kiosks and restaurants were closed at 2:00 a.m., with the terminal running on limited generator power.

Immediately upon deplaning, Josh turned on his handheld ham radio. He was disappointed to find all he could hear was static. Whatever had disrupted the power seemed to have messed up radio communication as well. After sitting at the gate for a while, Josh decided to search for a local police dispatch office. He thought there must be a police station at the airport. Maybe if they had a ham radio setup there, it would have better reception and a stronger signal, and he might be able to communicate with either Steve in San Diego or George at home.

When he finally found the headquarters, located in the main airport terminal, it was quiet though the young dispatcher looked harried. The bulk of the airport terminal had switched to generator power, yet not all areas were covered. With all the usual channels of communication down, he had been fielding walk-in callsfor several hours. People were coming in for all sorts of things, from needing medical attention and finding lost children, to cars that couldn't get out of the parking garage because the electronic gates were stuck in the closed position. He had even helped the airport maintenance crew assist some people trapped in an elevator. However, by the time Josh came in at 3:00 a.m. things had calmed down considerably.

Unfortunately, the man had no information for Josh. All he knew was that the usual ways of communication weren't working, and there was no effective emergency backup. He looked at Josh blankly when asked if the department had any ham radio operators.

As a blood-red sun rose above the city of El Paso, Josh walked out of the airport, hoping to find some way to get word to people in his life that he was okay. He had already put his family through one round of wondering if he was dead or alive and felt enormous guilt about that. The last thing he wanted to do was put them through hell again. He spent the day seeking help at the city's police and fire stations, which were all in turmoil. He learned there was a limited ham radio network in the city, similar to what San Diego had about six months ago, and the network that existed was not tied into any police or fire dispatch systems. After visiting the fifth firehouse in town, one of the dispatchers connected him with a friend who he thought dabbled in ham radio technology. Address in hand, Josh went to the man's house, only to be disappointed when he was told the man had passed away several months ago. Another dead end.

When North Becomes South

As evening approached, Josh decided to return to the airport in case power was restored but regretted that decision a few minutes after getting into a taxi. With traffic lights out, roads were snarled all over the city and tempers were flaring. "You sure you want to go to the airport?" his cab driver asked over the sound of beeping horns and swearing drivers. "It may take several hours to get there."

He told the driver to keep going, thinking to himself, "I have no place else to go." Eventually, though, the cab driver gave up and suggested he walk the remaining mile. It seemed the entire city was in gridlock. He finally reached the airport, only to find it in complete bedlam. He tried to make out individual voices among the deafening noise of chattering people but couldn't. Between babies crying, parents yelling at their kids and each other, and people milling aimlessly about, Josh realized there was no way he could get back to the gate area, even if power were restored. It was going to take days for authorities to sort out who was going where and figure out how to get people to their destinations. He felt strangely claustrophobic in this crowd of anxious people and wished he could talk to someone, but no one looked approachable. He had never experienced a mob at flash point, yet he suspected the situation at the airport was fast approaching that.

At least he hadn't checked a bag on his flight, he thought. Glancing around, he realized many people were camping at the airport for the night. He wondered if he should do the same. At the very least, it would save him the cost of a hotel for one night. Since there was no space indoors to sit, he went outside and found an isolated bench. He sat down, contemplating what to do next. How long should he wait here? He was starting to feel quite hungry. A few stores were open but from what he had seen, most of the shelves were already bare of food. He did have a few small snacks with him, but a handful of trail mix wasn't going to last him long. And what about water? Luckily, after the plane had landed, flight attendants had handed out bottles of water and snacks to the passengers as they were deplaning, and he still had about half bottle remaining. He had also gotten another bottle at one of the fire stations he'd visited. But what would happen when that ran out? He clearly needed a plan if this power outage didn't get resolved soon. He wondered if he would be better off in the city rather than here among the airport chaos. Idly, he pulled out his phone and his wireless ham radio and stared at them. While he could turn them on, neither device was capable of anything else. *So much for technology*, he thought. Sighing, he decided to attempt to get a few hours of sleep and make a plan in the morning.

Early the next morning he left the airport once again, opting to take his chances in the city though he still didn't quite have a strategy in mind. Exhausted, hungry, and with no idea of where to go, he was hoping for some kind of divine intervention when he came face-to-face with the border wall. Even though he'd seen pictures of it on the internet, the sheer enormity of it astounded him. It had clearly been hastily constructed and looked so out of place and imposing in what should have been a beautiful city. This is the true edge of our country, he thought to himself. Despite the fact that San Diego was a border city as well, the fencing there seemed a lot less stark.

"This wall will be our downfall," a man standing near him muttered.

Josh glanced at the man. He was short, with dark, swarthy features and appeared to be South American, yet judging by his speech, he had been in the U.S. for a long time. He was simply standing there, hands in the pockets of his long trench coat, staring at the wall, just as Josh was doing.

"I wish it wasn't here," Josh offered hesitantly.

"That makes two of us," the man said. "Though you may not realize the folly of it as much as I do."

"What do you mean?" asked Josh. For some reason, he took an instant liking to this man, the first person he managed to have a decent conversation with since landing in El Paso.

"My family was deported to Ecuador a few days ago. I should have gone with them but thought it better to stay here for a short while longer. Now I'm not so sure."

"I'm sorry," Josh said, at a loss for words.

The man looked at him. "No need to apologize on your part. I simply think we will all be regretting this construction sooner than we may have thought." He seemed lost in thought, then suddenly looked at Josh and smiled. "Sorry... I was mumbling to myself. My name's Pablo."

"I'm Josh,"

"What brings you here Josh?" asked Pablo.

"I'm actually not supposed to be here. I mean, I was traveling from San Diego to Boston when the power went out and our plane landed in El Paso. Honestly, I don't know what I'm doing here. Right now, I'm just wandering around, trying to find some way to communicate with family and friends and let them know I'm still alive."

"So, you are separated from your family as well," said Pablo slowly. "I guess we have something in common."

"Why didn't you go with them when they were deported? Could you have gone?" Josh asked.

"I could have, but I had a job here and we needed the money. I teach Spanish at the local university. I have a lot of connections here—friends who told me they could help us. But now, I'm not so sure. Many of my closest friends are science teachers, and they are all very worried about other things right now. Climate change and the movement of -"

"Earth's magnetic poles." Josh interrupted. Pablo looked at him with surprise. "I know about that," Josh continued. "We've been following it closely in San Diego, trying to get local people involved in preparations. I'm not a scientist, but I've been helping the San Diego Fire Department set up emergency communications. I have a lot of experience with ham radios."

Pablo studied him for a moment. "I wonder if one of my colleagues at the university might be able to help you or you could help him. I know a few people who have dabbled with ham radios. Perhaps, I can introduce you to them."

Now it was Josh's turn to break into a smile. "That would be great! I need to get in touch with my family, to let them know I am okay."

"I don't know how long it will take me to reach them. Where are you staying?"

Josh looked away. "Nowhere, right now. Last night, I stayed at the airport, but I'm sure not doing that again. It was insane there. Like I said, I don't have a plan." He thought back to a year ago, when he had slept on the beach in San Diego. While that hadn't been the first time he'd found himself on the street overnight, he had hoped it would be the last. He sighed. "I've slept out in the open before and I suppose I could do it again if needed."

Pablo was watching him intently. "My friend, in this city, it isn't safe to sleep on the streets—ever. Especially now, with people nervous about the power outage. Already, there has been looting downtown, and it is only the beginning. With my wife and daughter gone, I have extra room at my apartment. Why don't you stay with me until the power gets restored?"

"Really?" Josh asked. "Are you sure? I mean, we just met..."

"Yes, I'm sure," answered Pablo smiling. "You need a place to stay and I could use the company. It will get my mind off the worry about my family. I live in a small apartment above a bakery with the best scones in town." Josh's mouth began to water. He hadn't realized how hungry he was.

"Unfortunately, the shop is closed today," Pablo continued. "My landlord owns it and briefly opened yesterday to sell off all his baked goods from the day before. The line was unbelievably long. I imagine he's pretty much cleaned out by now. Luckily, though, I have quite a bit of food stored in my house. My wife and I have been stocking up for a while just in case something like this were to happen."

For Josh, true hunger had never been an issue. The concept of worrying about where his next meal was coming from was completely foreign to him. He had always assumed he could get something to eat, somewhere, even if it was a snack from a local convenience store. Suddenly, it hit him that might not be an option, especially if this outage continued for the next few days. He looked at this man he barely knew and felt overwhelmed with his kindness. How was it his own people were so hateful and bigoted? For a moment, he was ashamed to be American—ashamed of how badly his country had treated immigrants. Shouldering his bag, he turned and followed Pablo away from the wall.

Chapter 9
Three Days After

Brendan was worried. It had been three days since the blood-red sunrise, and according to all the compasses his students had, it was clear the magnetic north pole of the Earth was moving, and quite erratically as well. Furthermore, he had been unable to access the internet all week and his phone was out of service. While internet and Wi-Fi connections were often sporadic in his village, cell phone coverage was generally good, so this increased his worry even more. He wanted to communicate with his mom, and he especially wanted to talk to Josh and find out what had happened.

Despite his worries, however, he was amazed at how every other aspect of life in the village remained unaffected, so he tried to put his anxiety aside. He watched as his neighbors went through the process of planning Anjali's funeral. As difficult as it was, this too seemed almost routine for the people of this village. They were far more accustomed to death than he was. Everyone still rose early each morning and got their water from the well, and the foot traffic outside his window was relentless starting at 4:30 a.m.

The basics of life went on: cooking, cleaning, doing laundry, planting, harvesting, and for children, going to school. He was grateful for one thing; for the past few days, his physics students were attending class in record numbers due to their renewed interest in the compasses. Often students skipped school when they had more pressing chores to do at home, but lately they were all showing up with eagerness to learn more. As a class, they were monitoring the strength of Earth's magnetic field and were fascinated to learn how that field protected them from all sorts of dangerous, though invisible, radiation from outer space. It had been a good opportunity for Brendan to introduce some more advanced physics concepts and the students were absorbing the knowledge better than he had expected. He was amazed at what a little interest could do for learning.

Sitting on his porch after his morning classes, he was surprised to see a white van drive up the dirt road toward his house. Rarely did a car venture into the village proper, even though the town was situated along the main road that ran north from Troeburg through the country. As he peered at it, he recognized the TeachAfrica van. Usually one or two workers would stop by his house once a month to check up on him, deliver his anti-malaria medications and make sure things were going smoothly within the community. He was puzzled by their appearance as it had only been two weeks since their previous visit.

"G' Mornin' Brendan!" Brendan rose and greeted the two liaisons, Sam and Maria.

"Hi," he said. "What are you doing here?"

Sam and Maria exchanged a look. "I guess you don' know about what's going on in the world, eh?" Sam said.

"What do you mean?"

"There's been a big power disruption all over. We can' call anyone on the phone so we're visitin' all the villages to make sure you have everythin' you need right now."

"How big of a power disruption?" asked Brendan worriedly.

"We don' know, but it seems like it may be all over the place. Everythin's shut down right now. The TeachAfrica office sent us to tell you to stay in place, in your village, for the next few weeks until things get sorted out."

"But I was planning to go into the city this weekend to get money," said Brendan.

Sam handed Brendan a large wad of cash. "This should keep you in decent shape for a while. Banks are shut down right now, so even if you were to go to Troeburg, you wouldn't be able to take out any money. Nothin's workin', and the city is becoming a li'l bit of a powder keg. We want you to stay away from there. Just stay here. You are safest here. We talked to your landlord, and your rent is all set for a while. We think you will be better off here."

"Banks are shut down?"

"*Everything* is shut down," replied Maria. "It may get very ugly soon if this doesn't resolve and no one quite knows what the problem is. We want you to stay here, okay?"

"How can I communicate with you? What if I need something?" asked Brendan.

"We'll be coming back through in a few weeks," said Maria. She and Sam were both native to Loscoaya, but Maria had spent several years in the U.S. and spoke flawless English. "We're driving north to check on all the workers in villages there. That's the other thing. We may relocate some of them and since you have a two-bedroom house and you're closer to the capital, we may pull someone out of a more remote village and bring them here to stay with you for a bit. If we do that, we'll drop them off here on our way back."

"It shouldn' be too long. You have good neighbors who can help you in an emergency, right?" Sam added.

Brendan nodded slowly, thinking about the prescient nature of his dad's advice about finding a mom. He had a million questions and thought of telling them about Anjali, but Sam and Maria didn't have much more information, and they seemed anxious to get on the road. Brendan understood that. They had enormous ground to cover in the next few weeks if they were going to all the remote villages where workers were posted.

"In the meantime, stay here, in your village until further notice, okay?" Maria said. She had always been very motherly and protective towards him and Brendan appreciated that. She flashed him a quick smile and gave him a thumbs up as they drove off.

Brendan was left with Sam's statements racing around in his head *I guess you don't know about what's going on in the world…Everything's shut down right now… Big power disruption, all over… city is becoming a powder keg….*

How was this even possible? And what was happening farther away—at home? Were they experiencing a big power disruption as well? With thoughts of his family back home crowding his mind, he made his way to Anna's house. When he was home a few months ago, his mom had bought some newborn baby clothes and he had told Anna he would bring them over. It would be good for him to see the new baby, and he knew the family appreciated his presence.

His neighbors were indeed happy to see him. "Have you talked with your brother yet?" asked Talah.

Brendan looked at her, surprised she remembered, given all the activity of the last few days. They had lost a daughter and had a new baby to care for, yet they were always looking out for him as well.

"I haven't been able to speak to my family for a few days," he said. "There's been no cell phone service and no internet. And today, people from TeachAfrica visited and told me this is a big problem, maybe all over the world. I don't even know if my parents have power where they are."

Anna looked up. "That could be very hard for them, if they're not used to living that way, right?"

"You have no idea how hard it would be," he said quietly. He remembered talking to his mom about adapting to a changing environment and fervently hoped this wasn't the start of that for them. And what about Josh? "I don't even know if my brother made it home," he added.

"Well," said Talah, "there's no sense worryin' about that right now. I imagine phones will be working soon enough. At least here we're used to livin' with no current and no internet."

She was right, thought Brendan. Nothing seemed out of place here, even with *everything shut down*. He supposed this was one advantage of not being connected to the power grid—life didn't get too disrupted when the grid shut down everywhere else in the world. Yet his life felt like it was in such flux right now. How could he *not* worry about his brother and his parents?

Laurie

Rumors were flying all over the place. "The beginning of the end... the Apocalypse... power lost all over the world." It was impossible to get any information at all, let alone to know if that information was accurate or not. In the span of a day, they had gone from a world flooded with too much news to no news at all.

Police, along with those appointed to the neighborhood watch group, were going door-to-door to check on people, and outside, there were handwritten paper flyers on every tree and lamppost announcing a special town gathering at noon today. Laurie and Stan were torn. They wanted to be with Alejandro when he picked up his infant daughter, but they also felt like they should be at the meeting. Finally, they decided to split up. Since Stan had started much of the paperwork at the hospital, he went with Alejandro and Diego while Laurie carpooled to the meeting with her neighbors Lisa and Sally.

Laurie and Stan were also worried about their house. With banks, grocery stores and all retail stores shuttered, there had been some looting in town. Their recently installed state-of-the-art security system depended totally on technology and did not include a simple deadbolt lock on the door. Ultimately, they decided to lock everything they could and hope for the best. As a forlorn Alejandro got into the car with Stan, Laurie once again promised him she would help with Dawn and Diego as much as possible.

When North Becomes South

The meeting room was jam-packed—way more so than for a typical town meeting. When the town did its yearly business, town leaders struggled to get a quorum of voters to attend, but today, it seemed like the entire town was present. People wanted answers, though Laurie wondered how many answers this meeting would provide. She hoped things wouldn't turn ugly if people began to panic at some bad news.

The Town Manager stood up to address the restless crowd. He was a big, burly man, with a commanding presence and a deep, clear voice. Thankfully, a generator was running and there was a workable microphone. "Ladies and gentlemen," he began. "We know this has been a tough couple of days and we have been trying to get as much information for you as possible. Unfortunately, with the scope of this power outage, that has been extremely difficult. I want to first remind you that we have been in this position before. In fact, just last month, when power was shut down to the entire East Coast of the U.S. for a full week, we all survived. So, first and foremost, I urge you not to panic. We got through it then, and we'll get through it now." Laurie fidgeted in her seat as she listened. This outage was different. She knew it and she wondered if he knew it as well. Deep down, she felt like the entire town leadership was still in denial. If this went on for much longer than a week, their lives would all be in ruins. Already, their basic needs were not being met. Banks were shut down, as were retail and grocery stores. How much longer could they all hold on? She looked around and saw others were also annoyed. The restlessness of the crowd was palpable as people whispered to their neighbors.

Clearing his throat, he continued. "The difference with this outage, though, is that communication is also disrupted, so it has been tough to get any information as to how widespread it is and what exactly has caused it. Our local ham radio operators have been working around the clock, trying to get an idea of what is going on, but even that technology has been disrupted. Right now, those radios are only working over a short range. While we do have communication with neighboring towns, most of what we are learning is through a relay system and it takes time to get responses. I want to take this opportunity to extend our thanks and appreciation to all the radio operators. They're all volunteers, and they've done a heroic job of helping us gather information during this incredibly chaotic time. Without them, we would be completely out of touch with the rest of the world." There was a smattering of applause as Laurie scanned the room looking for George. She was sure he was there but couldn't spot him in the crowd.

As people began murmuring again, the moderator once again cleared his throat. Raising his voice, he instantly commanded attention. All side conversations ceased, as the crowd looked at him expectantly. He continued in what he hoped was a reassuring tone, "Here's what we've been able to piece together so far. We believe this is a worldwide phenomenon sparked by unusual sunspot activity several days ago. If any of you were able to witness a sunrise or sunset in the past few days, you may have noticed some red flares emanating from the sun. Experts here believe this event disrupted power grids everywhere. Those solar flares lasted for over two days, so they had the potential to damage every power substation on Earth."

There was a collective gasp from the crowd, as the seriousness of this news began to sink in. Laurie immediately thought of Josh. *Power grids everywhere...* Had his plane taken off before the power went out? Or was he still in California? She squeezed her eyes tightly closed, trying to block the nightmare unfolding in front of her.

"As terrifying as that may sound, it may be better than an alternative scenario, such as a nuclear blast from one of our enemies overseas. We are confident at this point that the perpetrator of this event was our sun, not a foreign country, and that our entire planet was affected. Our global enemies are as incapacitated as we are right now.

"The problem is because this is so widespread, we have no idea how long the power will be out. The people who need to fix it are all regular folks, like you and me, with families to care for and their own wellbeing to worry about. *Everyone's* life has been turned upside down. Getting a working infrastructure in place to do the work is a challenge. It could be another day, or a week, or even longer. Yet the last thing we want is for people to panic. We know you all need food and water, and we've set up an emergency system for people to obtain supplies from several local grocery and hardware stores. The police and other volunteers will be visiting each household and you will be assigned a number and a time when you can get what you need. Initially, we are operating this like a food stamp program. Every family will be given a voucher for rationed supplies based on the size of your household. For now, we ask you to keep any cash on hand that you have, and only use these vouchers.

"Remember, we are all in this together. We must apportion our supplies town-wide. That includes food, gasoline, and other necessities. As far as gasoline goes, we ask you to be judicious and only use your vehicles if necessary. I have talked with leaders in other nearby towns, and they are all doing the same thing. This may be a global problem, but for now it is up to us to deal with it locally." Laurie was paralyzed with worry about both Brendan and Josh. For her, the local problems paled in comparison to not knowing what was happening to her two boys. She thought Brendan was probably okay, but the thin thread that always connected them was communication, and without that, her worry increased a hundred-fold. And the uncertainty of Josh's whereabouts threatened to derail her completely. With an effort, she turned her attention back to the speaker.

"Finally, we are going to give a status update each day at noon until this crisis is resolved. This is where you should come for information. This is where you should come if you have a problem you can't figure out for yourself. There are numerous ham radio operators in town with access to police dispatch most of the time. That method may not be as quick or as easy as we would like due to magnetic disruptions, but it is still our best option for communication. Each neighborhood has a radio operator assigned to it and you can get that information here before you leave. However, we ask you to please let these operators do their local civil service job. I know you may be concerned with family in other parts of the country and the world, but for now, we need to focus on our needs here. There will be time down the road to broaden our vision and check on other communities.

"In closing, I want to thank you all for coming today, and I encourage you to stay calm and keep your wits about you. Together, we will get through this."

There was silence in the room as the Town Manager stepped down and the Moderator stood up. "I'm going to give you a few minutes to ask questions. We request you do this in an orderly way, like at town meetings. Please come forward to a microphone if you want to speak."

As a long line began to form at the microphone, one of the townspeople stood up on a chair. "You didn't tell us a thing," he shouted. "How are we supposed to survive with no running water and no power? What are our taxes paying for, anyway? We elected you to govern us, and it looks like you're all just passing the buck. What are *you all* doing to help us?"

"Sir, if you will get in line and go to the microphone, we'll address your question in order," said the Police Chief.

"Screw that, I ain't waiting in another line! I waited in line two hours for gas yesterday, and when I got up there, they said I could only get two gallons! How're you going to fix that?"

Mumblings of agreement came from the crowd. Police officers surrounded the man, pulling him off his perch as the townspeople became increasingly agitated. Everyone had a question and the mood was shifting from one of quiet listening to one of anger. The Town Manager, Police Chief, and Fire Chief patiently fielded questions as best as they could, yet rumors of widespread panic and looting in some of the nearby major cities had people on edge. As town officials confirmed those stories, people became even more upset. Someone overturned a chair, and soon, several others did the same. The atmosphere in the room was starting to turn ugly.

"STOP NOW!" yelled the Police Chief into the microphone.

Miraculously, the crowd quieted. "This is *exactly* what we are hoping to avoid. Our town is better than this! Where is your common sense? We know you're all stressed—believe me, we are too! But rioting here isn't going to fix things. Go home and be with your families. Organize your neighbors! Use your head!"

The message was clear: stay in place and everything should work out. But as they walked out of the building, Laurie was reminded of Brendan's question to her when he saw them stocking up on supplies. "*For how long?*" Did they truly have a strategy in place for long-term survival? The last time had only been a week, and by the end of that week, everyone's nerves were frayed, and that was with outside communication providing a timeline for repair. This felt totally different. She desperately wished Alejandro was in better shape to talk about this, as she had a premonition this was far more ominous than a short-term power outage. Six months earlier, both Alejandro and Sophia had been confident a major crisis was not imminent, but as she thought about the compasses malfunctioning a few days ago, she was convinced this event had affected the migration of the magnetic poles in a major way. Alejandro needed time to grieve and get his feet back on the ground, but she also felt they needed to know the extent of this crisis. He was the only one she could think of who truly knew what was going on.

On returning home, Laurie gathered the baby clothes she had purchased a few weeks earlier and she and Stan walked across the street to deliver them. A haggard and exhausted Alejandro opened the door. The past few days had taken a toll on him. Added to that, Diego had gone on a rampage after being unable to access the internet and was currently upstairs in his room sobbing.

As Laurie cradled baby Dawn in her arms, Alejandro invited them down to the basement. Despite the trauma of the past three days, he seemed anxious to unburden himself and glad Laurie and Stan were there to hear him out.

Many of the instruments were functioning on solar power, and they had about an hour of daylight left to look at them.

"Look at these maps," he said. "There was a solar flare a few days ago, causing magnetic north to jump almost ten degrees. That's huge! The movement has slowed a little since then, but it's still going faster than before and it's far more erratic.

"We see the strength of the field here," he continued, pointing to some other instruments. "It's weakening over much of the Earth, especially over the north and south poles, but strengthening over the equator. I believe as the poles migrate, the weak zones will continue to expand which means both the northern and southern hemispheres will become increasingly exposed to galactic and solar radiation. It's possible there could be a 'safe zone' over the equator that might stay protected for at least a little while. Leonard McFay talked about this a lot, but no one truly listened to him. If that's true, eventually, the only safe places on our planet may be south of us."

"How long would this take to happen?" asked Stan.

"It's so hard to know," replied Alejandro. "This is all uncharted territory in science. This flip of the poles has occurred hundreds of times during Earth's history, yet we have no way of knowing how long it took each time. Our best estimate has been anywhere from 100 to 1,000 years, but that's just a guess. Potentially, it could happen in 50 years, or 10 years. Or even shorter. Maybe there is a tipping point, and it's instantaneous. Truthfully, we don't know. All we can do is monitor the movement and chart the changes. Right now, there isn't much change in the magnetic field strength here, which is a good thing. So, I don't think we need to worry about that yet. But there might come a time when we may either have to move south or live underground for a while."

Move south or live underground? Laurie thought. *How were they supposed to adapt to that?* Once again, she felt like her world was being turned upside down.

Josh

Josh stared out the window of Pablo's second-floor apartment. He felt trapped. Just yesterday, he had woken up to the sound of glass breaking and loud footfalls on the ground. Peeking out from the side of the curtains, he had seen three men running with packages under their arms. Within seconds, they turned a corner and were gone from view.

"Pablo, wake up," he had called across the hallway. Pablo opened his door a crack. "Looters. Down on the street below. I think they broke into the bakery."

Pablo nodded. "I'm not surprised."

"Shouldn't we—" Josh checked himself as Pablo simply shook his head. He was about to ask if they should call the landlord who owned the bakery. No power. No cell phones. He had to keep reminding himself of that.

"I told you there would likely be looting, and the streets would be unsafe. I warned my landlord as well, and he said he would come this morning to board up the windows." Pablo said. "People are scared. Even in the best of circumstances many of them don't know where their next meal is coming from. They live paycheck to paycheck and have no safety net. Take away water and electricity and they may as well be living on a deserted island."

Staring out the window now on the third day with no power, Josh wondered how much more of this he could take. "What do you suggest we do today? Is it even safe to go out?" The day before, they had ventured out to search for Pablo's colleague, whom he thought dabbled with ham radios, but the man had not reported to work, and no one knew where to find him. One more dead end, thought Josh.

The police were out in force, ineffectively trying to direct traffic and keep order in the city. To Josh, it seemed not much had changed since his first day in El Paso when he rode in a taxi back to the airport. Amid horns beeping and drivers cursing, more than one officer yelled at them to go home and stay home. After looking at one closed business after another, they decided to follow his advice and returned to Pablo's house to wait things out. The message was clear: the streets were not safe. Josh wondered how secure the apartment was. Did anyone know of Pablo's stockpile of supplies?

"We need to stay inside at least for a while longer. Let the looters take their goods. There's not much we can do to stop it at this point. I have a lot of food stored up, and lots of jugs of clean water as well. It won't last us forever; hopefully, things will calm down in a few days. If not, I suppose we may have to scavenge a bit."

"Scavenge for clean water?" asked Josh. "How are we going to do that?"

"We shouldn't have to scavenge for water. Luckily, the University put in a well recently. That was one of the emergency measures they initiated when power was lost on the East Coast. It's driven by a generator, so as long as there is gas for the generator, the pump will work. It also has a manual backup. If generator power is lost, we can pump it by hand. Hopefully, it won't come to that, but you never know. We may have to scavenge for food, though. I don't know how long my supply will last."

"Pablo, do you really think this is, like, permanent?" Josh asked hesitantly. He knew this was serious but hadn't imagined power loss for good. "I mean, how much damage was done to the grid?"

"It's not about how much damage, Josh," Pablo replied. He spoke matter-of-factly, yet Josh wondered if he was starting to lose it. They had only known each other for two days, but those two days felt like a lifetime, and already Josh felt like he knew Pablo relatively well. Pablo continued with a hint of exasperation in his voice. "If you believe the rumor mill, this outage is massive in scope. It's possible many other cities in the country are experiencing this same thing, which means there needs to be a coordinated effort to repair the damage. Who's in charge? Do you think the President has a clue how to deal with this situation? Think about it. The utility workers—all the people who should be out there fixing this—are all suddenly in survival mode, caring for their families and making sure their own basic needs are met. So, right now, there is no organized workforce anywhere."

Josh considered this. Yesterday, it had been spooky walking around town. Everything was closed: banks, grocery stores, retail stores, restaurants, even gas stations. The few open ones were running on generator power and accepted cash only. Lines of cars stretched as far as the eye could see. Several of these stations also had convenience stores although their shelves were almost empty. With no banks open, people would run out of cash fast, and what then? No wonder looting had started. People were hungry and beginning to panic. Society was crumbling right before their eyes as the financial and retail world fell apart.

And what about other places in the country? As Pablo said, rumor had it this outage was massive in scope. Was there power in San Diego? Josh shuddered as he suddenly recalled the moment of the outage, something he had blocked from his mind. Moments after taking off from the San Diego airport, he was admiring the city below when the lights went out. So, yes, this outage did extend that far west. *And how far east?* he now wondered. Was it possible his parents in Connecticut had lost power as well?

As a tidal wave of worry threatened to engulf him, he was snapped out of his thoughts by the now familiar sound of breaking glass in the distance, this time followed by several gunshots and a police siren. He was beginning to feel like they were living in a war zone and wondered if they would ever escape. Where could they go? Was any place safe? Shaking his head, he muttered, "Guess we do need to stay in today." *All because of a loss of power for a few days,* he thought.

Chapter 10
Six Months After

The sound of birds chirping and chickens squawking outside roused Laurie from a fitful slumber. Time had new meaning now. They no longer used clocks. They woke when the sun rose and went to bed when it set. It was springtime, but though the days were warmer, there was an early morning chill in the air. Shivering, she quickly dressed, putting on her warmest sweatshirt, and went downstairs to stoke the fire. Fire was their friend. The constant blaze in the fireplace kept the house relatively warm, and they used it to cook as well as to keep a steady supply of boiled water from the well, since bottled water had long since vanished.

It had been a difficult week. Several days ago, Lisa told her their family was leaving town. Her youngest son, Kevin, had severe asthma and they recently ran out of medicine.

"Even with the medication, this past winter was challenging. I don't think he can live through another season like it," she confided in Laurie. "We're hoping a warmer southern climate will give him a better chance of survival."

Laurie turned away to hide her tears. Another loss, she thought. Why did everyone have to leave? Would Kevin truly be safer anywhere else? She wasn't sure it would make much difference and was tempted to tell Lisa so, but who was she to argue? It was probably better to keep those dark thoughts so herself. She would miss Lisa for sure and wondered if her own reaction was a bit selfish. Smiling sadly, she wiped her wet face. "I wish you didn't have to go! Who am I going to complain to about everything?"

"You're a survivor, Laurie," laughed Lisa, giving her a hug. "Mark my words, with your resilience and Stan's resourcefulness, out of all of us in this neighborhood, you and Stan will be the last ones standing."

That was about a week ago and she had not seen much of Lisa since. She wondered when they would leave. Peering outside this morning, she was glad to see the sun. It was a welcome relief after three straight days of torrential rain. Three days earlier a fierce lightning storm had hit George's house sparking a small fire. Miraculously the deluge of rain immediately following contained the damage, but the strike demolished all his ham radio equipment. George was beyond devastated. Even the limited amount of communication he had been able to provide had proven critical to the survival of the neighborhood and given George a purpose for his life. Without that, Laurie worried he would lose his will to go on.

The lightning storm also sparked several other fires in town and the air around their house had been smokey for several days, but weather prevented them from investigating. Now that the sun was out, perhaps she and Stan could take a bike ride to the center of town to assess the damage.

A movement outside caught her eye and she noticed Diego across the street with Lisa's son, Kevin. Laurie knew they had become friends in recent months. It looked as if Kevin was giving Diego a lesson on his bike. Laurie recalled when Kevin got that bike several years ago and proudly rode it around the neighborhood. She wondered if he was going to leave it for Diego. Apparently, that was one of the perks of remaining here, she thought a little guiltily. When neighbors departed, their discards became treasures to those left behind.

Diego

Kevin watched as Diego rode down the street. He hated to part with his bike but was happy Diego could make good use of it. He felt sorry for Diego whom he knew was a bit of a loner and hoped the bike would get him outside and at least provide him with something to do during the long days at home. Life could get pretty boring when you weren't in school and had no friends to play with.

Though Kevin was several years older, he and Diego had started hanging out together during the past few months. They had connected out of necessity, since there weren't many kids left in the neighborhood. To some extent, they had bonded over their mutual obsession with video games. When power went out and their electronic devices no longer worked, Kevin entertained himself by drawing cartoon characters. A few months ago, on a warm winter day, Kevin sat outside on his driveway with his sketch pad. Diego saw him drawing and stood watching for long time. "Whatcha doing?" Diego finally asked.

"Nothing really," Kevin replied. "I'm just doodling. I like to draw the characters from my favorite games."

"Can I try?" asked Diego. He sat down and joined Kevin, and soon the boys had created several pages of cartoons. Kevin considered himself a good artist, but he was astounded at Diego's ability. Diego had a sharp memory for the characters he used to see on his phone all the time, and he created lively scenes in which the entities appeared to jump off the page. As they were finishing up, some other boys in the neighborhood walked by and peeked at the drawings.

"These are so lame!" one of the boys exclaimed, laughingly pointing at Diego's sketches. As the boys strolled off, Kevin tried to tell Diego his drawings were amazing, but Diego simply shrugged. "You can keep them if you want," he said as he trudged home. Since then, Kevin had tried to get Diego to draw more, but Diego refused, though he enjoyed looking at Kevin's sketches whenever they got together.

"You're really giving this to me?" asked Diego now as he returned on the bike. He couldn't believe his luck. Kevin was one of the first friends he had ever had, and no one had ever given him a gift quite like this.

"My mom says we're leaving, and I can't take it." replied Kevin. "We're going by car and there's no room to bring it. It may as well get used. You just need to promise to take good care of it."

"I promise!" said Diego. "But I kind of wish you weren't going."

Kevin nodded. "I wish we weren't going too. But maybe it'll be better. At least it'll be warmer, and we won't have to spend all our days working on the farm."

"Yeah, lucky you. I hate that place! Seems like all we do around here is haul water, then go to the farm to pull weeds and plant the garden. I wish I could go someplace far away."

"Well, now you'll have the bike and can explore a little. Oh wait—I almost forgot. I have one more thing for you." He pulled a blank sketch pad out of his backpack, along with a pack of colored pencils. "I have a couple more of these you can have."

Diego looked at the pad. "You're giving me this, too? Why?"

"I think you should draw more, Diego. The sketches you did a while ago were amazing. I know those other kids made fun of them, but you can draw for yourself and never show them to anyone else. Because it's something you're good at."

Diego stared down at the pad. He was surprised Kevin even remembered that day. He had thought his sketches were good, but he didn't like when those other boys had laughed at them. That made him decide to never show his drawings to anyone. And what was the point of drawing for himself? Even so, he took the pad from Kevin with a mumbled thanks.

Josh

"Come Josh, we need to move quickly!" Pablo called from the end of the alley. They were almost to Pablo's apartment building and thus far had managed to avoid the throngs of people who threatened to take their food. They sprinted to the alleyway behind the bakery and seconds before reaching the door, Josh felt a tug from behind. He twisted around, falling backwards as a teenage boy ripped off his backpack. As he landed on the ground, both the boy and backpack disappeared into another alley. Josh stared after him. Pablo was already safely inside, but half their weekly allotment of food had been in that pack. Gingerly checking himself over, he stood up slowly. His hip hurt and he was bleeding from a gash on his arm, but he knew it could have been much worse. At least the boy didn't have a gun. Still shaking, he stumbled to the door and slowly crawled up the darkened stairway.

It had been six months since the power outage and much of El Paso remained in chaos. Everyone was in survival mode worrying about where their next meal was coming from. The initial violence of the first few weeks had finally tapered off once shelves were emptied. Those who survived had settled into a restless existence. Yet people would still do anything for food, including shooting others. Arresting people was futile, as the city jails overflowed and there was no way to feed all the inmates. El Paso had become a living hell.

The entire fabric of the city had changed. When the internet crashed, so did all organized society. There was no access to financial institutions. Wealth became a thing of the past. After all, if there was no record of your money, and no way to access it, what good was it? With banks closed, people couldn't get cash, and thus a simple bartering economy sprang up. People traded what they could for whatever they needed, and most of those needs centered on the basics of food and clean water.

Josh and Pablo at least had clean water available from the well at the university. For several months, they had relied on Pablo's stash of food, but that was almost gone. As Pablo had predicted, they had reached a point where they had to scavenge for food. This was almost impossible in the city, where everyone else was also hungry. They needed to figure out some other way to secure nourishment.

"I have a friend who lives on a farm across town. I helped him out of a bad situation about a year ago and he owes me. He might be able to help us out. I think we should pay him a visit," Pablo announced one day. Josh doubted anyone would help, but Pablo insisted he was a close friend, and this was the only way they could survive. Thus, several weeks ago, he and Josh traveled to the farm on foot and begged the owner to let them work there. Thankfully, he agreed. Now, once a week, Pablo and Josh made their way to the farm and spent ten hours doing the backbreaking and grueling work of planting, weeding and harvesting. In exchange, they received a week's worth of food. It was probably one of the better jobs in town, but the difficulty was getting the food home safely. This was the third time they had made the trip, and while the other two times had been harrowing, at least they had made it without mishap. Now they realized they had to be even more vigilant.

Despite all the hardships of the past six months, Josh maintained hope that he could reconnect with his friends and family. He was continually on the lookout for ham radio operators who might have contact with the outside world, but thus far he had come up against a wall. It seemed their entire existence was confined to Pablo's small apartment and their once-a-week forays to the farm. He knew this couldn't go on forever, but for the time being, at least, they had a little food each week which was more than most. Much as he was angry at the boy for stealing his backpack, he also realized they lived in a vastly different world now, where survival trumped all else. He was unsure how much longer he could go on like this, but for now, he didn't see any alternative. He was grateful for the fates that had connected him with Pablo six months earlier.

Often, he thought of his family and wondered how they were coping. He was sure they had also lost power. At least they lived farther away from the heart of a city, in an area with many more farms. He thought, too, of his brother, Brendan. He recalled his mother telling him Brendan had lived for the past two years in a tiny village in Africa with no running water and no electricity. How had Brendan managed, he wondered now? Was it possible for a society to grow and thrive when people were always concerned about where their next meal was coming from? He imagined the village where Brendan lived was far different from the hellhole El Paso had become. He wondered if Brendan was still in that village and how he was coping. From what he could gather from the rumor mill, this loss of power was worldwide, but what did that really mean? Was Brendan also affected?

Brendan

Brendan sat on his porch, quietly surveying the landscape. Suddenly, Ezra, one of his water-delivery boys came running around from the back of his house with an envelope in hand.

"Letter for you!" cried Ezra, waving the paper in the air. With no post office in town, letters were a rare event, and the last time Brendan had gotten information from the outside world was when the TeachAfrica liaisons had visited about five months earlier. Ezra eagerly handed him the letter, waiting patiently while Brendan fished a few coins from his pocket. The world economy may have collapsed, but here in this small village, cash still reigned.

As Ezra trotted off, Brendan gingerly looked at the envelope, addressed to him in neat script. His excitement grew as he realized it was from Leonard McFay in Troeburg. Brendan had written to McFay to inform him his three top students were graduating soon and interested in studying in Troeburg the following year. They wanted to know what was happening in the Capital. During the past few months there had been limited traffic into and out of Troeburg due to the gas shortage. Taxis no longer ran and the only way to get to Troeburg was by bicycle, a trip which usually took several hours. Brendan had sent the letter to McFay by bicycle courier several weeks ago and wasn't sure he would get a reply or how long it would take, as few people were making that ride, and reports coming back from Troeburg were somewhat disconcerting.

After the power grid shut down, there had been looting in the city, and people from his village preferred to stay away from the turmoil, though more recent accounts suggested conditions were improving. Brendan hoped McFay was still there and would be able to help them, but he didn't expect to hear anything soon.

Though the internet was still down, and cell phone service no longer existed, life in the village continued as it had for years. Brendan still taught at the school and was accepted as part of the community. The women's gardening circle was thriving, and they had plenty of food for all. Yet the lack of contact worried Brendan. He was monitoring the movement of magnetic north and could see it was behaving erratically. On the flip side, however, his magnetometer indicated the magnetic field was strong. He recalled both Alejandro and McFay stating that as the poles migrated, the safest place to be might be at or near the equator.

The other big change for Brendan was his new housemate. True to their word, Sam and Maria returned to the village about a month after the bloody sunrise. With them came Grace Evans and her dog, Flamingo, who now shared his residence. To Brendan, Flamingo looked like he had about 20 different breeds in his genetic make-up. He was a medium-sized black-and-white mutt with one blue eye and one brown eye. Brendan often found both the dog and Grace quite annoying. He had been used to having the house to himself, and he found the adjustment difficult.

Like Brendan, Grace had come to Africa after college to experience a new culture and had been in Loscoaya for the past year and a half. She grew up surrounded by animals on a farm in northern Minnesota where her family still lived. An animal lover at heart, she had adopted Flamingo shortly after arriving in her village. She was tall, with short cropped dark hair, and straight bangs lightly covering her chocolate-brown eyes. Although she told him she had once struggled to keep her weight down, life in Africa had certainly changed that. She was thin as a rail, but also strong. Brendan was amazed at how far she could throw a ball for Flamingo who had an infinite supply of energy.

Since dropping off Grace, there had been no word from the TeachAfrica office, which both he and Grace found worrisome. They heard rumors about power disruptions worldwide, yet nothing was confirmed. Try as they might, they couldn't get any reliable information. It felt like they lived in a tiny, protected bubble.

As Brendan sat down to read the letter, Grace walked up. His first instinct was to ignore her, but then he realized she might be interested in what McFay had to say. After all, she had family in the U.S. and had the same worries about what was happening in the world at large. He quickly skimmed the letter, glad to see McFay was willing to help his three students. McFay thought there would be some good opportunities for them in the city. As Brendan read on though, his heart sank.

"Listen to this," he said to Grace. He had previously told her about McFay, and their conversation on the airplane. He read aloud:

While things here in Troeburg are relatively stable, I wish I could give you more information about the rest of the world, and especially about your family back in the U.S., but I'm afraid I know as little as you do. As I'm sure you know now, there was a massive solar flare 6 months ago that lasted for 2 full days, destroying power grids all over the world. As far as we can tell, no place on Earth has yet been able to recover fully. The city of Troeburg is lucky because the new hydroelectric power grid was installed about 3 months before the outage, and the city wasn't yet dependent on it. While life here was slightly disrupted by the loss of power, much of the city had not yet been connected, so things carried on much as before. Officials have assessed the damage to the grid and are confident they can repair it and get it operational within the next 4 to 6 months. Believe it or not, this is one of the few cities in the world that can do this! Everywhere else, it seems people are dealing with massive destruction and an inability to adapt to a completely new lifestyle. Plus, it looks like the poles are migrating at a much faster rate than anticipated, and the magnetic field is weakening over the far northern and southern hemispheres. This may result in a large amount of radiation sickness which could force people to try to migrate toward the equator, though it may already be too late for many of them. I fear it may get worse, but it is so hard to predict.

I apologize for the lack of better news and will try to update you if I hear anything more, as I know this must be hard for you.

Wishing you all the best—

Leonard McFay

Chapter 11
Four Years After

With a sinking feeling, Laurie peered into the nearly empty freezer in the bunker. This was the last of their ten freezers of stored food. At least they had eggs from their chickens, but aside from that, from now on they would have to subsist on whatever they could scavenge day to day. She sighed as Brendan's words echoed in her head:

For how long?

The past four years had been a lesson in resilience in so many ways, yet now she wondered if it was all worth it. The neighborhood was in shambles. Once it became clear power would not be restored any time soon, people had left town in droves. The outage began as cold weather settled in, and though temperatures that November were mild compared to most years, many people feared the potential of a harsh winter. Laurie and Stan were among the lucky ones; they had solar panels on their house and could at least keep the heat, refrigerators, and freezers working. If the days were sunny and snowfall light, they felt confident they could survive the winter.

The town-wide voucher system had lasted for about six months, then fell apart as widespread panic set in. It became every man for himself, with a few pockets of people helping each other out. That first winter was brutal, and most remaining neighbors departed for warmer climates the following spring. No one quite knew what they would find, but they felt life would somehow be easier where the winters weren't as harsh.

Laurie looked at Stan in despair. "Maybe we should have left years ago, like all our friends." The few friends they had made in the months before the crisis had stayed for a while, but then one by one decided to seek a warmer and better place. The only one in the neighborhood who now remained besides Alejandro, Diego, and Dawn, was George who claimed he had nowhere else to go and was better off here where he at least had reliable neighbors. Moving to an unknown destination along with masses of other people seemed foolish to him.

She and Stan now quietly thought of all the families who had departed. Stan broke the silence. "We don't know if they are any better off. With no access to news, we have no way of finding out."

Laurie shivered. He was right, of course. When people left, it seemed like they vanished from the face of the earth and Laurie feared the worst.

"At least they left us their food," Stan continued. Many of their neighbors had quite a bit of stored food they could not take with them, and they either gave their food to the remaining families or left it in their houses to be scavenged. "That's kept us going for a long time."

Laurie nodded, though the thought filled her with guilt. They had felt safest here, with their stockpile of food and a routine that seemed to be working. They had made a life for themselves and did more than survive. Their chickens were thriving and providing plenty of eggs. They set up a hydroponic garden and some local farmers organized a weekly farmers' market where people could barter for what they needed, often paying for their food by helping at the farms. The farmer who raised goats turned out to be a godsend and baby Dawn thrived on the milk he provided. Much of the food they collected from the farms could be frozen and preserved for later use, so their stored food lasted longer. They banded together and they endured.

Yes, they had done well, thought Laurie as she looked in the freezer. Turning to Stan she said "You're right, that's kept us going for a long time. But now, this last freezer is almost empty, and yesterday I found out our favorite farm stand is closing soon, and the farmer is leaving with his family. With all the families with small children gone, Dawn and Diego are now the only children in the neighborhood." She struggled to fight back her tears.

"I know it's been hard but think of how much you've done for those kids." Stan said taking hold of her hands. With schools closed, both children had almost no structure in their lives, and Laurie had dragged Diego to the farm every day to help with chores. At least there were a few children there. Laurie had also realized Dawn was unusually bright and curious, and given her background as a teacher she took it on herself to give both children a rudimentary education. It gave her a sense of purpose and propelled her to find ways to do more than survive—to *adapt* as Brendan had said. Teaching Diego was challenging because the bulk of his elementary schooling had involved the use of interactive technology. He had a hard time reading and focusing on actual books. Yet though she struggled with Diego, she felt he was at least learning a few things and vowed to keep trying. And spending time with Dawn more than made up for her difficulties with Diego.

In Laurie's mind, Dawn was the glue that held them all together. She was their light in the darkness, the center of their universe. Wiping her eyes, Laurie smiled weakly at the thought of that, and as if on cue, she heard a knock on the door.

"Hi, Auntie Laurie!" said Dawn brightly. "Can you read to me this morning?"

"Sure," said Laurie, her face breaking into a bigger smile. Stan squeezed her hand as he rose to go tend to the well, and Laurie and Dawn settled in together. "Remember last night when we saw those beautiful lights in the sky?" Laurie asked. "What your dad called the northern lights?"

Dawn nodded. "Dad said the sky lit up in honor of my birthday."

"Well, I found a story about that. I'll read it to you now."

The night before, they had witnessed a spectacular light show, with the aurora borealis in full swing. That was happening with more and more frequency these days. Alejandro explained that the ability to see the aurora was linked to the migration of the magnetic north pole of the Earth and the strength of the magnetic field. As beautiful as it was though, he cautioned them about its darker side. Brighter lights signified a weaker magnetic field.

Even so, it was a dazzling show, and as a special birthday treat for Dawn, they had allowed her to say up late to watch with them. They all stood in awe, mesmerized by the lights dancing across the sky. After the show, Laurie found an old book in Brendan's room called *Legends of the Lights*. It was perfect reading material for Dawn. For the next several hours, Laurie entertained Dawn with all sorts of stories and tales about the aurora borealis. The girl overflowed with curiosity and peppered Laurie with one question after another. They learned that some Indian tribes believed the lights were torches used by friendly giants allowing them to see when they fished at night. They read a story from Finland about a mystical fox who threw sparks into the sky with its tail. They discovered that some people believed the lights were dancing spirits—some human and some animal ones—especially deer, seals, salmon and beluga whales.

"What do *you* think the lights are?" Dawn asked Laurie when they had finished.

"I think they are a way of communicating with people who aren't here with us right now," said Laurie slowly.

"You mean dead people? Like my mom?" asked Dawn.

"Maybe, and others as well." Laurie replied. She looked at Dawn. At four years old, Dawn didn't really understand what death meant, though she knew her mother was dead. What did that mean to her, though? She hadn't ever met her mom, really, so how could she miss her? Given her unique upbringing in this crazy, chaotic world, did she even realize other kids had moms who were alive? "Maybe dead people, and also other people we love who are still alive but too far away to talk to."

Dawn was quiet for a moment. "Can people on the other side of the Earth see the lights, too?" she asked.

"I don't know," said Laurie. "That might be a question to ask your dad. But I do know one thing. People on the other side of the Earth *can* see the moon at night. And it is the same moon we see." That fact always comforted Laurie at night when she wondered how Brendan was doing. They had formed a pact years ago when Brendan first left home. They would use the moon to think of each other, and each would know the other was thinking of them whenever they saw the moon—the *same* moon no matter where they were on Earth.

Brendan

Brendan was excited. Today, his three top students from four years ago, Janice, Ian, and Cyrus were visiting, and they had prepared a demonstration for the entire school. After graduating high school, the trio had been admitted to the university the following year and all three were now working with Leonard McFay. Magnetic north was moving a lot, changing position almost daily. It had become more erratic and unpredictable as time went on, and these students were collecting data to track and predict its movement.

Everyone gathered eagerly, especially Brendan's current students who loved to monitor the compasses. Four years after bringing them from the U.S., these instruments remained a hit in his 12th grade physics class. This seemed to have a trickle-down effect as more and more students were motivated to learn math and physics in the earlier grades. His two water-delivery boys, Theo and Ezra, came. Even four-year-old Debrak was there. Raising Debrak had indeed become a community effort and Debrak was present at most gatherings that happened in the village. Brendan had established a special bond with him, and the child now sat on his lap as Cyrus began speaking.

"The Earth is a giant magnet with two ends, called poles," Cyrus began. "There's a force between those poles that affects all sorts of things on the ground."

"Like what?" asked one of the kids watching.

"Like it protects us from damaging radiation from outer space. It's like armor," said Ian. "It's invisible, but it's all around us. We can' see it or feel it, but animals can. I noticed a long time ago my dog always pees lined up with the north and south magnetic poles. I don' know why, but he jus' does that. Where the magnetic poles are is important to animals and important to us."

The three former students talked about how Earth had "true" north and south poles and "magnetic" north and south poles, and these were different. True north and south, they explained, never moved. Those were specific places on the planet. Magnetic north and south poles moved however, and that movement was causing problems with things here on Earth. The compasses showed where magnetic north was at any given time. They laid out all the compasses and the kids gathered around to look at them. The needles all pointed neatly in the same direction, which was magnetic north, even though true north was a completely different direction.

After the demonstration, while Brendan stayed to talk with Ian, Cyrus, and Janice, Debrak stared at the compasses, transfixed. He seemed to be talking to himself. Occasionally, he spun around in a circle, then returned to stare at the needles.

"Why are they moving?" he asked. Everyone stared at Debrak. He had sat through their talk, but still, this didn't seem like a typical question from a four-year-old.

"What do you mean?" asked Cyrus

"I can feel it moving," said Debrak. "The magnet. It's like it keeps pulling at me, wanting me to turn toward it."

He spun around again, five times with his eyes closed, before stopping and standing facing directly toward magnetic north.

"How'd you do that?" asked Ian. "I bet you peeked and opened your eyes."

"No! I can jus' feel it!" claimed Debrak.

On a whim, the three older students decided to play a game. They put a blindfold on Debrak, then spun him around and keeping the blindfold on, they then asked him to turn toward magnetic north. Time after time they tested him, and each time, Debrak managed to line himself up perfectly. Finally, Brendan had to step in and save Debrak, as he was starting to get very dizzy.

"It certainly is a mystery," he said. "Maybe someday you can use him in your project. But for now, he needs to get home to eat something and rest up. His family is planning a big birthday celebration tonight."

Brendan walked Debrak home, then returned to his own house to relax for a while. It was mid-afternoon, and everyone in the village was sleepy from the day's heat. Here during the dry season, the temperatures could easily get into the upper 90's during the day, and today was particularly scorching. He had learned a long time ago to live without air conditioning, but on this day, he wished he had something to help him cool off. An ice cream cone would be nice.

As he approached his house, he saw his housemate, Grace sitting on the porch with Flamingo. The dog danced around Brendan's legs until finally flopping down for a nice belly rub. "Flamingo, behave!" commanded Grace, and the dog immediately sat up at attention. Brendan had to admit she had a way with the dog.

For the past four years, he and Grace had shared a small house on the edge of the village. The TeachAfrica liaisons had brought her there so they could consolidate operations, but eventually the company went out of business, and Grace and Brendan were left to fend for themselves. When she first arrived, Brendan found both her and the dog super annoying. He felt like both of them were always around. Privacy was hard enough to come by in this village, and he valued his alone time. Plus, he was bothered by the fact that everyone in town assumed they were a couple, and he spent a good part of the first year making a point of telling people they were "just housemates." Over time, though, he began to appreciate her company more and more. As he looked at her now, he couldn't really imagine life without her. He thought about how much his life had changed. He had to admit he liked talking with Grace, and he felt as if he could talk with her about things other people in the village had a hard time understanding.

He sat down on the worn-out sofa and Flamingo jumped up beside him. "I heard your students' presentation," said Grace. "They were pretty impressive."

"They were," agreed Brendan. "I'm proud of them all. It's amazing how much they understand of the world now just from living in the city. Listening to them reminded me of how different things are here. Especially when they were talking about the way the movement of the magnetic poles caused so much disruption worldwide. The younger kids had no idea what they were talking about. Nothing has really changed here."

"Because there wasn't anything here to ruin. Loscoaya didn't depend on technology, especially in the outlying villages." Grace replied. "Remember, this country had no access to technology until about ten or fifteen years ago."

"You're right," agreed Brendan. "Added to that, the power grid in Troeburg was only minimally damaged. I guess we were lucky this country was turned away from the sun when the worst of the damaging rays from the solar flare hit. It's hard to believe Troeburg has a power grid now, and apparently the rest of the world doesn't. But that's what McFay continues to say."

Grace listened intently. She enjoyed these quiet conversations with Brendan. It had taken them a while to get to know each other, but she now felt Brendan was one of her closest friends in the village.

"Cyrus told me today that not knowing where and how fast the poles are moving is making it impossible to recover fully," he continued. "They can't get ahead of it. He also said that even though the magnetic field around the northern and southern hemispheres has been weakening, the field around the equator keeps strengthening, and this is protecting Loscoaya's power grid from further disruption as the poles keep moving. Eventually, that may change, but for now, with a capital city with a working power grid we are probably one of the luckiest countries in the world."

"Well, here in our village, not having power isn't really an issue," said Grace. "They were never on the grid here. They never depended on technology the way we did. How can you lose something you never had?"

Brendan nodded. "You're right. This event may not be having a huge effect here, though they have had their share of challenges over the years. Think about how they lived through civil war that destroyed their houses. And how the Ebola Virus killed so many people. The people here are incredibly resilient." His thoughts drifted to home. Not a day passed when he didn't think of home for at least a few minutes. He wondered if his parents had that same resilience.

"For some reason, I keep thinking of home today," he said.

"Me too," she replied. "I think it's because today is the 4-year anniversary of that bloody sunrise." Grace had told him that the people in her village, like his, had been mesmerized by that event.

The two of them sat in silence for a few moments, lost in their thoughts of how that event altered everything for them, even though little changed for the local villagers. Brendan recalled the first months after the solar storm, when he realized power had gone out all over the world and he couldn't communicate with his family back home. He remembered George, the ham radio operator in his neighborhood, and wished he had learned more of that technology, as his brother Josh had done. Brendan had always been jealous of Josh's interest in that. Now he wondered if he should have followed his brother's lead and gotten more involved at the time. It probably wouldn't have helped him because he had no equipment, though he might have brought some equipment with him if he had studied it earlier. He sighed, realizing it didn't make any difference now.

Thinking of Josh simply made him angry. He still couldn't forgive his brother for all the turmoil he had caused in the family, and he couldn't imagine any scenario in which Josh could be forgiven. His adopted mom, Talah, had tried to get him to keep an open mind, but the more time went by, the more entrenched Brendan became in his views of his brother. It didn't matter that his parents had absolved Josh of any wrongdoing. As far as Brendan was concerned, what Josh did was indefensible. Occasionally he wondered if Josh was still alive and felt a twinge of guilt that he hadn't been a better brother, but it was quickly replaced by anger.

Brendan looked at Grace. Her presence calmed him whenever he started to go down the path of anger toward his brother. Although they remained purely housemates, Grace was starting to grow on him and occasionally he wondered if they might become a "couple" as the people in his village called them, though given his adamant public denial for several years, he wasn't sure how to make that happen. He certainly enjoyed her company and occasionally wondered what she felt about their relationship. As far as he could tell, Grace seemed quite happy with the way things were, but at times he had caught her surreptitiously looking at him when she thought he wasn't aware of it. Yet comfortable as he felt around her, he was scared to bring it up. He felt like he could talk to her about almost anything except this. What if he was imagining those looks? What if she laughed at him?

At any rate, they were together now. Maybe they had been thrown together by random events, or maybe it was fate, but as far as Brendan was concerned, they were lucky to be together. The town management offered them each a small salary and a house to live in, and the two of them decided to stay given that they had nowhere else to go. With no airplane travel, and no ability to communicate with family back home, they felt they had no choice. At some point, they hoped to learn more of what had happened to their families. Somehow, each of them had faith their families were surviving and eventually they would be reunited with them.

As much as he enjoyed Grace's companionship, today Brendan felt like he needed some alone time. He got up and went into his room. Grace had long since learned to give him space when he needed it, and he was grateful for that.

Though he thought of his mom and dad every day and hoped they were safe, it had become easier for him to put those thoughts aside during the last few years. Occasionally, however, he was overwhelmed with memories that threatened to crush him. Today was one of those days. He rose and opened a small box on his desk, removing a worn piece of paper. It was a letter his mom had written three and a half years earlier. They had sent it by boat, and miraculously it had gotten to him, delivered to him by the two TeachAfrica liaisons, Sam and Maria, on their last visit to his village three years ago. It was the only communication he had had with his family since the solar flare incident.

Gingerly, he unfolded the letter and read it over. Written in his mom's beautiful script, he appreciated the fact that she had been a teacher and had learned to hand-write, especially since his own handwriting was atrocious in comparison.

Dear Brendan,

I don't know if you will ever get this letter, or even if we will ever be able to send it, but I feel like I have to try. I am writing this by hand, as a way of adapting to our new way of life. While we do have solar panels on the roof of the house and can at least run our computer, conserving whatever electricity we can get has become a major priority right now.

You probably know that we had a huge power outage about six months ago, and as I am sure you can imagine, things turned to chaos quickly. Some people were more prepared than others, but none of us really expected this to happen so soon, and we were all caught pretty much unawares. Right after the outage, many neighbors left because winter was approaching, and they didn't think they could survive the cold. Dad and I stayed, figuring the solar panels on our house and the insulation we put in would help us get through. It was tough, but we managed. Your father is one of the most resourceful people I know. He is incredibly handy with tools and has done a lot of work to keep our house safe and secure against the elements. We have plenty of food right now, especially since neighbors who are leaving have been giving us all their stores. I know you thought the chickens in our yard and all our freezers in the bunker were not such a good idea, but at least we had enough food to last us through the winter, and we still have a decent amount which we are supplementing by joining forces with some local farms. We even have extra eggs to give to neighbors! We don't know how long it will last, but our hope is that this will pass, and life will get back to normal at some point. Though I am not sure what normal is any more. All the things that seemed so important a few short months ago have paled in comparison to just keeping our day to day lives going.

Who could have imagined the loss of power and internet could cause such turmoil?

When the power went out, banks closed, stores closed, gas stations closed, and people panicked. The town leaders tried to keep the peace and it worked for a short time, but with no money and no knowledge of how long this would go on, our world fell to pieces. The devastation here now defies description.

A few weeks ago, there were some massive thunderstorms here. Our neighbor George's house was struck by lightning and all his radio equipment was destroyed. He is devastated. The storm also sparked an enormous fire in town, and our skeleton crew of a fire department was unable to fight it. Miraculously, our neighborhood was spared— even though George's house was damaged, the torrential rain helped to control fire from spreading here. But in other parts of town, the fire burned for a long time. Finally, three days of solid rain put it out. Much of the town was destroyed. Cars were abandoned and left out to rust on the sides of the road. Houses are empty and many have been completely cleared out by looters. The only way to get around town is by bicycle and that works during the summer but will become impossible next winter. I'm scared, but Dad assures me the house is sturdy, and we are planning to stay for now. We have nowhere to go, really, and figure we will just hunker down and survive.

Our neighbors, Sophia and Alejandro, had a baby girl, born on the day the power went out. I still cry when I think of this and it's hard to even write about it. It was an *emergency and I tried to help with the delivery, but something went dreadfully wrong. Sophia died shortly after because she lost too much blood and couldn't get a transfusion. That should never have happened here! We have all been trying to help raise this baby, named Dawn. She is a real jewel and is the one bright spot in our sea of darkness right now, though often I look at her and just see Sophia.*

One more thing, and this is probably the most painful. Josh never made it home. We were so excited at the prospect of seeing him, and then the power went out everywhere and now we once again don't know if he is alive or dead. I try to keep the faith. At least I know he didn't mean to hurt us when he disappeared. I wish I could explain the circumstances to you, but it is too hard to write about.

Last night, I looked at the full moon and thought of you. Is the moon full where you are right now? I hope you are safe, and that communication will be restored soon so we can at least know you are okay. Please don't worry about us. . . we will be fine. We are learning to live with less, as you so clearly told us we had to do.

Both Dad and I love you more than you can imagine and have faith that someday we will see you again. Until then—stay out of trouble!

Love,

Mom

Brendan fingered the letter as he thought of home. Four years! If he could have sent them a letter in reply, he would have, but he had no idea how. Were they even still alive? After hearing today about how Earth's magnetic field was weakening, he wondered if they had finally decided to move. And what about Josh? Where had he been hiding for so long and why hadn't his mom told him the details?

He had read the letter countless times over the last three years, and usually it gave him a sense of comfort. But today, all he felt was loss and despair as he realized he would likely never get answers to all his questions. Overwhelmed with grief, he sank down on the floor and wept.

Josh

For four years, Josh and Pablo worked at the farm one day a week in exchange for food. They had no choice if they wanted to eat. It had once been a small fully automated dairy farm. With no power, it was impossible to keep up with the milking and the cows had long since been sacrificed for meat. The homestead now supplied a large variety of vegetables: soybeans, corn, lettuce, strawberries, tomatoes and potatoes. The area could provide food for many people, but because of the gas shortage, all planting, weeding and harvesting had to be done by hand. The work was backbreaking and grueling, and during the summer it was brutally hot. Even though today was relatively cool, Josh thought an ice cream cone would be nice. He couldn't remember the last time he had had one of those.

Each time, they had to navigate their way home with bags of food through a maze of deserted houses. It was an excursion they were both tired of. Usually, they traveled back to Pablo's apartment at night, as the cover of darkness seemed safest. They had adopted that idea after getting mugged several times in broad daylight. It seemed counter-intuitive at first, but it worked. Most nights, they managed to avoid being robbed because no one else in their right mind dared to venture out into the streets at night.

"I wonder if our life is ever going to change," Josh said to Pablo as they made way up the darkened stairs and into the equally dark apartment. "Will we ever feel safe outside?" El Paso remained in chaos, and aside from a fear of looters, disease was rampant. Because the infrastructure of the city had been destroyed so rapidly, there was no organized way to fix it. Food, especially, was in short supply, and the only way to get it was to travel outside the city proper, as Josh and Pablo did each week. Added to this, more people were flooding into the city daily, hoping to move farther south into Mexico. Unfortunately, the wall that had been so proudly erected to keep people out was now imprisoning them. Just as Pablo had predicted four years earlier, it was an endless stream that got worse with each passing day, though Josh couldn't for the life of him figure out where people were coming from.

Most were fleeing from the harsh northern winters, which were difficult to survive in without electricity and especially heat. Many of these migrants talked about seeing the northern lights as far south as Kansas, which worried Pablo more than anything. Even though the University had shut down due to lack of power and internet, he had kept in touch with some of his science colleagues. Many of them had moved away, but the few who remained gathered occasionally to discuss the problems they all faced.

"The lights are a sign of a weakening magnetic field," he told Josh more than once. "If the poles continue to move closer, we may be in danger here."

Josh was all for moving. The "few days" that Pablo had offered for him to stay at his house had turned into weeks, then months, then years. They had stayed because they weren't sure where to go, and here at least they had a routine that allowed them to survive. Leaving meant a lot of planning, especially for food and water along the way. And where would they go?

After the power outage, Josh had desperately searched for some way to communicate with the world outside of El Paso. He missed his family and George. He missed Steve and Amigo. And if he was honest with himself, he missed Marguerite as well. He didn't know if that relationship would have gone anywhere, but it felt like she was snatched away from him before he had a chance to find out.

Pablo's contact at the University had disappeared, but finally, about a year after the outage, he found a man with a working ham radio set up in his house. It was more powerful than Josh's handheld unit, though it was still limited in reach and could only transmit over short distances. But the fact was that they *could* communicate, and ham radio operators all over the country were beginning to organize and relay information. Encouraged by this, Josh attempted to connect with both George on the East Coast and Steve on the West Coast, using the same relay method he had employed to contact George before everything collapsed. It had worked once; maybe, just maybe, it would work again, although Josh had to acknowledge that circumstances had changed dramatically.

The process involved relaying a message from radio to radio until eventually the message could be delivered to the recipient, either by radio, email, phone or regular mail. Since email and phone were out of the question, and regular postal mail no longer functioned, Josh could only hope George or Steve had access to radios, or someone who lived close to either of them would get the message and deliver it in person. It was a long shot, but worth a try.

The man was willing to help for a fee. He expected payment in food every time they sent a message and made it clear that if a reply ever came back, payment would be expected for that as well.

While Josh wrote to Steve and George, Pablo also drafted a message to his wife's cousin in Ecuador hoping to reconnect with his wife and daughter who had been deported just days before the power outage. He still felt enormous guilt about sending them off alone. They sent the messages off, listing Pablo's apartment as a return address, and six months later, when they got no response, they repeated the process. They had been doing that every three months since and thus far, nothing had come of it. Josh had sent his last message about two months ago.

This morning, as he stared out the window, there was a knock on their door. Pablo opened the door to a wafer-thin boy holding a piece of paper. It was the son of the ham radio operator. The boy couldn't have been more than six years old. Dangling the paper, he said, "My Pa says this is for you, but you need to give us some food first." He held out his hand. Pablo shook his head. It seemed that parents often used their children in this way. It was much harder to say no to a starving six-year-old than to an adult.

Chapter 11 ~ Four Years After

Josh handed the boy a bag full of corn kernels and the boy dropped the note and ran. Pablo handed it to Josh, who simply stared at it. Finally, after four years, they had some contact with the outside world! It was a type-written message from Steve. He quickly scanned it, drinking in this news from the outside world.

Josh,

I was amazed to get your letter. Things have been so insane here that I have barely had time to think about anything besides our day-to-day survival. San Diego has been hit especially hard because we are on the coast and have been struck by numerous coastal storms, and many people have moved inland. Luckily, my house sits on a hill, so we've been protected from the worst of the weather, but it's been one calamity after another. Earthquakes have been occurring frequently here as well. Mostly they've been small tremors, but they've been scary and unsettling. I want to let you know that the ham radio network you set up has been amazing! Radio operators have been instrumental in helping us deal with all sorts of local problems. Most of the communication is short range, but through their relay systems, we have learned much about what is happening in other places as well. It seems like they are becoming more organized across the country as people adapt more to this new reality. Our city owes you a huge debt of gratitude.

More and more people are moving south. Everyone is trying to go across the border into Mexico. My scientist friends are telling us we may want to do this as well. It seems the movement of the poles is wreaking havoc on our atmosphere, especially farther north. Right now, they are saying that the closer we can get to the equator, the better. I have some important news for you. Remember my sister, Marguerite?

Josh paused and looked up. How could he forget? They had gone out for several dates the week before the power outage, culminating in a night Josh wished he could re-live. He smiled now as he remembered that. He had sworn off women for almost a year, and his feelings for Marguerite had taken him completely by surprise. Reading this now brought those emotions tumbling back. He remembered wondering if maybe things with her would be different from his former habit of one-night stands. But what he read next stunned him:

Well, she had a baby girl about three years ago and guess who the father is? I never saw any photos of you as a kid, but I would be willing to bet that little Jessica is an exact replica of what you must have looked like.

I don't know if there is any way for you to get back to San Diego, but since communication has opened up, maybe it will be possible. Judging from the date on your letter, it took about a month for your message to reach me. You said you had tried before, and this was the first one to come through, but with our improved communications network hopefully we can keep this channel open.

I know this is a lot for you to digest but write back to me if you can.

Steve

He handed the letter to Pablo and sank down onto the sofa. Memories of the night he spent with Marguerite came crashing down on him. He had felt a true connection with her and thought that maybe the relationship could go somewhere. Well, clearly it *had* gone somewhere, just without him. Suddenly he felt like he was at a crossroads. As much as he appreciated Pablo's friendship and the security of a place to live, his life had been in limbo for a long time. He needed to re-connect with people from his past. And he knew he couldn't do it here. He felt a renewed sense of urgency.

"I want to go to San Diego," he blurted. "No... I *need* to go to San Diego. I know we've talked about it before, and we keep coming up with excuses not to go. But I have nothing here and things aren't going to get any better. In fact, it's just going to get worse. Look down there at all the people! The city is bursting at the seams, and sooner or later, it's going to explode. Either we will be killed in a riot or catch a disease or something else disastrous. I know you feel safe here, but for me, it's no longer about being safe. You can come with me or not, but I need to go."

Pablo studied his friend. "I know how you feel, Josh. I, too, have a family elsewhere. You're right that I feel somewhat safe here, but this isn't really my home either. My home is in Ecuador. My family is there. I would give anything to go there, but I don't know how we can do it." Pablo thought of his wife and young daughter, Elena, who would be eleven years old now. He wondered what she looked like. He remembered his wife spending hours braiding her hair long straight beautiful black hair. Did Elena still let her do that? Most of the time, he managed to tuck those memories away, but when they surfaced, it was with a vengeance.

"I should have gone with them," he said now with a heavy voice. "The worst part of it all is not knowing if they are okay."

"If we can get to San Diego, we can get to Mexico and then to Ecuador much more easily," Josh pressed. "There's no wall there. I bet people are crossing the border there easily. We need to make a plan and do it."

Josh looked down at the street below, noticing a lone biker in the distance. There had to be a way for him to get to California. He thought of Steve and the project to stash supplies in the desert for migrants who had crossed the border from Mexico. And as he contemplated that, an idea began to form in his mind.

Laurie

The friends all gathered to see the light show once again, and since it was Dawn's actual birthday and she had stayed up once, it was impossible to get her to bed without at least a short peek. Only Diego was absent, as he preferred to hide out in his room much of the time. Dawn pointed to a bright star on the horizon at an angle to the lights. "What's that star called, Daddy?" she asked.

"That's Polaris, the North Star," responded Alejandro. "It sits directly over the North Pole of the Earth and is one of the brightest stars in the sky. Sailors used to use it to navigate on the open ocean. They would steer toward it and know they were heading due north."

"But north is *that* way," said Dawn, pointing directly at the dancing lights.

"Well, not exactly," replied her dad. "That's magnetic north, which is different from true north. The Earth is like a giant magnet, and magnets have a top and a bottom, just like the Earth has a north pole and a south pole. People think of the north pole of our planet as the top, but the magnetic north pole of our planet doesn't quite line up with the actual north pole."

Dawn looked up at him with her big brown eyes. "But why is the top of the magnet moving?" she asked. Everyone stared at Dawn. Maybe she had overheard some of their conversations, but this certainly didn't seem like a typical question from a four-year-old.

"What do you mean?" asked Laurie

"I can feel it moving," said Dawn. "The lights. It's like it they keep pulling at me, wanting me to turn toward them."

"Well," said Alejandro, "I think you have had enough of this for tonight. How about I put you to bed and we can talk more about this in the morning, okay?"

"Okay," agreed Dawn yawning. With one last wistful look at the lights, she went inside with her dad.

Alejandro returned a few moments later. "Dawn told me about the stories you read her today. She really liked them."

"Yes," said Laurie. "She is so quick and eager to learn new things."

"There are some other legends, though, that you may not know about," he continued. "Did you know 'aurora borealis' actually means 'dawn of the north'? Aurora was the Roman goddess of the dawn. In medieval times, the lights were thought to be omens foretelling of war and famine."

He faced Laurie and Stan. "I'm worried. I've been monitoring the magnetic field closely and it's weakening around here. That's why we see the lights so much. Magnetic north is getting closer to where we are, and as it approaches, the field may weaken even more. The aurora is another sign that things are changing. As beautiful as the lights are, this is a bad sign for us. Pretty soon, we may not be able to travel safely outside at all."

"You mean, we may need to stay indoors or go underground?" asked Stan. This was something they had talked about over the past few years, but they still thought they had plenty of time to prepare. "How soon is 'pretty soon'?"

Alejandro shrugged. "Everything about this has been so unpredictable from the start. We have no previous data to go by. This phenomenon hasn't happened in over 700,000 years. We still don't know if there will be a tipping point and then an instantaneous flip, or whether it will simply keep up a steady pace for years. And the movement could stall or shift at any time. All we know is that the poles are migrating, and the magnetic field seems to be weakest wherever the north and south poles are. But as far as we can tell, the area around Earth's actual equator seems to have a stronger magnetic field. It's almost like all the power of the field is being stored in a band around the planet's middle. Perhaps that will remain strong, or perhaps not. All we know now is that it would be safer for us to all move south."

Laurie contemplated that. She remembered the mass exodus of many of their neighbors and wondered what became of them. Most people just left, never to be seen again, but occasionally, people did return and told tales of chaos and trouble to the south as more and more people congregated at the southern border. People desperately wanted to get into Mexico, but unfortunately, the wall that had originally been built to keep immigrants out of the country was acting as a prison keeping people in. The only way to get south at this point was by boat, either to Central or South America, or across the Atlantic to the southern coast of Africa. Or possibly to travel across the U.S. to Southern California where the wall hadn't been finished. All those trips were fraught with danger, and Laurie and Stan had been reluctant to even consider any of those options. Now it looked like they might be forced into it.

"Sophia once told me she didn't want our children to grow up underground," said Alejandro. "She wanted them to feel the grass under their feet and the sun on their faces. To know the rain and the wind. If we stay here, we may never see daylight again."

"It sounds like you have already made up your mind," said Stan.

"Not completely," replied Alejandro. "But I am seriously considering it. I thought about going to South America, where Sophia and I came from. We both had family there, but I don't even know where they are any more, and South America hasn't been very welcoming to Americans, so you might have a harder time there. I've heard rumors that Africa has a more open border policy though. And I also heard rumors that Leonard McFay is in Loscoaya and has set up some sort of research facility. And Brendan is there, right? Maybe we could all try to go there instead. What do you think?"

Laurie and Stan glanced at each other. "This is a lot to digest all at once," said Stan slowly. "We don't even know if Brendan is still there or if he is okay." Laurie shot him a glance. Even though she thought of Brendan all the time, she and Stan rarely talked about him these days, and it was painful to hear Stan voice her own fears.

Prior to the power outage, they had sent several packages to Brendan by boat across the Atlantic, and he always got them, even though it took several months. About six months after the outage, they saved up several cans of gas, drove an hour to the shipping port and sent a letter to him the same way. It was a daring move done at a time when everyone was trying to conserve gas as much as possible, but they were desperate to communicate with Brendan and let him know they were okay. When they reached the port, a boat was almost ready to sail, and the shipping manager told them boats departed for Loscoaya on or about the 15th every month. They had only made that trip once and had no idea if the letter ever reached its destination, though perhaps if those boats were still sailing, they could take passengers as well.

Stan saw the tears in Laurie's eyes and turned to Alejandro. "It sounds like we have some time at least. How about we think about it a bit?"

Laurie felt completely overwhelmed. As memories of both Brendan and Josh assaulted her, the added thought of leaving left a pit in her stomach. She couldn't imagine living anywhere else. This was their home. They had raised a family and were comfortable here. They had adapted, sort of. But on the flip side, they needed to look at the handwriting on the wall. Their stored food was almost gone. Local farms were closing. And if Alejandro and his family left, they would be essentially alone in the ghost town of their neighborhood. Maybe it was time to consider leaving. But... to Africa?

She took one more look at the northern lights. In the book, she had also read about the Menominee Indians of Wisconsin who believed the lights were torches used by giants who were guiding spirits of great hunters and fishermen, while the Inuit of Alaska believed they were the spirits of the animals they hunted. Whether they were ghosts of the hunters or the hunted, the spiritual power of the lights could not be denied. Were the lights a harbinger of bad things to come if people stayed in place? Or were they perhaps dancing across the sky to show movement was necessary for survival in this world?

Diego

Diego lay on his bed, crying. Even after four years, he missed his mom terribly. How could they all be down there, celebrating Dawn's birthday? It was *because* of her birth that his mother was gone. Didn't they know that?

Ever since his sister was born, the world revolved around her. He remembered how Laurie used to drag him day after day to the farm to collect milk for her. How they forced him to work on the farm in order to "pay" for the milk and whatever other food they needed. Four years ago, his whole life was turned upside down and nobody seemed to care.

Hauling water, going to the farm to plant and weed the gardens, listening to his little sister babbling like a brook. He was so done with this lifestyle. What he really wanted was to go back in time four years to the virtual reality he used to enjoy. The memories had somewhat faded, yet he could still feel the satisfaction of playing on his electronic device, destroying alien spacecrafts or winning crazy roller-coaster road races against friends who lived in houses across town. *He hated this life!* The sea of technology that he grew up in had been stripped from him, and he resented it.

The first few months after the outage were a living hell for him. He spent much of the time alone in his room sobbing and rarely ventured outside. His father, overwhelmed with a new sister in the family, never seemed to care or have much time to devote to him anyway. While Laurie tried to get him to do some schoolwork, he had little interest in the books she chose for him to read. Aside from the trips to the farm, everyone ignored him. Eventually he became friendly with Kevin across the street, and for a while, life improved. Until Kevin left.

He thought back to the day Kevin gave him the bicycle. At the time, he hadn't genuinely appreciated the value of that friendship. He was so thrilled with the bike that he didn't bother to think about the loneliness that would ensue. Now, he wondered a little guiltily what had happened to Kevin and if he was even still alive.

After getting the bike, he started making frequent forays out of the neighborhood. With no traffic and few people on the road, he enjoyed a newfound freedom. At twelve years old, he wanted to get as far away from home as possible.

About six months ago, he biked farther than usual and met with another girl who also worked at the local farm where they spent much of their time. She took him to a different farm where pot was growing wild and introduced him to smoking weed, which he found a great way to pass the time. Most afternoons he was there by himself, but once he encountered a group of older kids partying. Not wanting to look like a baby, he joined them and ended up spending the night there. He wasn't sure what they were drinking or where they had gotten alcohol, but the next morning he regretted his decision, as he woke with a raging headache and felt horrible. He felt even worse when he returned home later in the day to a furious Alejandro. His father took away the bike for a few weeks, but later decided it was better for Diego to be out in the fresh air rather than confined to his room all day. Alejandro also thought maybe Diego was making some friends, so he let his son have a little more freedom.

The day he got his bike back, Diego hopped on it and took off, hoping to spend a little more time at the farm only to find the entire farmhouse and surrounding land had been burned to the ground. He sat on the burnt-out grass and sobbed openly. His supply of weed was gone, and he could no longer use that as an escape. Upon returning home, he ran up to his room and refused to come out or talk to anyone for several days.

On this night, as he looked out at the northern lights, he cursed the forces that had made his life so empty. The dancing lights looked so bright and dazzling like his sister, and his life felt so dull and colorless. He thought if he could wish upon a star, he would wish to go far, far away from this place to somewhere completely new and different.

Chapter 12
Five Years After

Laurie, Stan, George and Alejandro gathered in Alejandro's kitchen. For the past year, the four of them had been debating where they might go if they left town. George was in favor of Central or South America, but Laurie, Stan and Alejandro were leaning toward Africa. Although the trip to Central America might be shorter and less treacherous, they had heard numerous reports of people being turned away at various borders and ships barred from docking in foreign ports.

"I still can't imagine going to Africa," said George. "Far as I can tell, no one in their right mind would even consider it. Much as I hate to separate from you, I think I'm going to take my chances and travel south along the coast to Florida. Maybe from there, I can catch a boat across the Gulf of Mexico."

"I know it's crazy," agreed Laurie. "But we think we might have a better chance of being accepted in Loscoaya, especially if we can somehow get in touch with Brendan."

"Five years ago, there was a cargo ship going to Loscoaya each month, and recently I heard through the grapevine it might still be running somewhat regularly," piped up Stan. "I have no idea how the ship would be powered, but somehow that country is thriving, and they want building materials that our country can supply. If we can get to the seaport and a ship is due to sail, maybe we can bargain our way onto it."

"I'm willing to go to the port to check it out," said Alejandro. He had been pushing for this for a long time. He turned to Stan. "How about we take our bikes and see what's going on there?"

Laurie and Stan had driven to the port once, four years earlier, to send a letter to Brendan. It was a 50-mile trip along roads that had once been good highways. Now, with no gasoline, cycling had become the transportation mode of choice and the roads were in disrepair, but Stan and Alejandro agreed to ride there in the next few days and see if they could arrange passage on a ship for their families.

"Well, good luck to you all." said George, shaking his bushy head as he rose to go home. "It's a damn shame we need to split up, but I can't see going to Africa."

The port city was a ghost town, eerily empty save for a few rabbits and mice. During the past five years, intense coastal storms had flooded the region multiple times, leaving pothole-filled roads and rubble everywhere. Most of the houses had been deserted and left to decay. Roofs were caved in, windows were either boarded up or broken, and siding and paint were peeling. Abandoned cars with flat tires and multiple dents littered the side streets as if a massive tidal wave had swept them up from one of the beachside parking lots. The port itself was uncannily quiet as no others were looking to make this trip. The ship's captain, a big, burly, Loscoayan man, eyed them suspiciously.

"Why you want to travel to Loscoaya?" he asked with a thick accent. "This is a cargo ship." As far as Stan and Alejandro could tell, the ship was carrying supplies that had been looted from deserted businesses. Stan wondered if the shipping company was bringing things from this former developed nation to be sold for cash overseas. Crazy as that seemed, he had to admit it would probably be a lucrative business if Loscoaya still had a working economy.

"My son lives in Loscoaya," Stan told him. "We want to go south for warmer weather, and this is the only way we can do that."

"My nex' shipment is solar panels, and there won' be much room. But I may be able to squeeze you in the cargo hold. How you want to pay me?"

"We can give you our bicycles once we get there," Stan replied. And maybe we can bring you a few solar batteries for storage, if they aren't too heavy and we can get them here."

The captain's eyes lit up. Having some extra batteries would be a boon to him. "This ship runs on solar and wind power. Is a new technology developed in Loscoaya. The biggest problem is energy storage. The more battery storage we have, the better the trip. So, I'll let you on as long as you bring me some batteries. But I'm warning you, the trip will be hard and uncomf'table. I don' want anyone complainin' I didn' warn you ahead of time."

Back home, they started to pack. How do you leave your life? Laurie wondered. How do you leave the place where so many memories are stored? What do you take with you and what do you leave behind to rot and decay? In the span of a few years, they had gone from being affluent citizens of one of the most developed countries in the world to refugees in every sense of the word. They were running from an environmental disaster with only what they could carry on their bikes and didn't know what they were running towards.

Laurie had seen what happened to all the abandoned houses in town and shuddered as she thought of what their house would look like in a few years. Would they ever return? They needed to leave now with the idea they probably never would. It was time to start a brand-new chapter of their lives, though they had no idea what the future would hold. Sure, they hoped to find Brendan in Loscoaya, but with communication as difficult as it was, they couldn't count on anything anymore. It was certainly possible they would arrive and be completely on their own. They could only pray they would be welcome in a new land.

A few days before leaving, Stan brought their chickens to the one remaining farm in the district. All of them were still laying eggs, and he hoped the farmer would take decent care of them as these birds had been a godsend to them for the past five years. He bartered with the farmer and obtained a decent supply of freeze-dried food for their journey.

The day of departure finally arrived. Laurie and Stan looked back at the house one more time and then looked at one another. At least they had each other, and Alejandro and little Dawn as well. Unfortunately, they also had Diego, who had grown increasingly surly over time. If he wasn't talking about the electronic games he used to play, he was complaining about how difficult life was and constantly trying to get away with doing less. They all hoped the trip might change him in some way, yet Laurie had her doubts. As they prepared to leave, they could hear Diego yelling at his father.

"I don't want to go!" he cried. He stormed out of the house, hopped on his bike and rode down the street. Alejandro shook his head and watched him go. "He'll be back in a few minutes, I'm sure," he said quietly. "Let's get moving and see what he does."

An advantage of being the last in the neighborhood to leave was being able to scavenge quite a bit from their former neighbors' houses, including several decent bicycles, one with a child's trailer for Dawn and another with a trailer they could put some batteries on. They had obtained the batteries by looting the local hardware store, though neither Stan nor Alejandro felt guilty about it given the store had been abandoned years ago.

It was early morning and they wanted to leave soon so they could reach the coast by mid-afternoon. Before departing, though, they had one stop to make. They knocked on the door to George's house and were surprised to see him fully packed and ready to go. "I thought you were waiting a few more days before heading to Florida," said Stan.

"Well, changed my mind," said George. "I'm going with you. I just couldn't see being all alone." With that, he turned and said one final goodbye to his house. As they left, Diego came riding down the street as Alejandro had predicted and joined their little caravan.

When North Becomes South

Travel by cars was a thing of the past, since gasoline couldn't be used after two to three years of storage, so they encountered no road traffic. The silent highway wound past numerous empty towns—devoid of people, though full of abandoned buildings and houses in total disrepair. Occasionally, they saw a decent-looking house along the road and Laurie wondered if anyone still lived there. Had everyone fled? Surely, there must be pockets of civilization, as there had been in her hometown. Yet, the only living things they saw during the 50-mile ride were birds and an occasional rabbit.

They reached the port late in the afternoon and were disappointed to find their departure delayed by several days due to dire reports from incoming ships of a storm brewing at sea. With no satellite communication, the captain had no choice but to rely on these eyewitness accounts. Thus, they were left to fend for themselves for a few days. They needed shelter, especially given the forecast. Since most houses and buildings had been abandoned long ago, there was no shortage of places to stay though they had to choose carefully as many of the buildings were dangerously crumbling. Finally, they found a small cottage near the boatyard that had been thoroughly looted and was mostly empty, but the roof looked sturdy and the windows were intact. It was probably one of the last houses in town to be abandoned. The storm that had been at sea swept in, battering their shelter with hurricane-force winds and torrential rain. Thankfully, the roof didn't leak. They hoped and prayed that once this storm passed, they would have smooth sailing.

As the ship finally left port, Laurie had a sinking feeling they had made the wrong choice. Solar panels took up most of the deck space on the boat, leaving just a tiny area for the passengers to be aboveboard. Most of their time would have to be spent in the cargo hold also packed with supplies, though they were able to carve out a small nook where they could at least lie down. They had thin mattresses and bedding scavenged from nearby houses, but with no windows it was dark, dank, and musty. How were they going to manage in this tiny space for the next six weeks? Laurie reminded herself they hadn't had a choice. If they had remained at home, it was only a matter of time before they wouldn't have been able to venture outside at all, and they would have ended up imprisoned in their own house. She was determined they wouldn't end up entombed here. They had gotten this far, and they would survive.

Three days into the trip she wasn't so sure, as all of them except Dawn and George were struck with a seasickness so intense it felt like a journey through hell. The stench in the cargo hold quickly became almost intolerable, but there was not enough space on deck for all of them to stretch out at the same time. For day after endless day, they took turns above and tried their best to ride it out, even as their spirits crumbled.

Miraculously, though, both Dawn and George weathered the rocking of the boat with no problem. Unbeknownst to any of them, George had served for several years in the Navy and had valuable experience with celestial navigation. He proved to be a huge help to the captain, who drafted him as part of the crew. Dawn also managed to stay healthy and grew more animated as the trip progressed. Ever since the first appearance of the northern lights a year earlier, Dawn had seemed anxious, constantly talking about a feeling of being pulled by some invisible force. She had developed a headache a few days after they first viewed the lights, and it never seemed to go away completely. In fact, it got progressively worse as the appearance of the lights became more frequent. Alejandro had tested her many times in his lab, and to his surprise found she had an unusual ability to sense the location of magnetic north. This was a skill many animals possessed allowing them to find their primal nesting places and return to those same places year after year. As far as Alejandro knew, this capacity had never been documented in humans, yet Dawn had it in spades.

During the past few months, Laurie, too, had noticed that Dawn seemed more listless. She often complained of feeling itchy, as if she was being hit by invisible little pellets. When Laurie asked Alejandro about it, he said he was worried. "She seems to be unusually sensitive to the magnetic field," he had told her. "But I'm not exactly sure what she is reacting to. All I know is that as the strength of the magnetic field around us is diminishing, she seems to be getting weaker."

Once on the ship heading south, she perked up significantly She was captivated by all the ship's instruments and quickly became a favorite of the ship's captain. Being the only child in her neighborhood, Dawn had spent a lot of time in her father's lab and had a surprisingly good understanding of navigation for a five-year-old. So, while Laurie, Stan, Alejandro, and Diego suffered in the cargo hold, both Dawn and George worked with the crew to keep the boat on track. George also helped with all the daily chores of keeping the boat afloat. With a skeleton crew, the captain appreciated them both.

"My Little Bird," the captain called out to Dawn. "Come tell me which way is north?" His face vacillated between a huge grin and an even larger scowl, depending on circumstances. He had a scowl now as the ship's compass readings were erratic and kept changing, making navigation difficult. During the daytime, when the North Star wasn't visible, the ship's compass was his best navigation tool, but on this trip, it wasn't working. He knew magnetic north and true north didn't align, but he also roughly knew the declination and with George's help, he could generally calibrate the readings. It seemed the shipboard navigational instruments were also affected by interference from some highly magnetized cargo on board. Yet for some unknown reason, the magnetized load had little effect on Dawn. Somehow, she was able to sense magnetic north much more accurately than the compass, and with George's calculations, they could determine true north far more precisely.

Dawn closed her eyes and pointed. George did a few quick computations and the captain sighed. It looked like they were quite a bit off course, but he trusted them and changed the heading. He had doubted her ability at first, but after a few days of veering off course and having to readjust at night when the stars appeared, he realized she was indeed giving him better readings than his shipboard instruments.

Down below in the cargo hold, the small band of passengers struggled mightily, barely clinging to life. With limited space above board, they took turns getting fresh air. They forced themselves to drink water and lived on saltine crackers they had miraculously scavenged from a recently abandoned convenience store near the port. Finally, after three brutal weeks of travel, during which Laurie more than once thought she would rather be dead, they emerged from the boat on the southern coast of West Africa. Haggard, sick, and barely able to move, they collapsed on the dock. While George and Dawn gathered up their meager supplies, the rest of the group huddled nearby, looking like drowned rats. Their hair was streaked with sweat and their clothes tattered and dirty, barely fitting on their wasted bodies. The ship's captain looked at them sadly and shook his head. He ordered the crew to give them some buckets of fresh water so they could sponge themselves off, and they each managed to find some relatively clean clothing in the small knapsacks they had brought with them.

"I tol' you it would be rough," he said. "I wish it could have been a little better ride for y'all. But at least you made it here and yer all still alive."

The group looked so pathetic that the captain took pity on them. "Tell you what," he continued, smiling his big signature smile and pointing at George and Dawn. "Your batteries worked great and this guy here and your li'l girl help me so much that I'll let you keep your bicycles. You'll need 'em to travel. And I'll give you some help here." He handed Stan a piece of paper. "This here is the name of a place you can stay nearby 'til you get your strength back. Is my cousin's guesthouse. He'll put you up for a couple nights if you tell him I sent you." With that, they left the docks, hoping people here would be more welcoming to them than people in their country had been to immigrants a few years earlier.

Somehow, now, they needed to find Brendan. Their only plan was to first locate the site of TeachAfrica, assuming it was still in operation. Hopefully, the organization was continuing to function in some capacity and there would be people who could help.

They were surprised at how vibrant Troeburg was and stunned to see the city had a working power grid. Even their guesthouse had electricity! After all they had heard about the worldwide power outage, this seemed so disconcerting. Hadn't this been a "developing" country just a few years ago, while their country was thriving?

The guesthouse run by the captain's cousin consisted of two tiny rooms in a ramshackle building near the port, but they were grateful simply to be off the ship. At least the owner gave them space and fed them a few meager meals of rice and beans in exchange for some trinkets Laurie had brought from home. After a couple days rest and more than a few bucket showers to clear the stench from their bodies, they felt much stronger and ventured out to barter for some cheap, clean clothing.

The central marketplace for the city was a kaleidoscope of colors and movement, smelling of smoked fish, barbecued chicken, and human sweat. It was a short bike ride from their guesthouse, and they were shocked to see so many people gathered in one location. With the worldwide gas shortage, there were few cars in the city, yet people were milling about everywhere, walking, selling and shopping, making bicycling tricky. Street vendors hocked everything from cheap costume jewelry to colorful print dresses and shirts. Many stalls contained brightly colored lapa or cloth that could be sewn into clothing, but they were also able to find a few items already tailor-made, and after a few small purchases, they left the market and headed off in search of the TeachAfrica headquarters.

The street address they had for TeachAfrica was near the central marketplace and they found the building easily. To their dismay, however, it was now occupied by a Loscoayan-owned storage company. A lone security guard sat in a booth at the entrance, looking completely unconcerned. When they explained they were looking for the TeachAfrica headquarters, or anyone who had worked there in the past, he simply shook his head. "They all lef'. Years ago. I na' no where they gone," he said in broken English. "Maybe try this address. This the owner of Loscoayan Storage." He scribbled an address on a scrap of paper and handed it to them. Dejectedly, they realized it was clear across town and would probably take them several hours to find. Tired and hungry, they got on their bikes and began the trek, stopping along the way to get food from some street vendors. Skewered chicken was a favorite staple, along with fufu (a concoction made from boiled cassava leaves) and banana fritters. After the weeks of near starvation on the boat, they were all grateful for any kind of food. Once again, they were astounded by the sheer number of people on the streets. Everyone was outside selling something or other. Women and children alike carried buckets of goods on their heads, and market stalls bustled with activity in stark contrast to the deserted port city they had left behind in the United States. Nervously, they realized they were the object of multiple stares. People simply gaped at them, pointing excitedly as they rode by. Women held tightly to their children, whispering in their ears. Laurie wasn't sure what they were saying, though she suspected it was not very flattering. It seemed their pale white skin created quite a sensation among the city folk.

They left the market district and continued along pothole-filled roads, past numerous run-down buildings, many of which had been damaged years ago during the civil war and never repaired. Collectively, their mood became somber and was made even more miserable by the constant whining of Diego, who continually reminded them this entire venture was plain stupid.

Feeling like they were on a wild goose chase, they finally found the address, a rickety house located in an equally decrepit neighborhood smelling of rotten fish. Cautiously, they knocked on the door, aware of all the stares they were continuing to attract. "Who der?" came a voice from inside. The door opened, and a portly man with ebony skin and a big round face appeared. He stared at the six white strangers on his doorstep, then immediately turned to close the door.

"No, wait!" cried Stan. "We need to speak with you. It's about the building you own—the Loscoayan Storage Company building."

"Wha' about it?" asked the man, turning back to them.

"We're looking for someone who may have worked there before, someone from TeachAfrica who owned the building several years ago."

"Oh… you looking for TeachAfrica people? They all lef', years ago."

"But do you know where any of them went? We want to find our son and they are the only ones who can tell us where he might be."

The man thought for a moment. "Your son work fo' TeachAfrica?" he asked. Laurie and Stan nodded. "They used to do good work here. They help our country a lot. My cousin tol' me they were very helpful in his village. 'Til the collapse."

Laurie and Stan nodded again. "Our son was here when the collapse happened. He worked in a remote village. We're trying to find him."

Once again, the man thought for a moment. "I na' no where any TeachAfrica people ended up, but you know the name o' the village?" Laurie told him and he nodded. "This village is not too far from this city. Maybe only abou' 40 miles but the road is full o' holes." He looked at the haggard group and then at their bicycles. They were obviously a sorry lot. "Too far for you to go today, and it's dangerous for you to be out on the streets at night." He rubbed his hands together. "If you have anything to pay me, I suppose I can let you stay here tonigh' and give you directions to get there in the morning. It'll prob'ly take you most o' the day." Laurie and Stan were grateful for the few items they had brought from home. They offered him some old jewelry, along with three small solar-powered flashlights and he seemed happy with that.

He opened the door to his home, a spartan two-room apartment. The group entered cautiously, not quite sure what to expect. Could they trust this man? Laurie had a moment of panic as she looked at the rotting boards and the shored-up roof. The house was sorely in need of a facelift, but at least it was shelter, and the man seemed friendly enough. If anything, he should be afraid of them, but he didn't seem worried.

Despite the outside appearance of the house, the inside was remarkably clean. The smell of a stew cooking in the kitchen was a welcome relief. Compared to the ship's hold where they had lived for six weeks, this place seemed palatial. Gratefully they entered, once again thanking their lucky stars the people in this country were so welcoming. They quickly settled in and prepared for what they hoped would be the final leg of their journey.

Brendan had once told them that when family members visited people in his village, they often gave no advance notice. It was common practice for relatives to simply show up unannounced. Brendan thought this was because of their belief in Voodoo and spirits that somehow might jinx travel plans. By showing up unexpectedly in Brendan's village, they would be adhering to the local traditions and customs. They could only hope Brendan was still there.

Josh

Josh looked around the apartment that had been his home for the past five years. As much as he appreciated the safety the building offered, he had felt imprisoned in El Paso since the moment he arrived there. He was now itching to carry on with his journey. Due largely to communication difficulties with Steve, it had taken the better part of a year to plan this trip. The idea was simple, based on stories Josh had heard of mountaineers attempting to summit Mt. Everest. He recalled reading how climbers would typically start at base camp and make many short climbs to establish and supply sub-camps along the route, allowing them to camp overnight before they made their final push for the summit. Josh figured if he and Pablo could do the same en route to San Diego, they could eventually manage a multi-day bike ride.

The journey from El Paso to San Diego was 750 miles, and they hoped to ride about 50 miles each day. Assuming Steve successfully hid supplies for them at strategic points for the last half of the trip, Josh and Pablo needed to stock enough hidden camps for about 350 miles, a trip of about seven days. From there, they would be dependent on whatever Steve could prepare for them. For months, he and Pablo made numerous forays by bike to stash food and water along their proposed route. They found several abandoned barns that looked like decent places to sleep, and they planned to carry a small tent. The last leg to their seventh campsite would be the most grueling, but over time they managed to stockpile enough supplies so they would be able to spend a few nights resting there before venturing further.

A month before their planned departure, Josh received a message from Steve saying he was about to make a trip to prepare the final campsite, describing the location in detail. Josh replied immediately, giving Steve their estimated departure date. He was hoping to get a confirmation from Steve that the last site was indeed stocked, but it never came. They could only pray the message was received and Steve had managed to get things ready for them on his end. Now they were ready to go. Unbeknownst to Josh, on the same day he and Pablo set out on the first leg of their journey west to San Diego, his family was departing on bikes for their trip east to Africa.

The first few days were uneventful, as they traveled over hilly terrain on roads devoid of all motor traffic. They passed a few other cyclists and pedestrians, though it was unclear where people were going. Most people kept their heads down and didn't seem particularly interested in talking with them. It felt eerie to be biking on an Interstate highway that was once a major trucking route for the entire country. It still seemed unfathomable to Josh that the loss of power had created so much devastation.

"I can't understand why people haven't been able to rebuild," he said to Pablo one evening as they sat around the campfire. "It's been five years, and you'd think the country was destroyed by a nuclear bomb. With all the crumbling buildings and overgrown side roads, it looks like a wasteland out here."

"It does seem crazy," Pablo agreed. "We were clearly too dependent on our gadgets. Individuals can survive some hardship, but whole cities that depended on things like mass production of food and sanitation couldn't keep going easily. Our society wasn't prepared for this. Everything was mechanized, and when the technology fell apart, we had no backups."

Josh thought about this. "I wonder how other countries around the world are dealing with this. I mean, there must be places in the world that are thriving."

"I'm guessing the most successful spots are ones that didn't rely on technology to begin with. Maybe rural villages where they never had electricity and running water. Areas that didn't have internet access, so they wouldn't miss it when it fell apart. You can't miss what you never had. At least not in the same way as those who depended on all that stuff."

"I wonder if we can find a place like that," Josh mused, half to himself. Maybe moving south to a rural village in Central America wasn't such a bad idea.

As they neared the end of their sixth day of travel, they noticed ominous clouds building in the distance. That night, they slept in an old barn and were grateful for the shelter as they awoke the next morning to torrential rain. Josh peeked outside. Massive puddles had formed on the road.

"Guess we'll have to wait a day before going on. There's no way we can ride through this."

Pablo agreed, happy to have an extra day of rest. "My legs are so achy that I wanted to slow down anyway. Luckily, we stashed an extra day of food here. But we only planned on a possible one-day delay. If the rain continues, we might have a problem."

Thankfully, the next morning dawned bright and sunny and they were up early, making a push for their seventh campsite, where they planned to rest for three days. This portion of the ride was quite hilly, and they knew it would be challenging. Despite all the biking they had done to prepare for this trip, it was taking a toll on them physically and they were looking forward to a respite. On reaching the campsite however, they were bitterly disappointed to find that animals had raided their stash of food.

"Probably coyotes or wild dogs," murmured Josh, as he looked around. It hadn't been much, mostly boxes of old cereal, stale crackers, and some nuts and seeds. But the animals had scattered it all over the surrounding landscape, leaving crumbs and little bits of cardboard everywhere. At least they had an intact jug of clean water. They needed to conserve this, though, in case they couldn't locate their next campsite. Josh was worried that even if Steve had successfully stocked it, they weren't sure exactly where it was and how far it was from their current location.

Hungry and tired, they collapsed into the tent, not even bothering to light a campfire. They planned to get up early and push on, and both fell into a fitful sleep, only to be awakened by coyotes howling in the distance. The symphony got closer, until the animals were prowling around just outside their tent, growling and occasionally scratching at it. Josh and Pablo had each experienced fear before yet being confined inside a flimsy dark tent with wild animals pacing outside induced a whole new level of terror. Trembling silently, they wondered if they would survive the night. Finally, Josh could take it no longer.

"Get out of here!" he shouted as loud as he could. "Scram!" He wished they had collected rocks or something to throw, but all they had were their voices.

Pablo joined in. "*Vete!*" he cried out in Spanish. The animals paused for a moment, and Josh and Pablo renewed their yelling, stamping their feet to sound as threatening as possible. Finally, the beasts departed, but their howling continued all through the night. Josh thought of the Mexican migrants for whom he had put out food and water years earlier. Did they even have tents? Or did they have to sleep out in the open and take their chances with the wild animals that abounded in the desert? He shivered at the thought.

The next morning, they once again arose early, but with a lot less gusto than previous days. Up to this point, they knew where they were going each day and what to expect, as they had done the route before. Now they were venturing into the unknown. What if Steve had trouble getting supplies to the last campsite? What if that site had also been raided, either by animals or other people? Josh struggled to suppress those questions and keep his fear under wraps.

That day, as they biked past abandoned farm after abandoned farm, Josh once again couldn't help wondering what happened to all the people. The devastation was still incomprehensible to him. Entire barns had collapsed. Most houses looked as if they hadn't been cared for in years, with broken windows, torn siding, and vines growing up to the sagging roofs. The entire countryside was empty. How was it possible everyone had disappeared? The whole world seemed to have collapsed in the span of a few years. After living in the hellhole of El Paso for the last few years, Josh thought he would be numb to all this; but his worry and anxiety kept growing.

"Tornadoes went through here," said Pablo. "Either that or some extraordinarily fierce windstorms. I'm guessing once that happened, people fled."

"Yeah, and they went to the cities that weren't equipped to handle them." Josh replied, thinking about how El Paso was overflowing with people.

Mankind had created all sorts of devices to make life better and easier, and *everyone* took them for granted. No one bothered to consider how to feed a city of over a half million people without electricity. Or how to farm a thousand acres of land or manage herds of thousands of cattle without gas for vehicles or electricity to operate machinery. Automation had allowed the world population to grow and evolve in specific ways, and without that technology, civilization, as they knew it, was doomed.

Late in the day, they began looking for some of the landmarks Steve had given them. Luckily, many road signs were still up, and they found the stash without incident. Gratefully, they saw it was intact and they tore at the meager supply of food. A few ancient granola bars, an old jar of peanut butter, and some dried fruit had never tasted so good. After a night's rest, they pushed on and for the next four days, they were easily able to locate the places where Steve had prepared campsites for them. It was hot and the traveling was grueling, but they knew they were getting closer to their destination.

Finally, late in the afternoon of what they hoped would be their last day of travel, they reached an area of the desert, not far from where Josh had left water for migrants years ago. This was where Steve had told them he would set up the final campsite. Josh remembered this area well and marveled at how he used to think nothing of driving this far out of the city. Being able to get in a car and go anywhere was one more luxury he had always taken for granted.

The supplies should have been there, but they couldn't find them. As they wandered around in the heat of the late afternoon sun, all they could find was a single jug of water. Through eyes parched from the sun, Josh squinted at the blurry landscape. Somehow, this wasn't the right spot, but neither of them had the energy to go on. Tired, weak and hungry, they collapsed onto the ground, unable to muster enough strength to pitch their tent. Josh thought they were only about twenty miles from their destination, but that seemed light years away to them.

He must have dozed off, because when he awoke, it was completely dark. Pablo was lying nearby, sound asleep. Josh ate a few crackers, trying once again to get up enough energy to set up the tent. On one hand, it would give them a little sense of security, especially given their experience with coyotes the night before but on the other, it was a clear, moonless night and the nighttime sky was extraordinarily beautiful. In the end, he decided he was simply too exhausted. After all, it wouldn't be the first time he had slept under the stars.

Brendan

After five years of sharing a house, Brendan and Grace finally decided to marry. Once announced, their wedding became a community affair with everyone chipping in for the festivities. The villagers loved to party, and though they were poor, they spared no expense when it came to celebrating an important occasion.

"I don't know why it took you so long to figure this out, Brendan. We all knew this day was coming almost from the moment Grace moved in!" Anna laughed.

Brendan blushed. As his feelings for Grace had grown, he had been hesitant to voice them, but once he took the plunge, he and Grace had never looked back.

The normally quiet town was abuzz with activity. The scent of charcoal fires filled the air, mixed with the delicious odor of roasted potato greens. Children kicked a football around, and Brendan and Grace were showered with the gift of their neighbors' company.

The ceremony was about to begin. The townspeople stood in a huge circle, with Grace and Brendan in the center, both clad in matching colorful African clothing, handmade by the village tailor from the finest African lapa Talah could find.

Suddenly, there was a commotion in the field, and the circle parted. Brendan looked up and blinked. A ragged group of people was walking toward the celebrants.

I must be dreaming, he thought. He blinked again, and the image remained. "Oh my God!" he exclaimed. "I can't believe it!" Breaking away, he ran towards his mom and grabbed her in a great bear hug, tears rolling down his cheeks.

"How…?" he began. He was so flustered that he didn't even know what to ask.

"It doesn't matter!" said Laurie. "Let me look at you!" She took a step back and gazed at her son. He had grown up, filled out, and looked like a full-fledged man now. Gone was the scrawny kid she had sent off to Africa. Her mouth dropped as she looked at Grace, who looked stunning in a perfectly fitted African gown.

For a moment, the villagers were silent. "Mom! Dad!" he yelled. Turning to the gawking villagers, he hollered "My parents are here!" He hugged his dad, pulling Grace along as well.

"This is Grace," he said. "I would have brought her home to meet you sooner, but, well, you know, circumstances kind of got in the way."

"Welcome to the family, Grace" said Stan a little sheepishly, taking her hands. "It looks like we crashed your wedding."

Grace smiled as Brendan struggled to find words. "I truly never thought I'd see any of you again! The best wedding present ever!" he finally exclaimed.

"I'm not sure what we expected, but it definitely wasn't this!" said Laurie, finally finding her voice. Smiling, she turned to Grace as well. "I look forward to getting to know you."

Suddenly everyone started talking at once. Stan turned to Brendan. "Maybe you should get on with the ceremony. Then you can properly introduce us to all your friends."

The village elder held up his hand to silence the gathering. The entire village looked at Brendan and Grace expectantly. With a huge smile on his face, Brendan took Grace's hand, and together they moved back to the center of the circle.

Once the formal ceremony was completed, the party broke out in full force. African music played loudly on boom boxes most likely stolen from looted houses in foreign countries. Palm wine flowed liberally, though neither Brendan nor Grace had developed a taste for it. Everyone wanted to meet the newcomers and the exhausted little group was showered with all the affection the townspeople could muster. It was several hours before they could retreat to the relative privacy of Brendan's home. While Grace and Laurie went inside to talk and get to know each other, Brendan sat on his porch with the rest of the group, grateful they could finally have a quiet conversation. Flamingo curled up in the corner, eying them all suspiciously. Finally, he got up and sat by George, who quietly scratched his ears.

"We came by boat," began Stan. "We had to leave home because it wasn't safe there anymore. The Earth is changing, the magnetic field weakening, and we worried that if we stayed, soon we wouldn't be able to go outside at all. So, we decided to take a chance and come here."

Brendan looked at Alejandro. "I was so sorry to hear about Sophia," he said. "I really liked her. I wish I could have gotten to know her better."

Alejandro simply nodded. He looked much older than Brendan remembered and more weathered. In fact, they all looked older. But none of that mattered because they were here, in his town. He still couldn't quite believe his eyes.

Finally, Alejandro spoke. "I've been tracking the magnetic field for the past five years and it's wobbling all over the place. Yet now, it seems magnetic north has come down just above the equator and magnetic south is just below it. For some reason, right around the Earth's middle, the field is stronger than anywhere else on the planet, so at least for now, this is the safest place to be."

Brendan nodded. This was exactly what his former students had told him.

Alejandro continued, "Sophia and I used to talk about this possibility, years ago. She told me she never wanted our children to live underground, to not be able to see sunlight."

Brendan nodded again, observing the two children huddled in the corner of the porch. They were clearly exhausted, but they were eyeing Flamingo with great interest. He recognized Diego from six years ago, though the boy had changed from a pudgy eight-year-old into a burly teenager. Brendan remembered how difficult he had been years ago and hoped he had matured. He turned his attention to Dawn. "You must be Dawn," he said, getting up and kneeling in front of her.

"How do you know my name?" she asked.

"My mom wrote to me about you after you were born. I remember that because we have a boy here in this village who was born on your same birthday and I thought that was pretty cool." Dawn stood, twisting back and forth, hugging a stuffed bear who had been her constant traveling companion. She stared at Brendan. She wasn't sure what to make of him, or of any of this. Diego looked around with disgust. "Where are we all going to stay?" he grumbled. "We can't possibly all fit here!"

"Diego, watch yourself!" said Alejandro sharply. "Brendan hasn't even invited us to stay here and if you're not careful, he may not. But if he does, at least we will have a roof over our heads!"

Brendan thought about that. The house had three rooms—well four if he counted the little storage room—which was considered average for this village. Often, families of eight or more would crowd into houses smaller than this. It would be tight, but they could do it, though he wasn't sure what Grace would think. It wasn't exactly what they had planned for their wedding night.

At that moment, Grace and Laurie joined them on the porch. "We've been looking at the different rooms and trying to figure out if everyone can stay here," said Grace. "If we empty the storage room, Dawn and Diego could sleep in there. Then we'd have a bedroom for your mom and dad, and George and Alejandro can sleep in the front room. It'll be a squeeze, but we can make it work. Families here do this all the time." Gratefully, Brendan looked at her and smiled. In his mind, there had been no question everyone could stay with them, but he thought it was a lot to ask of Grace. Looking at her now, he was overwhelmed with love for her. He wondered why it had taken him so long to figure that out.

While they were talking, Flamingo sidled over to the two children. Cautiously, Diego reached out a hand to pet him. Flamingo inched closer. "If you rub the top of his nose, he'll do anything for you," said Grace.

"Watch." She rubbed the dog's nose, and he immediately went into a trance. Dawn giggled. "Can I try?" she asked. Soon, both Dawn and Diego were curled up with the dog, and the three of them fell fast asleep.

As they sat on the porch, they were joined by Talah and Anna carrying bundles of clothing in their arms. "We thought you might want some clean clothing after your long journey," said Talah. The women dropped off the clothes and left after inviting them to dinner at their house the following evening. Looking at the pile of clothing, most of it hand-sewn, Laurie was overwhelmed by their generosity. Once again, she was struck by how warm and hospitable these people were to them, and she was embarrassed by how her country had treated immigrants over the past decades. She had even played a part in that, she reflected now. When Sophia and Alejandro had first moved in, had she made any attempt to get to know them? Had she welcomed them to the neighborhood? With shame, she recalled how little she did for them during their first few months in town. The opportunity had been there to help them feel accepted, and she did nothing. She realized now that each of them had the power to make a difference in the lives of others. She had learned many things on this journey thus far, but as she looked at the pile of clean, dry clothes, that one fact stood out more than any others.

Josh

Josh woke up with a raging headache and a wet tongue licking his face. Rolling over, he blinked at the morning sun and looked around. For a moment he was completely disoriented. *I must be dreaming*, he thought. He was lying on a sand dune and couldn't for the life of him remember how he got there. Amigo was tugging at his sleeve.

Suddenly, he sat bolt upright. "Amigo! You found us! I wasn't sure I'd ever see you again!" He couldn't believe his eyes. He grabbed the dog in a big bear hug. If Amigo was here, Steve wasn't far behind. They had made it!

"What's all the racket?" Pablo groaned, opening his eyes. "Is that a *dog* on your lap?"

"It's my pal, Amigo! He has the best sense of smell of any dog in the world. He must have tracked us here."

A few moments later, Steve appeared. Josh and Pablo looked up gratefully. "I came up here yesterday thinking you might be arriving. But when I saw no sign of you, I camped at the site we left for you. It's just over that hill. If you'd gone another few hundred yards, you would have found it."

Josh tried to stand and hug his old friend but was too weak to move. As it was, it took all his strength just to sit up and pet Amigo. He gripped the dog for dear life.

"Am I glad to see you!" he exclaimed hoarsely. "I thought this was the end. We couldn't find the campsite and finally gave up looking and collapsed here. Honestly, I don't think either of us could have made it another hundred yards."

"And I'm not sure we can now if we don't get something to eat," said Pablo weakly. "My body feels like it's wasted away."

"I can take care of that," said Steve. He pulled a meager supply of food from his backpack. "Amigo must have smelled you. He took off before I had time to gather more. It isn't much, but hopefully it'll give you enough strength so you can make it to our tent. Marguerite came with me and we have a lot more food and water there. You can rest there before we head back to my house."

At the mention of Marguerite, Josh's head shot up. "Marguerite is here with you?" he asked. He suddenly realized how much he wanted to see her and how scared he was. When he closed his eyes, he thought he could picture every inch of her, but he wondered how much of that was real and how much was in his imagination. He had no idea what his feelings for her would be, given they hadn't seen each other for six years.

"She's here. She wanted to see you before you meet Jessica. We left Jessica back at my house with my wife and two boys."

Josh and Pablo gratefully accepted the food. They gobbled down several hard-boiled eggs each. "I can't remember the last time I had one of these," Pablo said.

"We have chickens at the house, so eggs are a major staple for us," Steve said. "It's been challenging to find things to feed everyone—especially my two growing boys. We've worked out some surprisingly good systems with local farmers, though. At least we have enough to subsist on."

After eating and resting a bit longer, both Josh and Pablo felt much stronger, "Do you think you can make it over that hill to our campsite?" Steve asked.

The two men stood up and nodded. "As long as we take it slow," Josh said. He was dragging but desperately wanted to get to the house. He was still grappling with the idea of being a father and wondered what his daughter would be like. What had Marguerite told her? And what about Marguerite herself? Given how confused he was about his own feelings, what could he expect of her?

To Josh's surprise, Steve picked up his handheld radio. Josh knew more powerful radios still worked at times, but he had given up on his handheld device years ago.

"I'm calling my wife to let her know I've found you and we'll be back sometime tomorrow," Steve said. "This radio works over a short range. When the magnetic field is stable and with no interference, communicating with someone 20 miles away usually isn't a problem."

Josh barely heard what Steve was saying. He was still thinking of Marguerite. She was there, at the campsite, a few hundred yards away. He was starting to get cold feet. What could he possibly say to her? With every message he had sent to Steve, he thought of also writing to her, but never followed through. It brought him back to the time when he had wanted to communicate with his family for years and didn't, because he didn't know what to say. That same feeling of shame from ages ago bubbled to the surface.

"Feeling ready to go?" Steve asked. Josh thought of saying something about his misgivings but kept silent. He turned to Steve and nodded.

Marguerite was standing outside the tent as they approached, scanning the horizon for a glimpse of them. When Josh saw her, his heart skipped a beat. She was every bit as beautiful as he remembered, and he felt completely tongue-tied. Should he hug her? Maybe shake her hand? He was completely at a loss as to how to greet her.

"Hey," he began.

"Hey," she replied. It was a start. "It's good to see you Josh." She smiled and Josh's heart melted.

"I'm so sorry," he began, fighting to keep his distance. "I never meant for things to turn out this way…"

Marguerite stepped forward and took his hand. She looked into his eyes.

"There's no need to apologize. None of this was your fault. I never blamed you. I was at the airport the morning after you left. I had a flight out to Colorado, remember? Of course, no planes went. It was chaos there. I tried to find out what happened to your flight but couldn't get any information since all the computers were down. With no communication, it was impossible to find out where your plane wound up."

Josh nodded, briefly recalling the moments before the outage, and the chaos of the airport in El Paso the next day. *I thought of you moments before the lights went out,* he wanted to say. But he held back the words. Aloud he acknowledged, "I should have written to you though when I sent messages to Steve. But I didn't know what to say."

"Well, that makes two of us," she replied. "I thought of writing to you as well but didn't want to pressure you. I didn't know what to say either."

For a moment, they simply stood there, hands clasped. Josh took a deep breath. "How about we try to start fresh? Like pretend we're meeting for the first time."

"Very well." Marguerite dropped his hand and turned toward Steve, who had been keeping a discreet distance. "Steve, come introduce me to your friends!" she commanded.

"Oh, sorry," Steve said. "Marguerite, this here is my friend Josh, and his buddy Pablo from El Paso." Turning to Josh, he said with a wink, "And this is my sister, Marguerite. She came to visit me from Colorado and ended up staying for the last six years."

"Pleased to meet you, Marguerite," said Josh, taking her hand again. Just touching her electrified him. She flashed him a dazzling smile, then turned and greeted Pablo.

For the rest of that day and into the night, the four of them rested, snacked on what little food was available, and talked about the state of the world, catching each other up on what was happening in their respective communities. San Diego didn't seem much better off than El Paso, except that Steve lived outside the immediate city limits and was less affected by crowds of people. Steve told them there had been a huge influx of people coming from the north, and it was becoming clear they would evenutally all have to move further south. He and his wife had already started making plans for that journey, though they still had a lot of details to work out. Chief among them was how far south they should go. As evening approached and Steve and Pablo got deep into conversation about the possibility of going to Ecuador, Josh and Marguerite went for a walk.

"Tell me about Jessica," he said to her as they looked out at the stars.

Marguerite took a deep breath. "Well, she's five years old now, and talks up a storm. She loves to read, and we're all trying to stay a step ahead of her. Her curiosity is insatiable."

"What does she know about me?" Josh asked.

Marguerite hesitated. "You have to understand she hasn't had a normal childhood, like what you or I had. San Diego's still mostly in the dark ages. There are no organized schools, and she never plays with other children. The only kids she knows are her cousins, Hale and Joey, and they are a lot older. So… the idea of every family having a mom and a dad isn't something she understands. I mean, she probably picks that up a little from books we read, but for her, it's not like she misses having a dad around in the way she would if she were at school with lots of other kids who have that. Does that make sense?"

Josh nodded. "How will you introduce me to her then?"

"To tell you the truth, I'm not sure," said Marguerite. "I wasn't sure how I'd feel about you, so I haven't thought much about what to say to her. I guess I want to sort out my own feelings first before bringing you into the mix."

Josh turned to face her, grabbing her shoulders. "I have to see her. I came all this way, and I need to see my daughter."

"Of course, you can see her," said Marguerite. "All I'm saying is I don't think we need to tell her right away that you're her father. Get to know her a little. We can say you're a close friend of Uncle Steve's and you're visiting for a while. Give her time to get to know you."

"You're right," said Josh. "I don't mean to be pushy. It's just been so overwhelming for me."

He hugged her close and inhaled her scent. She had told him she needed to sort out her feelings for him, and he owed her the chance to do that. But as he stood there with her looking at the stars, he felt himself tumbling slowly over a cliff with no way to stop. In a sense, he was in free fall, yet somehow, Josh knew that he had finally found his way home.

The following day, they woke early, ready to bike the final 20 miles to Steve's house. Once the sun rose, it wouldn't take long for the temperature in the desert to skyrocket, and they wanted to reach the house well before that.

Josh felt a twinge of excitement as they topped a hill and saw Steve's ramshackle house in the distance. He remembered this place well. As they rode down the dirt road to the house, two boys and a girl came running out. Amigo raced ahead to greet them. Josh got off his bike slowly and stared at the little girl who was gazing up at him. Steve had written that he thought she looked like a miniature version of Josh, but when Josh looked into her deep brown eyes, all he saw was his mother.

Chapter 13
Seven Years After

By some miracle, everyone except Diego was out of the house for the afternoon. Brendan and Grace sat on the porch quietly talking, while Diego lay in his room napping. Life was hard in Loscoaya. Between hauling water, cooking over a coal stove, doing laundry by hand and simply making sure they all had enough to eat, they had their hands full. Added to that, both Brendan and Grace were still teaching in order to fulfill their contract with the village so they could keep their house. Since the arrival of his parents, squeezing six additional people into their little house had proven challenging for all. And now, with Grace pregnant and due in a few weeks, they looked forward to welcoming another mouth to feed with a little trepidation.

"When Debrak was born, I wondered how my neighbors did it," said Brendan. "Their house was already over-full, and then they had a new baby, and somehow they managed to squeeze him in. We've talked about this over and over, yet I still don't know how we're going to manage."

"We'll make it work somehow," said Grace. "People here have done this for hundreds of years. Remember, Alejandro won't be here for the next couple of months, so that's one less person in the house. Maybe Dawn and Diego can also go stay with him for a few weeks."

When they first arrived in Loscoaya, Alejandro had been thrilled to discover Brendan had met Leonard McFay. McFay had dropped out of sight shortly after making the recording they had viewed years earlier. Even though there were rumors he was in Africa, no one knew for sure what happened to him. And now, here he was in Loscoaya, in the capital of Troeburg only a mere 40 miles from where they were living.

Brendan's former students, Janice, Ian and Cyrus, were still working with McFay on a project to predict the movement of the magnetic north and south poles. Given his expertise, Alejandro desperately wanted to help with that as well, though he thought Diego and Dawn would be better off in the village rather than in the chaotic city of Troeburg. The city wasn't far, but it was difficult to get to, especially with a worldwide gas shortage. Most people made the trip by bicycle, and it often took a full day. Alejandro worked out an arrangement with McFay to spend a month in the city and a month back in the village with Dawn and Diego. With the help of Brendan, Grace, Laurie, Stan and George, he was confident the two children would be well taken care of. It wasn't ideal, but it allowed him to continue what he considered vital work, while keeping his children safe. For the next couple of months, he planned to stay in Troeburg to give Grace and Brendan a little more space in the house, providing Dawn and Diego agreed. For the most part, Dawn appeared to be adapting well to life in the village and although Diego was struggling, he told his father he would manage.

"Don't worry, Brendan," Grace continued. "Just be grateful you have your family here to be part of all this. I would give anything to have my parents and my brother meet our new addition to the family."

"I know," replied Brendan. "I wish I could have met your family as well."

For a few moments, they sat quietly, each lost in their own thoughts. Grace grew up in Minnesota and as far as she knew, her parents still lived there. She had received no word from them since the great power outage, and though she knew many people in the United States had moved south, she was unable to get any real information about what was happening in the northern part of the country. Her brother was in Ecuador at the time of the outage, and she thought it most likely he was still there. But she had no way of knowing that either, and although she tried not to dwell on missing them, sometimes it was plain hard. At least Brendan knew how she felt. Even though his parents were here now, he still didn't know about the fate of his brother, and he could remember the years when he had no contact with any of his family.

When he finally learned what happened to Josh, it was hard to hear, and he felt enormous guilt. He, too, had been in Boy Scouts for a while and heard rumors about Reggie but never paid them much attention. By the time Reggie was a Scout Leader, Brendan was far less involved. He spent hours talking to Grace about it, replaying scenes from his childhood in his head. All the times when he could have asked Josh what was going on but didn't. Grace helped him see it wasn't his fault or Josh's, and over time, he realized Josh was the victim of a predator, and neither he nor Josh were to blame. At least he wasn't so angry anymore. He deeply missed his brother and often wondered if he were still alive somewhere. George was convinced Josh had survived, and he and Stan were attempting to build a radio hoping they could somehow contact him. Or, if they couldn't find Josh, perhaps they could locate Grace's brother in Ecuador. Years ago, George had taught high schoolers in the radio club how to build a ham radio, and he knew he could do it again now if he could just get the right materials. Both George and Stan were excited about the project, though to Brendan's thinking, it was a pipe dream. However, he supposed anything that kept his dad and George occupied was a good thing.

In the meantime, life went on in their village much the way it always had. As he had told his mom years ago, all they could do was try to adapt as things changed. At least he had Grace and the rest of his family.

Diego

Diego swore under his breath as his sister came into the room. He hated sharing a room with her. In fact, he hated everything about this place. He desperately wanted to return home, where at least he had his own room and wasn't constantly expected to do chores. He still wished he could go back in time to the way life had been before the power went out.

Back then, he had friends. Maybe his parents didn't realize it at the time, but the hours he spent on his phone and with video games weren't always solitary. He texted friends and he played games, sometimes with himself and more often with others. They had contests and battles and fights. Maybe they weren't playing with each other face to face, but they were still interacting. His friends understood and accepted him. That was a huge part of his life, and when the power went out, he lost it all.

And then there was his little sister who seemed to make friends with everyone. Sure, she had a tough time here initially. But, after a few months of settling in, everyone loved her. And the more they loved her, the more isolated he felt. He wanted to fit in but didn't know how. In his younger years, he always connected with his friends by text messaging, but he couldn't do that here and he found conversation with other kids awkward. He had grown up with a completely different way of relating to people.

Recently, he started playing cards with some older guys in town and yesterday they snuck him some palm wine. "Is good for you!" his new friend Carl exclaimed, laughing as he poured him cup after cup. "Will take away all your worries!"

It was one of the few times since being in this godforsaken place that he could honestly say he had a good time. He stumbled home late in the afternoon and went directly to bed, mumbling something about not feeling well. While it was a lie at the time, he woke this morning with a raging headache, the likes of which he had never had before. His sister coming into the room made it far worse.

"Diego, wake up!" said Dawn. "We need to get to school!"

"Shut up!" he shouted, pulling the sheet over his head. "Go away and leave me alone."

Maybe it was time to leave this place. Yesterday, one of the guys talked about traveling to another village where there was better food and more women. Diego wasn't sure about the women part, but the food sure sounded good. He was sick of the same food here day in and day out. And he was sick of everyone being on his case about going to school. Why? What difference did it make? His newfound friends hadn't ever gone to school and they all seemed happy enough. He had just decided to stay in bed all morning pretending to be sick when his stomach lurched violently. No pretending needed, he rolled out of bed, ran outside, and immediately threw up.

"I'm not going to school today," he announced as he tumbled back into bed. Laurie, Stan, and George watched him go and shrugged. "That boy is trouble," said George. "He's so unhappy here, but from what I remember, he didn't seem happy before the Event either."

"The Event" was what they now called the power outage which had changed their world. It had seemed so innocuous at the time—just another disruption in a string of them that season, except the power never came back on. It clearly marked a turning point in the history of the Earth. They had all done their best to adapt, except Diego who seemed unable to let go of his old life, even after all this time.

"You're right he didn't seem happy, even before," said Laurie. "But I think the problem is deeper. He barely said more than one word to me in the six months I knew him before the Event. I was at his house a lot and he always had his head buried in his phone. And when the power went out and he no longer had his phone as a crutch, he couldn't function. It was hard enough for us adults, but we at least had some memory of what it was like to live before the digital age. Diego never had that. He had a brief friendship with a boy in the neighborhood, but then they moved, and he was alone again. I wish there was a way to help him now. I wish he had some friends."

"Be careful what you wish for," said Brendan. He had entered the room at the tail end of the conversation. "Grace told me she saw him yesterday playing cards with some of the 'bad boys' in town."

"What do you mean 'bad boys'?" asked Laurie anxiously.

"You know… the group of guys in town who never do much of anything except hang out and occasionally cause trouble. Some of them never went to school and some were former students of mine who were officially in school but never came to class, never studied, and didn't graduate high school. Their reputations aren't great. Diego was with them all day yesterday. They may not be the best role models for him."

"I don't know what to do," said Laurie softly. "He's sixteen years old, and we have absolutely no control over him. Do you think you can talk to him, Brendan?"

Brendan blew out a breath. He had been hoping it wouldn't come to this. He liked Alejandro and Dawn a lot, but didn't have a clue how to reach Diego, and he didn't particularly want to try. Thinking back on his first two years of teaching, he remembered how jaded he felt and how he vowed not to feel bad for anyone who didn't pull their own weight. Instead, he focused his energy on helping those students who genuinely wanted to learn and were willing to put in the effort to do so. But then he remembered Josh. Maybe if he had paid more attention and been a better brother, Josh would have talked to him and he could have helped.

"I'll try, but don't get your hopes up. I don't think he'll listen much to me," said Brendan slowly. "I'm not sure I can say anything that will really make a difference. I think I'll give him a little time right now though and see if I can catch him when he's feeling a little better."

Several hours later, Brendan knocked lightly on the door to Dawn and Diego's bedroom. "Can we talk?" he asked.

Lying in bed, Diego pulled the sheet up over his head. Brendan sat down on the lone chair in the room, wondering how he had gotten into this situation. Why did his mom think he could make any headway with this kid? For a while he was silent, trying to figure out the best way to start.

"What do you want?" asked Diego.

Best to dive right in, he thought. "I saw you yesterday, down by the old school, with Carl and Michael."

Diego pulled the sheet off his head and stared at him. "So?" he asked.

"I know them. They are not very trustworthy people. I guess I just want to warn you to beware."

"They're my friends," said Diego stubbornly. "They're the only people in this stupid village who will talk to me."

"Are they really your friends, Diego?" Brendan asked softly. "Or are they looking to get something from you?"

"What do you mean?" asked Diego. "What would they want from me?"

"They probably like that you are younger, and they think they can boss you around, for one thing. Maybe get you to do their dirty work for them—things that might be dangerous or that they just don't want to do."

"I don't know what you're talking about," said Diego. "They haven't asked me to do anything."

"Not yet, maybe. But they will. And I don't want you to get into trouble. You may think you are the same as they are, but you're not. Believe me when I tell you those guys are only out for themselves. If they think you can somehow help them improve their way of life, they are going to grab at that. You need to be careful."

"Why should I believe you?" asked Diego. "You think you're big stuff here around town, with all your education. You're always talking about how important education is and how everyone needs to learn more. Well, I

206

don't agree. I think it's a waste of time. What's it going to get me, anyway? Education won't get me out of this hellhole."

"Is that what this is about, Diego? Getting out of this place?"

"Well, duh... of course. Do you think I want to stay here for the rest of my life?"

Brendan shook his head sadly. On the one hand, he understood how Diego felt. This was certainly not the life any of them had envisioned. But here they were, and they could either make the best of it or fight it. He had chosen to make the best of it, he realized. And Diego—well thus far he had chosen to fight it, but was that a done deal? Brendan wasn't so sure. Once again, he thought of Josh. *I couldn't help my brother*, he thought to himself. *But maybe I can make a difference with Diego.*

Brendan pressed on. "You can certainly leave here, Diego. No one's holding you prisoner. But I doubt you will find much else beyond this village. I know you have memories of life before, of a quite different existence, but the world has changed. It's up to you whether to change with it or not. The memories you have, the times when everything was handed to you on a platter, those times aren't coming back. No matter how much you wish for them."

Diego stared at him as he continued. "I once had a smartphone. I miss it too sometimes. I never played the sophisticated games you had, but I used to play Mario Kart and Dungeons and Dragons constantly. World of Warcraft too. At some point though, I recognized it wasn't real. My uncle died in a car crash and I suddenly realized people didn't simply come back to life after driving their cars off a cliff. I gave up the games shortly after that and started living my life. Now I can see the games were simply a way to fill up some empty holes. I had to find a different way to fill those holes."

"Carl and Michael fill those holes," said Diego. "They understand me."

"Do they really?" asked Brendan. "Or do you think they do because you so desperately want them to? One thing I've learned of people here—they are great at reading other people and giving them what they think they want. I'm not saying you're wrong about them, I'm just saying be careful. They may not have your best interests at heart."

With that, Brendan left the room, leaving Diego to ponder what he had said. Brendan didn't feel like he had made a dent, but it was the first decent conversation he had ever had with Diego, and he supposed that counted for something.

Diego was torn. He had already decided he would sneak out to visit his newfound friends that afternoon, before Brendan had knocked on his door. Much as he hated to admit it, the conversation with Brendan rattled him. Carl and Michael had been kind to him. They accepted him. Why shouldn't he consider them his friends? It never occurred to him they couldn't be trusted, and part of him resented Brendan for even saying that. Yet, now he wondered. Could he trust these people? How well did he really know them? All day yesterday, they talked of a big plan to get lots of money, and they made it sound so easy. Diego wanted in, and they were more than willing to accommodate him. They had a plan and he was part of it. It had been a long time since he had felt like he belonged. Damn Brendan for trying to ruin it for him.

Getting up from bed, he made his final decision. He was his own man. No one was going to boss him around. And besides, he hated having five parents in addition to his dad. Why did he have to listen to them, anyway? None of them were his "real" parents and his dad wasn't around. His mind made up, he quickly dressed and peeked out the bedroom door.

Amazingly, no one was there. In this house, there was always someone, somewhere (usually his sister, who followed him around like a puppy dog). Quietly he slipped out of the house, grabbed his bike, and made his way down the dirt path to the appointed meeting place.

Carl and Michael were waiting for him, along with two older men he had met the day before. They all greeted Diego heartily and he immediately felt like he had made the right choice. He *belonged*.

As the day turned to dusk, the men laid out their plan.

"Is simple," Carl said. "There's a lone house between here and the nex' village over. Is far from the road and far from any other people. I been checkin' it out over the pas' two weeks. There's two brothers an' a teenage boy in high school, an' I know their schedule. I seen them recently around town boastin' about how they scored a great deal in Troeburg las' week."

Michael chimed in. "Yest'day, their booth at the market was suddenly filled with all sorts o' stuff. They mus' have a big stash in their house, and we gonna take some of it. We can't sell it near here, so we got to travel 'round for the next few weeks to distribute it."

"All we need to do is get into the house, get the goods, and get out quick as possible," continued Carl. "Diego, you're our getaway man since you have the best bike."

Their plan positioned him near the house ready to take the goods, which would be in one backpack and two side duffle bags which could fit on his bike. Their plan was to throw it out the window. Once he had it, he was to hightail it out of there as fast as he possibly could. They had a rendezvous point set up at an abandoned house about three miles away, where they planned to hide everything until they could figure out the best way to distribute it.

Diego glanced sideways at Carl who looked oddly suspicious. "Wha' you lookin' a' me for?" Carl asked, shifting his position. Was he hiding something? Diego looked away. Much as he was getting excited about this new adventure, Brendan's words still jiggled around in his head. "Be careful of them," he had said. He snuck another glance in Carl's direction and caught a glimpse of Carl pocketing a gun. "Don't worry 'bout it man!" said Carl. "I na' gonna use it. Is jus' for show."

Diego shook his head. He wanted to trust these guys, but the first seeds of doubt were sown. It was beginning to dawn on him this was not a video game in which you had many lives. This was real. This guy had a real gun. Maybe this was what Brendan had meant.

"I'm not sure I want to go through with this," he stammered. He started to turn, but Michael blocked his way.

"You think we can let you go now?" Michael asked. "Now, when we jus' tol' you the whole plan. We been workin' on this for weeks—weeks! We ain't about to stop now. You leave now and the plan is ruined." He turned to Carl. "C'mon, let's go. It'll be dark soon."

Dawn

Dawn watched as her brother snuck out of the house. She was glad he was out. At least now she could get into the bedroom they shared. She didn't understand why he was so mean to her. For the most part, she tried to stay out of his way, but it was hard in this small house. Yet then again, most of her friends shared rooms with their siblings and sometimes with cousins and aunts and uncles too. While she dimly remembered having her own room in a much bigger house, privacy was not important here and she was young enough not to be bothered by the lack of it.

At the moment, she wanted to get into the room and find a book she had promised to show Debrak. During the past year, they had become friends even though he was opposite her in many ways. He was so sure of himself and all the other kids worshiped him, while Dawn was shy and kept to herself. He was loud and boisterous—a big boy for his age with a commanding presence; Dawn was quiet, reserved and petite and could almost disappear into the background. He was clearly comfortable around kids his own age, whereas Dawn much preferred adult company. For the first five years of her life, she had been sheltered by the few adults who surrounded her. Initially, Dawn avoided Debrak as much as possible, but then they discovered they had the same birthday and that each of them had a mother who had died on the day they were born.

"Everyone here say the day I was born, the sun rose blood red," said Debrak. "They all thought it was a sign from the gods and maybe it was my mama's blood." Dawn had never heard the story of the bloody sunrise, and she was fascinated by the descriptions. Could it have been the blood of *both* their mamas?

Every year on that date, the town held a celebration, and one year ago, when Dawn and Debrak turned six years old, they were at the center of it. People sang and danced, and the town's chief spoke of how they thought the bloody sunrise signaled the end of the world as they had known it, but there they were, six years later and all was well. The town was thriving. They had new people in town. They were aware of food shortages in other parts of the country and the world, yet their village was doing fine, and new merchandise was coming in from Troeburg each week. More and more people had solar panels put onto their houses, and it seemed like the sun, which had threatened them six years ago, was now more friend than foe. The occasional rumors and stories about how difficult things were in other parts of the world had little effect on their day-to-day life.

It was during that celebration that Dawn and Debrak discovered they had something else in common. Two years earlier, on Debrak's 4th birthday, some of Brendan's students had introduced a new game in town that quickly caught on. They called it the "magnet game."

They showed the children a compass and let them see the direction of magnetic north. Then they blindfolded them, spun them around a few times, and keeping the blindfolds on, asked them to turn toward magnetic north. Debrak was considered the champion at this game and everyone knew it, but all the other kids liked to play as well. Dawn didn't particularly want to play, but since she was a guest of honor at the celebration, she couldn't easily avoid it. Reluctantly, she allowed them to blindfold and spin her around. The townspeople all fell silent as she stopped, facing directly north. She was the only person (adult or child) with this ability other than

Debrak. There were small murmurings in the crowd as they tested her several times and each time, she stopped and faced the correct direction.

"Somethin's up with both those children," one of the women said. "No one else can do that. Must be some sign from the gods." The comment quickly sparked rumors that Dawn's presence in the village must be due to some heavenly force.

That party was a year ago, and with their mutual birthday coming up once again, Dawn wanted to give Debrak the book Laurie had shared with her on her fifth birthday. She remembered it because that was the night the northern lights appeared for the first time; the night her dad had told her the lights were dancing in honor of her birthday. She often wondered if the lights were connected to the bloody sunrise, and she had tried to describe them to Debrak, but he didn't understand what she was talking about.

As she held the book in her hands, she shuddered now as she remembered how the lights had affected her. She recalled feeling an annoying pull when they first appeared, followed by a constant sense that something was wrong with the air all around her, like she was being bombarded with invisible little pellets. As the lights got brighter and brighter each night, she felt weaker and weaker. She continued to feel worse until they got on the boat and traveled south, away from the disturbing nighttime lights.

Since being here, she felt fine and had almost forgotten that feeling, though recently, she experienced little pangs of it. Occasionally, she felt itchy and uncomfortable in the same way she had before they moved to Africa. Even now, her body felt tingly. And just yesterday, Debrak mentioned to her he had been feeling strange lately and described a similar feeling. Sometimes they had talked about how they both thought they had some extra sense, a way of feeling the world that was different, but neither of them could put it into words. Dawn wondered if this might have something to do with the bloody sunrise on the day they were born. She wasn't sure if the lights had anything to do with it, but she wanted to share this with Debrak and see if he had any other ideas. With the book tucked under her arm, she walked down the path to Debrak's house.

Laurie

Laurie and Brendan strolled through the mango forest on the edge of town. They followed a dirt path, skirting numerous fields of cultivated eggplant, bitterball, and cassava, until they reached the forest, where trees were dripping with mangos and avocados. The air smelled fresh, as a brief shower had just passed through. Now the sun was shining, and birds were happily chirping. It was the end of the rainy season and for these few weeks they could enjoy a few showers before the land became parched and the air brutally hot.

"Do you miss it, Mom? What you used to have?" asked Brendan.

Laurie was quiet for a while. "I don't know. It's all such a blur in my mind now. We've lived through three separate lifetimes. There was the time before, then the five years after when we stayed in our house, and now our life here. If you had asked me ten years ago, before all this started—if you had given me a snapshot of our life now and asked what I would prefer—I would have laughed. Of course, I would have preferred everything we had then. There would have been no question in my mind. Yet now… I see how little we had then and how much we have now. How about you? Do you miss anything from back home?"

"I miss being able to get in a car and drive anywhere, I guess. But here, there's no place I feel like I need to go to. And I suppose I miss watching TV and movies sometimes."

Laurie laughed. "Your dad and I watched TV almost every night and sometimes barely talked to each other. Dad would get home from work and dinner would be made for us by our resident robot or delivered by an Uber driver, and we'd sit and vegetate. At the time it was so comfortable, but now as I look back, it was like we weren't even really living. So... I guess, no, I don't miss it. I rather like what we have now. Sure, we have to work the land, and cooking is hard. We have fewer choices about what to eat and it's hard to do laundry and keep things clean. But it's just the way everyone does things here. We have the basics. Dad and George are enjoying making furniture and especially trying to build a radio. And I've had time to write lots of children's stories. They may not be published, but kids here sure love to read them. Thanks to you and Grace working here, we have enough food to survive, we have a roof over our heads, we have people here who care about us and we care about them. What else could we want?"

Laurie plucked an overripe mango off the tree as they walked. "I remember buying frozen mangos at the grocery store and keeping them for months in our freezer. Then pulling them out to make a smoothie and gulping it down without even tasting it."

"Dad told me recently he never thought you would survive that first year," Brendan said quietly. Laurie looked at him in surprise. Stan had never shared that with her before. "He was so worried, wondering about how you would manage. Where would you get food, and clean water, and heat in the winter? Would the well work and provide enough for your needs? You had done a little preparation, but when it happened, when it became real and everything changed overnight, he was terrified."

"It was a scary time," Laurie agreed. She thought back to those first few months. She had certainly felt adrift, though she had always thought of Stan as her anchor in the storm. "Witnessing the desolation after just a few years, how buildings simply collapsed from lack of upkeep. Then there were those massive fires in town that couldn't be controlled because no one was left at the Fire Department."

For a while, they were both quiet, lost in their memories. Laurie hadn't thought about those fires since she had written about them to Brendan years ago. Seeing their once-bustling town in ruins, seeing the houses of friends turned completely to ash. The Town Hall and library wiped out. And where were the people? Few remained to witness the devastation, save themselves and a dwindling number of townspeople. Suddenly, the reality of what had happened in the world came had come crashing down. This was to be their future, their world from here forward. Nothing would be the same.

She and Stan had spent some time at the site of the former library, sifting through the rubble, seeing if there were any books worth salvaging. Miraculously, they found a small collection of children's books, fully illustrated and intact. Somehow the fire had skirted around one small section of the children's department. Laurie salvaged what she could of these. Most of the other books were so charred they were beyond recognition. It was one of the few times Laurie had seen Stan cry. He loved to read, and the library had been like a second home to him. He could easily spend hours simply browsing the stacks, looking for the next thriller to check out.

"That time at the library was the one and only time I saw your dad break down," Laurie told Brendan now. "He was always so positive, always optimistic that things would somehow work out. And he always seemed to have some sort of plan in mind. But when he saw those books burned to ashes, it was like a part of him burned up as well."

How many other libraries, how many museums and archives had been destroyed? How many other towns across the country had suffered fires like this or flooding from torrential rains? Was it enough that they personally had survived? Thinking about it now made them both sad.

"I wish we could have brought all those books with us so the next generation of kids could know what it was like," Laurie said, half to herself. She had seen the blank looks of children like Dawn and Debrak and all those who had been born after the Event whenever they talked about things like computers and cell phones and laptops. It was one of the things that had been so difficult for Diego when they first arrived in Africa, as no one knew what he was talking about when he referred to his games. It was as if they had come from a different planet, and in a sense, they had. In many ways, they had all lived in a virtual reality for much of their lives. It was almost impossible to explain that reality to those who had never even experienced the act of looking at a screen and having it come to life.

"I love that you're writing stories for the children," Brendan offered. They enjoy reading them. And our new baby will love it as well."

Laurie smiled at the thought of that. She and Stan were going to be grandparents! Over the past year she had come to think of Grace as her own daughter, and she was grateful they had this time together, hard as it had been. She did worry about the delivery, though. Grace was due any day now, and they had some highly experienced midwives in town, but Laurie couldn't get the memory of Sophia out of her mind. Not wanting to worry Brendan with those thoughts, she turned to him and said brightly, "Let's get back to your wonderful bride. She probably has her hands full with everyone at the house."

As they circled back to Brendan's house, they saw Stan running toward them. "Come quickly!" he cried. "It's Diego. He's been hurt."

Diego

They ran into the house to see Diego lying on the floor, writhing in pain. His face was bloodied, and his arm was bleeding. Brendan's neighbor Anna had some nursing training and was tending to him, cleaning his wounds and bandaging him.

"What happened?" Laurie asked Stan.

"We don't know yet, but it looks like someone attacked him."

As Brendan came in, Diego looked at Brendan and managed to get out the words. "You were right. They were not my friends." Then he closed his eyes and went quiet, succumbing to the herbal sedative Anna had just given him.

"What did he mean?" asked Laurie. "Who did this?"

Something clicked in Brendan's brain. "The robberies," he said. "I'm not sure, but I bet they are connected to this."

During the past few weeks, there had been a rash of small burglaries in town. They were minor incidents, but it had upset the townspeople to think someone among them would steal from them, given what little they all had and how much of it was shared. Brendan heard through the grapevine this was also happening in other nearby villages, and everyone was little uneasy.

Ever since their talk a few weeks ago, Brendan had been watching Diego closely, and noticed he was staying out late and skipping school. He was also avoiding Brendan as much as possible, which Brendan found frustrating. As far as Brendan was concerned, Diego could stew in his own juices.

The day before, however, Diego had pulled him aside wanting to talk. "I'm scared of Carl and Michael," he said.

"What do you mean? Have they threatened you?" asked Brendan.

"Maybe a little," mumbled Diego, unable to look Brendan in the eye. He refused to give any more detail and when Brendan pressed him, he went silent. Disgusted, Brendan repeated what he had told Diego earlier about his newfound friends not having his best interests at heart. Diego remained mute. "If you have something to tell me Diego, I'll listen, but otherwise there isn't much I can do." Now he wondered if Diego had been involved with Carl and Michael in the recent spate of robberies. Had they hurt Diego because he wanted out?

For two days, Diego lay in his room, unwilling to see or talk to anyone aside from Anna, who checked on him periodically, and Grace who brought him food. Even Dawn moved out of the bedroom and slept in the common room.

While Diego convalesced, Brendan did a little investigating around town and learned that Carl and Michael had disappeared, along with several of their friends. With a little more snooping, he found that indeed, Diego had been seen with the group frequently during the past few weeks. It wasn't hard to put two and two together, and Brendan finally decided it was time for another talk.

He knocked softly on Diego's door, and when there was no answer, peeked in. Diego was sitting up in bed, drawing on a sketch pad.

"You look much better," Brendan offered, glad to see Diego sitting up. Aside from a bandage on his arm, he looked healthy.

"You were right," Diego said finally, staring down at his pad. "I was stupid to think they were my friends." He hesitated, then looked up pleadingly. "Carl attacked me." The words came quicker now. "They were so friendly at first, then when I said I wasn't sure about things, they refused to let me go because I knew too much. They forced me to help and got bolder and bolder. But I got more scared. Last week, they wanted me to do a job that really frightened me, and I refused. Carl started hitting me but then the others pulled him away and I ran. I think I passed out as soon as I got here. I'm afraid of them, Brendan. I know way too much and now you do too. There's no way I can hide from them. I want to leave town. If I stay here, they'll eventually come after me."

"You're not going anywhere right now," said Brendan. "Except maybe to the local police. They want these robberies solved and they'll protect you," Brendan said.

"Are you sure?" asked Diego. He looked at Brendan pleadingly, wanting reassurance. "I'm scared, but I also don't want them to get into trouble because of me. I wish there were another way."

He looked down at his sketch pad as a tear fell from his eye. Brendan glanced at the pad. He did a double take. "What do you have there? Did you draw that?"

"I'm just doodling," Diego said with embarrassment. He quickly flipped the pad, but Brendan had already seen it. "Come on, I want to see. It looked amazing!"

Slowly, Diego turned over the book and Brendan stared in awe. "Are there more?" he asked. Diego nodded and turned the page. As Brendan looked at page after page of caricatures, he was immediately taken back to his teenage days. Diego had recreated an entire universe of video game characters from ten years ago. Brendan was astounded.

"Diego, these are incredible. I had no idea you could draw like this!"

Diego merely shrugged. "It's just something I like to do to pass the time," he said.

"I wonder if you could sell these at the market. You could get a lot of money for these. I bet the kids in this village would absolutely love them!"

Diego looked at him. It had never occurred to him that people would buy his sketches. "Really?" he asked. "You think people would actually pay for these?"

"These characters are all in fashion here. Look at all the old t-shirts that are sold at the marketplace. Those images are everywhere. I definitely think people would buy them!"

As an idea began to take shape in Diego's mind, there was a sudden commotion from the other room. "Brendan, come quickly," Laurie cried. "I think Grace is going into labor!"

Brendan looked at Diego. "We'll finish this conversation later," he said, dashing out the door.

Diego leafed through his sketch pad. For the past two days, he had been sketching non-stop, and he felt an incredible sense of peace and fulfillment. Suddenly, he understood what his friend Kevin had meant years ago when he gave him the sketch pad and told him he could draw for himself. Drawing was what he was meant to do. And now Brendan said maybe others would buy his work. Was that even possible?

He looked around the room, feeling suddenly emboldened. On a whim, he got up, tucked some of his sketches under his arm and quietly snuck out of the house. No one saw him leave as the family was all gathered in Grace and Brendan's bedroom. He was nervous as hell but felt like this was a step he had to take. He knew his former cohorts had been hiding in a neighboring village for a few days and he hoped they would be there now to hear him out.

He stepped into a clearing and came face to face with Carl. "Well, look here. If it ain't our li'l snitch."

"I'm not a snitch, Carl," he said with a shaky voice. "If I was, you'd all have been arrested by now."

"What are you doing here?" asked Michael. "Did anyone follow you?"

Diego shook his head. "I have an idea and I want your help. It's a business idea—a way to make some money. But if you agree to help me, you have to agree to give up stealing for good."

"Why would we do that?" asked Carl.

"Because with my idea, you'll make more money and it'll be more lawful. You won't have to worry about being arrested."

The four men looked at each other. "Go ahead, what's your plan?" asked Devon, one of the other gang members.

Diego took a deep breath. He wanted to show his sketches but was terrified of once again being ridiculed. He closed his eyes and heard Brendan's voice in his head, "These are incredible!" Slowly, he opened his sketch pad. "I have these drawings," he began as the group gathered around to look. "I'm thinking of selling them, but I need a sales team."

"Where'd you get these?" asked Michael. "They look like original drawings of the things we see on our t-shirts!"

"They *are* original drawings," Diego replied. "*My* drawings."

"You did these?" Devon asked incredulously. "They are amazin'!" Everyone nodded vigorously. "How much you want to sell them for?"

"That's where I need you," explained Diego. He looked around at the group of men. "You see, I can draw these—lots of them, but I know nothing about how to sell them or even how much to sell them for. I need help. If you all help me sell these, I'll give you a percentage of whatever they sell for, but you have to first promise me, no more stealing."

"These here are worth a fortune," murmured Michael. "I bet we could sell these for big bucks!"

"That's what I'm hoping," said Diego. "Will you help me? We can set up a legitimate booth at the market. If so, and if you can promise me no more stealing, I promise not to go to the police. What do you think?"

Josh

Josh and Marguerite sat comfortably on Steve's porch, with Amigo between them and Jessica on Josh's lap. Steve and his family were off foraging for food, hoping to augment the meager supplies they had stored in the house. Josh thought back to when he had first sat here, the night he had told Steve about his childhood trauma. That seemed so long ago. Life had certainly taken some twists and turns since then. While it was not easy here, at least they had enough food to survive, and they had each other. Josh was grateful for that, and for the way his relationship with Marguerite had blossomed. They had indeed become a family, though he often thought wistfully of his family back east and wondered if they were still alive. And he thought of his older brother. He knew Brendan was in Africa seven years ago. Did this calamity extend to the other side of the globe? It seemed incredible to him that he had no way of knowing. What he did know was that on their continent, northern latitudes were no longer safe. Scientists in the northern hemisphere of the United States and Canada were sounding the alarm, telling everyone who would listen that the closer they could get to the equator, the better. During the past year, countless people had migrated south to San Diego, driven by fear of radiation exposure as the magnetic field over the northern hemisphere weakened. Some people opted to remain at the border, though large crowds pressed even farther south.

"I wonder how much longer we can stay here," Josh mused. "Steve thinks it is only a matter of time before we will start to feel the effects of the weakening magnetic field here in San Diego. Pretty soon, we'll also have to head south."

"Pablo wants to go to Ecuador. He's been pushing for that ever since he found out his daughter is alone there. I know he wants us to go with him, but it seems like such a risky trip," said Marguerite.

"It's riskier to stay here," Pablo said, walking toward them. "I've decided to go. Remember when we were in El Paso and you told me you had to come here?" he asked Josh. Josh nodded. "Well, I'm telling you now. I *have* to go there."

Josh understood what he was saying. Years earlier, when Josh had repeatedly sent messages from El Paso to both his family back east and to Steve, Pablo had also tried to communicate with his wife's cousin, Emanuel, in Ecuador. But he never got a reply. On reaching San Diego, he found the equipment Josh had set up years ago was still working, and it was more powerful than the radio they had in El Paso, so he kept trying. Finally, after months of hearing nothing, he received a message from Emanuel with some bittersweet news. His wife had died on the trip to Ecuador, but his 15-year-old daughter, Elena, had survived. She was currently living with relatives in a remote mountain village. Pablo was overwhelmed with grief and guilt.

"I should have gone with them," he sobbed when he got the news. "I should never have let them go alone."

"It's not your fault, Pablo," Josh tried to console him. "How were you to know things would turn out the way they did? None of us could have predicted what happened."

Pablo shook his head. "I let them down. Both of them. I have to get to Ecuador—to see my daughter again, to let her know I didn't abandon her. She was so young when they left...."

That conversation took place almost a year ago and since then, Pablo had been plotting and planning for this trip. Communication continued to improve during the year, and he and Emanuel exchanged several messages. Emanuel had a friend living in the port city of Esmeraldas. If Pablo could get there, this friend could assist him in reaching the village where his daughter lived. Pablo realized that while many people were migrating south into Mexico on foot, if he wanted to go as far as Ecuador, it made more sense to journey by boat.

Now, Pablo faced Josh and Marguerite. "I found an Ecuadorian captain who is willing to take a few passengers. He seemed to like me, especially when I told him of my daughter."

Josh and Marguerite looked at each other now. Maybe it *was* time to leave. "I don't want to live underground for the rest of our lives," Marguerite said quietly. "Our daughter deserves better."

'The only problem is he can only take four passengers," Pablo continued. "We wouldn't all be able to go together." They had discussed this many times with Steve and were loath to separate, but this was an opportunity they needed to carefully consider.

When Steve returned, Josh pulled him aside. "Pablo's found a boat that can take him to Ecuador and we're thinking of going with him," he said. "But the boat can't take all of us. He only has room for four passengers."

Steve studied his friend. He had been afraid it would come to this. For a while now, they had all been talking of migrating south to Mexico, though they knew it might not be far enough. It was clear the farther south they could get, the better, and they might not have another chance. He hated to part ways with his sister, his niece, and his closest friend, but knew this plan probably made the most sense. And so, it was decided; Pablo, Josh, Marguerite and young Jessica would make the trip to Ecuador by boat, while Steve, along with his wife and two boys would travel to Mexico by foot. Both journeys would be fraught with danger, but unless they were prepared to live underground, they all needed to go and there was no way they could stay together.

The following day, Pablo, Josh and Marguerite went to the boatyard to meet the captain and finalize plans. Marguerite eyed the captain with distrust. He was friendly enough to Pablo, but his long greasy black hair, beady eyes and unkempt mustache all combined to give her a visceral feeling of dislike, especially when he looked at her with a lazy grin. Sleazy was the best word she could come up with and she suspected she would have to be careful around him. She watched as Pablo and Josh negotiated the terms of the trip. He pointed to Amigo, who was sitting quietly at Josh's side. "Is he coming too?" he asked with a bit of a leer.

Amigo let out a low growl as Josh's face registered a look of surprise. "We were planning on it, as long as you'll take him," he replied. He was hoping Amigo could go with them, though Steve had promised he could take the dog on foot if needed.

The captain broke into a broad grin. "Sure, I'll take him! So... we have a deal?" The men shook hands and walked off the dock, as the captain called after them. "One week from today. Be here on the dock at 5:00 a.m. sharp!"

"I don't know, Josh," said Marguerite as they walked away. "That man is trouble, and the way he looked at Amigo was downright scary. Maybe we shouldn't bring Amigo with us."

"It'll be fine," Josh reassured her. "Amigo can take care of himself. I actually feel better having him with us for security. He's super-protective of Jessica."

He had a point, Marguerite thought. No stranger could get close to Jessica without Amigo's permission. For that matter, Amigo was protective of them all, and it was clear Josh had made up his mind. Yet even so, she had a strange foreboding about taking the dog with them and vowed to herself to keep a close eye on him.

Saying farewell to Steve was one of the most difficult things Josh ever had to do. Every other time he had left someone in the past, he either left without a goodbye or thought it would be short-term and didn't consider the possibility of never seeing them again. This time felt different. As much as he tried to make light of it, he felt tears form in his eyes as he hugged his friend goodbye.

"Stay well," Steve said to him. "And take good care of my sister and niece!"

Josh held up hand in salute. "I promise," he said, turning quickly away, waiting as Marguerite and Jessica said tearful goodbyes as well. They were embarking on a new phase of life, but at least they had each other.

On board the tiny boat, they were crowded into a small cabin for sleeping, but once underway could move freely about. They cruised along the coast, anchoring in protected harbors of Mexico for the first three nights. This gave the captain and crew an opportunity to sell some of their cargo of fish. During those stopovers, they remained on the ship; however, they didn't mind as the trip started out comfortably enough and they had a plentiful supply of food caught by the expert fishermen who crewed the ship. After all, this was primarily a fishing vessel, so food was not an issue.

As the boat hugged the coast, it was less susceptible to the whims of nature. They enjoyed calm sailing and reveled in the sight of the crystal-clear blue water. "Dolphins!" squealed Jessica, pointing at the graceful creatures as they swam by. She was standing on deck with Marguerite and Amigo. Just then, Marguerite felt the hair on the back of her head stand on end. She turned and spotted the captain strolling toward them, leering at her with a crooked grin. He brushed against her, snaking his hand around her waist and making her skin crawl. It took all her self-control not to slap his hand away; though she wanted to, she realized they were on the ship by his good graces, and she didn't want to anger him. She was grateful for the presence of Amigo who gave a low threatening growl. The captain shot Amigo a menacing look and walked on. After that, she kept a tight hold on Jessica and was rarely out of sight of either Josh, Pablo, or the dog.

On the fourth day, as they prepared to head to sea towards Ecuador, the captain got word of a major tropical storm and decided to anchor in a sheltered bay for several days until the storm passed. He let his small group of passengers off the boat, leaving them to fend for themselves and find lodging in the tiny fishing village. The villagers welcomed them, allowing them to sleep in a dilapidated barn for several nights. They were grateful to be off the boat when the storm roared in with deafening thunder and brilliant bolts of lightning. Even though the barn roof leaked, at least the ground beneath them was stable. They managed to find some dry spots to rest in, and the sturdy walls protected them from the fierce wind. Marguerite, for her part, was happy to be away from the captain's lascivious stares.

Finally, the storm passed, and they returned to the boat, ready for the final leg of their journey. The boat headed for open water and the week-long trip to Ecuador. They had no idea what awaited them there, but at least they would be temporarily safe from radiation exposure and Pablo had a chance of reuniting with his daughter. They knew if the magnetic poles reached the equator, there would be no place else to run. Maybe this was the end of the line in terms of migration, and perhaps in the future they would all have to live underground, but at least they would have time to prepare.

As the winds calmed, the remainder of the trip was smoother than expected. They relaxed into the shipboard routine and were grateful for the relative ease of the trip, hardly willing to believe their luck. Marguerite managed to avoid the captain, and the days melted into one another, as rhythmic as the rise and fall of the ocean waves. Clear sparkling days were followed by starlit nights, during which they gazed in awe at the inconceivable number of stars. Night after night, little Jessica peppered them with questions about the stars and constellations. Josh remembered how his mom, being a teacher, always had a large collection of books on these topics and he reached back into his memory, trying to recall stories to tell her. He related tales from his childhood about how Orion the hunter stood up against Taurus the bull, or chased after a hare with his two hunting dogs, Canis Major and Canis Minor, and he taught her to identify those constellations. Mostly, though, they simply sat together and gazed at the sky, hoping for a future in which the open air, sun, and stars wouldn't be just a memory.

Finally, after a week of sailing, they reached their destination. As Josh and Pablo gathered their few possessions from their tiny cabin, Marguerite stood with Jessica at the bow of the boat, watching as the crew lowered the gangplank. They had made it! She breathed in the salty air and let it out with a sigh of relief. Just then, she sensed something behind her, a hot breath on her neck. Not wanting to alarm Jessica, she turned slightly as the captain slid his hand under her shirt and up her back. Out of the corner of her eye, she saw Josh and Pablo running toward them with Amigo in front. "Amigo, stop!" commanded Josh. But it was too late. Amigo lunged at the captain, and a shot rang out. The dog fell to the ground.

"Noooooo!" cried Josh. He was by Amigo's side in an instant.

"I take him as payment," the captain smirked. Josh and Pablo were aghast.

"Pablo, help me!" Josh yelled, struggling to lift Amigo up. Together they dragged the still body of Amigo off the boat. Marguerite and Jessica grabbed their few belongings and ran quickly behind them. The captain glared at them, muttering angrily in Spanish. Josh shuddered at the thought of what he had intended to do. Luckily, there was a crowd of people on land, and the captain was reluctant to fire his weapon recklessly. Quickly they carried Amigo off, praying the captain wouldn't follow them and they could find a place to hide. Gently, they laid the dog down in a small clearing behind a few dilapidated buildings. The bullet had gone into Amigo's chest, and the dog was barely clinging to life. "Amigo, I am so sorry," Josh sobbed. You did nothing wrong!"

The dog opened one eye for a moment, before taking his last breath. Marguerite hugged Jessica tightly, as Josh whispered in Amigo's ear. "You saved my life more than once. I promise I will never forget you."

Chapter 14
Ten Years After

Laurie, Grace and Brendan sat on the porch, watching little Benjamin chase a lizard along the porch railing. In the background, they could hear George and Stan muttering to each other as they tinkered with their radio. "It's hard to believe he'll be three years old soon," Laurie said.

"I know," replied Grace. "So much has happened, yet so little has changed around here. I wonder if life in this little village will ever be different."

Laurie pondered that. She remembered her big house and the solitude she used to endure. In one week, it would be exactly ten years since the power went out and their lives changed forever. In hindsight, she could see how removed she had been from the Earth and the natural cycles of life, yet she never realized it at the time. You can't miss what you've never had, she mused to herself. Aloud she said, "It'll change over time, I'm sure. But it'll never be what we all grew up with."

"That's true, but then again, no one ever goes back to their childhood way of life," Brendan chimed in. "I'm sure life will be a lot different for Benjamin when he gets to be an adult. There should be plenty more opportunities for him. Look at how Diego has thrived."

Diego had indeed undergone a major transformation after his confrontation with Carl three years earlier. He had turned his sketch hobby into a full-fledged business and was teaching drawing classes in the village as well. He was even working with Laurie to illustrate a few of her children's books.

Laurie smiled, thinking how proud Sophia would be of him. It was good he found a niche. But then Laurie's thoughts turned to Dawn. Lately, she had noticed Dawn was more withdrawn and that worried her.

Dawn

It was a week before her tenth birthday, and the townspeople were planning a grand celebration. Dawn, however, felt anxious. As her birthday approached, she started experiencing debilitating headaches. She spent more and more time in bed, often saying she felt too weak to get up and go to school. Laurie tried to talk to her, but Dawn became increasingly withdrawn.

Now, as she lay alone in her room, she thought of her brother. Somehow, he had managed to become successful. She was glad things were working out for him, but she also felt a little envious. She remembered back to the day three years earlier when Benjamin was born. That was a few days after Diego was attacked, and when he recovered, he seemed like a different person. Dawn didn't understand how he could change so quickly, and at first, she didn't trust that change; however, after three years, she had to admit Diego was much easier to be around. She just wished he had more time for her. Lately, he was always out with his friends, and now with their father away in Troeburg for a month, Dawn felt very alone.

The night after Alejandro left, Dawn awoke at midnight with a strange yet familiar feeling. Unsure of what had disturbed her, she quietly got up, slipped outside, and stood transfixed staring at the horizon in the direction of magnetic north. Far, far away she saw an eerily recognizable glow, faint but clearly there. *The lights!* she thought. *They are chasing me.* As she turned around to go inside, she saw something even more distressing. Directly across the sky, on the opposite horizon, was another set of faint and dancing lights. *Two sets of them? How could that possibly be?* she wondered. And then she remembered one of Laurie's books they had read long ago, the one she had shared with Debrak. It had described two arrays of lights in the sky—the aurora borealis (northern lights) and the aurora australis (southern lights). She ran inside, crawled back into bed, and yanked the sheet over her head. Five years ago, she had felt horrible when one set of lights was tugging at her. How would it be now with two?

The next morning in school, Debrak pulled her aside. "I need to talk to you," he began. "I felt something last night. It was like what you used to tell me about. It woke me up, and I didn't know what to do."

"Did you see the lights? she asked.

Debrak looked at her questioningly. "Lights? No, I was in my room in bed. I didn't see anything."

"Tonight, if it happens again, go outside, and look both north and south, *magnetic* north and south that is." They both smiled at that, because they both knew that magnetic north and south were now almost directly east and west. "You'll see them dancing across the sky. I think they have something to do with how we are feeling. I wish my dad were here to talk to about it."

With Alejandro away, they decided to consult with Brendan. That night, everyone gathered outside to see if the northern and southern lights were visible. Sure enough, there they were, faintly visible on the horizon.

"It's beautiful!" exclaimed Talah, who had come over to watch with Debrak.

"It may be beautiful, but it's not good," replied Brendan grimly. "It means the two magnetic poles are getting closer, and the magnetic field around us is weakening. The weaker the field, the brighter the lights. Alejandro told me they've been concerned about this for quite a while, but they were hoping for a slower progression."

"But I thought the field around the equator was stronger," said Laurie.

"It has been for a long time, but at some point, that may change, as the magnetic north and south poles align over us. And it looks as if that's happening already. We don't know how this will play out. We know this has happened hundreds of times in Earth's history, yet we still don't know the details of how the flip occurs. Is it slow, over a period of years or decades? Or is it instantaneous? All we know is things are changing rapidly now, and we have to deal with the consequences day by day. And one day, we may have to move underground to avoid damaging radiation."

Laurie, Stan, and George stared at each other. After all they had gone through to get here, it didn't seem possible they were facing the same fate they had fled from five years earlier. "We have no place else to run to," said Stan. "This may well be the end of the line."

Josh

As he tinkered with his homemade radio, Josh questioned if they had made the right decision. He had his family and Pablo was reunited with his daughter, yet life was hard in this village, which had defied progress for eons. In many ways, he felt they had traveled back in time to a period when modern conveniences could barely be imagined. He remembered the trip from El Paso to San Diego when he and Pablo had wondered if places like this existed. He was grateful they did, and equally grateful he and Pablo had found one of them.

Prior to their arrival in Ecuador, they had been worried about entering the country, but with power and internet out worldwide and many people migrating from their home countries, immigration had become the norm. Pablo's cousin, Emanuel, had told them that the country had an open border policy and thankfully they found that to be true.

Josh thought back to his conversations with Pablo during their long bike trek from El Paso to San Diego. It seemed the prediction they had made then had proven accurate. In Ecuador, as in the rest of the world, major cities were crippled and unable to handle the scale of the disaster, and much of the infrastructure of the country had collapsed. Everyone was migrating away from the cities. The only safe places to live were primitive villages, and luckily for them, Pablo's daughter had found refuge in one of them.

They all suffered from the trauma of losing Amigo, especially Jessica who had never lived a day without the dog. Each night, she cried herself to sleep hugging a stuffed teddy bear that had been one of Amigo's favorite toys. Despite their grief, they managed to find Emanuel's friend who had agreed to guide them to the village where Elena lived. For a month they trudged with her along dirt-packed trails, wondering if they would ever reach their destination. After a long and tortuous trek, they arrived in the village high up in the mountains. Given Pablo's family connection, they found themselves embraced by the community, enabling their simple survival. Now, as Josh sat on the porch of his adobe hut, he heard Marguerite in the background reading to a small group of townspeople. She and Jessica were slowly adapting to village life, and Marguerite had taken it upon herself to teach English, captivating both children and adults alike with her stories of the outside world, where things like large houses and buildings, cars, airplanes, computers and telephones were completely foreign.

For Josh, though, simple survival wasn't enough. He was restless and wanted to know what was happening in the rest of the world. Did anyone else survive? Where was his family and where did Steve end up? He and Steve had talked about how they might reconnect, and he hoped George was still out there somewhere. For this reason, he was building a ham radio with enough power to reach long distances. It was a painstaking process and he was close to finishing. He was convinced that when he could communicate with the world beyond the village, doors would open that they couldn't even imagine now.

The previous night as they sat around the campfire, they noticed faint lights on the horizon. The village people were scared. They had never seen anything like this, and they wondered if the spirits were angered in some way.

"It's the northern lights and southern lights," Pablo explained patiently. "In other parts of the world, these lights are seen all the time. It is considered a beautiful thing."

He didn't want to frighten them further. Privately, though, he and Josh were worried. The magnetic poles were coming closer, and the people here were helpless to defend against any increased radiation exposure from a weakening magnetic field. The best they could do was to move their families into a small group of caves in the mountainside. There was no place else to run to, and this made Josh even more desperate to get his radio working. He needed to know what was happening elsewhere, if there was an elsewhere still left.

Alejandro

At the research lab in Troeburg, Alejandro met with a team of scientists. Thinking back to what had happened in the U.S. when magnetic north got closer to them, he recalled how weak Dawn became after the northern lights appeared regularly night after night. He was concerned because she was experiencing some of those same symptoms again. When he mentioned that to the group, Ian's ears perked up. He was the student in Brendan's class years ago who noticed his dog always peed facing north or south, and from there, he had gone on to study the magnetic field with a particular interest in how animals reacted to it. He had also seen how both Dawn and Debrak consistently "won" at the magnet game. They always knew where magnetic north was.

"Many animals sense the earth's magnetic field much more than mos' people," Ian said now. "Not only the direction, but the strength too. I've wondered 'bout the way they both feel that pull. Maybe they can also feel the field strength and that's what's botherin' Dawn now. Maybe you should bring them both here for some studies."

Ian thought about why Dawn, and now Debrak as well, might be so weak. It seemed counterintuitive. If the children were simply sensitive to Earth's magnetic field, why would they weaken as the field weakened? What, exactly was the connection? And then it hit him—maybe they were sensitive to more than the magnetic field. Perhaps they were sensitive to radiation in general. According to Alejandro, both Dawn and Debrak had recently complained of feeling constantly bombarded by little pellets. Was it possible they were feeling invisible electromagnetic radiation which would be stronger now that Earth's defensive shield was weaker? If so, then shielding them from that radiation was critical.

He shuddered at the thought of this. Since it was invisible and most people couldn't feel it, it was easy to ignore, even though their instruments told them radiation exposure was increasing. For the general population, apparently the radiation had to reach a far higher level before people would feel the effects and be spurred into action. Most people, especially here in Loscoaya, didn't trust scientists when it came to things they couldn't see and feel.

Aloud, Ian said "I wonder if Dawn and Debrak are super-sensitive to all radiation. If I'm right, the best treatment for them would be to put them in a safe room for a while, to shield them from increased exposure."

The team of researchers in Troeburg had been concerned about the potential for increased radiation exposure, and construction of several protected underground bunkers had already begun. One was completed but hadn't yet been tested. Eager to test both the rooms and Ian's idea about Dawn and Debrak, Alejandro returned to the village to collect both children. When Dawn saw him coming across the field, she ran to greet him. He grabbed her in a big bear hug, lifting her off the ground and spinning her around. *How light she is!* he thought. *Has she lost even more weight?* Setting her down, he looked at her anxiously.

"What are you doing here?" she asked. "You just left three days ago. I thought you'd be gone all month."

"I'm only here for a short time," he replied. Her face fell. "I came to pick something up and bring it back with me. Two things, actually. Would you and Debrak like to come to Troeburg for a few weeks? They have some people there who may be able to help you feel stronger again."

"Debrak, too?" she asked. "Both of us?"

"Yes, we want both of you to come. What do you think?"

It didn't take long to get both children packed up. Given their weakened state, however, traveling proved to be a much bigger problem. Ordinarily, the 40-mile bicycle ride would have been manageable for Dawn and Debrak, yet they were both far frailer than Alejandro had realized. They left early the following morning to give themselves the full day to travel. It was a grueling trip, since both children could only ride about ten minutes at a time, with substantial periods of rest between. As the day wore on, Alejandro wondered anxiously if this was indeed a good idea. When they finally arrived in the city about eight hours later, both Dawn and Diego collapsed, falling into deep sleep.

They were immediately carried down to the newly constructed safe room—a basement bunker located in one of the houses near the University. Then, everyone waited. Both children were almost comatose on arrival and no one knew for sure how long it might take for them to recover, or if they would recover at all.

For three solid days, both children slept deeply, awakened every few hours by Alejandro or one of his colleagues just enough to get a little water into each of them. Finally, on the fourth day, they were able to sit up and eat a small amount of food. Over the next few days, their strength returned, but Alejandro worried about taking them out of the safe room. This one-room bunker needed to be their home, at least for the immediate future. With great sorrow, Alejandro thought back to Sophia's words to him years

235

ago, telling him she didn't want her children to live underground. Tears formed in his eyes. Had he completely failed her? Would Dawn ever be able to go above ground again?

Alejandro wondered if that fate might be in store for all of them. It was exactly what Ian had realized a few days ago and was quite sobering to think about. They knew the magnetic field was weakening because they had instruments that measured it. However, the average human being couldn't feel this. For some reason, perhaps because they were born on the day of the great Solar Superstorm, Dawn and Debrak were unique in their sensitivity to it. No one else sensed it, but if the field continued to weaken, eventually they would all feel the effects. And even though they couldn't sense it now, were they all being exposed to increased radiation to the point of danger? How long would it be before they would all have to live underground?

A Second Superstorm
November 11, 2031

For ten years, the sun has been relatively quiet. The few solar storms that have erupted have been directed into outer space, but now, another superstorm arises and once again, particles of hot, molten gas head directly for Earth. As happened ten years earlier, radioactive particles emitted from the storm hit Earth's atmosphere, causing a massive disturbance of the magnetic field.

Earth's magnetic poles have been moving rapidly for the past ten years and already shifted almost 90 degrees. Magnetic north now sits just seven degrees above the equator and magnetic south is seven degrees below. The magnetic field above the northern and southern hemispheres of Earth has weakened to almost nothing, leaving much of the surface of the planet uninhabitable. The only region protected by the magnetic field is a small area around the equator, though that band is shrinking as the poles begin to align with the equator.

The force of this superstorm causes the shift that scientists had thought would take centuries to occur in a matter of days. On Earth, the poles suddenly flip. North moves south of the equator and south moves north, crossing paths and starting to move slowly away from one another.

It will be decades or perhaps centuries before the poles finally settle in their new resting places, where they will likely reside for several hundred thousand more years. Over time, Earth's protective magnetic field will expand back around the planet and the small clusters of people who sought refuge at the equator will move and repopulate the world.

Brendan

A week after Dawn and Debrak went to Troeburg, the townspeople prepared a great celebration to mark the tenth anniversary of the bloody sunrise. Every year, the myths surrounding this day had become further embedded into the culture of the community. During the week leading up to the big day, everyone gathered each night to look at the northern and southern lights. Although beautiful to behold, rumors about them were beginning to spread. The two sets of lights danced in opposite directions, leading people to believe they were spirits fighting for domination of the heavens.

Brendan felt strongly that the townspeople should not be outside, but the villagers were bubbling over with enthusiasm and would not be contained. Quietly, Brendan reminded everyone in his household that the brighter and more dazzling the lights, the more hazardous it was to be outside. It meant the magnetic field was weakening and they were at a far greater risk for radiation exposure. At least in the house with a metal roof, they had a bit of protection. But though he tried to explain this to the villagers, most of them had little regard for the scientific reasons behind the light show. They preferred to make up their own stories involving witchcraft and magic, and the big debate in town was whether the increasing intensity of the lights was a good omen or a bad one.

On the evening of the celebratory day, while Dawn and Debrak remained in the safe room in Troeburg, people in the village gathered in the field by the public high school. The sun was setting due west and the northern lights would soon be visible in the eastern sky, so all eyes were focused east. Suddenly, a small child turned and pointed toward the setting sun.

"It's bleeding!" she cried. And indeed, the sun was beginning to glow orange, and then red, just as the rising sun had done ten years earlier. The villagers watched in awe, mesmerized by the flashes of fire emanating from the setting orb.

As day turned to night, the lights on the opposite horizon began to dance. They got brighter as the sky darkened, and a shimmering, moving show began. Eventually, both the northern and southern lights lit up the sky with an intensity never before seen. Brendan, Grace, Laurie, Stan, Diego, and George remained indoors, hoping the solar panels on the roof of Brendan's house would block some of the incoming radiation. They watched as the townspeople stood in the field, rooted in place.

Brendan paced restlessly around the house. "I wish we could get them to all go inside," he said. "Every minute they are out there increases their chances of radiation sickness. They may not feel it now, but it might come back to haunt them years from now."

George stared at him. "Sonny, if this continues, none of us will likely be here days from now, let alone years. And honestly, I'm not even sure our flimsy roof is giving us much protection. I say, let 'em have their fun. You tried your best to warn them the past few days and those who are out there didn't listen. You can't save the world."

Brendan was silent. George was right, he thought. If this went on for more than a few days, they would all be subjected to huge levels of radiation. There was truly no way to avoid it. As his dad had said a few days earlier, they were at the end of the line, with no place else to run. He felt like a trapped animal with no energy left to flee. How could you fight the forces of nature?

For several hours, the townspeople watched as the lights continued to brighten. The villagers caroused in the field, singing, dancing and beating on drums. Inside Brendan's house, the little group simply listened.

Suddenly, when the lights were at maximum intensity, everything went still. The silence was eerie and surreal. Brendan pulled aside a curtain to peek outside and saw nothing but black. The lights had disappeared, leaving the village in complete darkness.

Josh

For the past week, dancing lights had appeared in the sky each evening, and every night they were brighter. Josh was worried. He and Pablo took their families to a nearby cave and planned to stay there until Josh could get his radio working and obtain more information. A handful of villagers followed them, but the bulk of the townspeople preferred to stay outside night after night, witnessing the glowing spectacle.

The opening of their cave faced west, and from their perch high up in the mountains, they watched in awe as the sun turned blood-red. Pablo's daughter, Elena, cowered in the corner. She was a strikingly beautiful girl, with long straight black hair and eyes that were almost as dark. At seventeen years old, she should have been out socializing with friends, enjoying herself as she matured into a beautiful woman. Instead, she was curled into a ball, breathing shallowly and shaking. When she looked up, her deep, dark eyes had a haunted look. Since arriving in Ecuador, she had bonded with Pablo a little, but the trauma of losing her mother was still with her. Added to that, for years, she had been raised by a very spiritual family and the thought of evil spirits terrified her.

Pablo tried to reassure her. "This is not because of evil spirits, Elena. The sun is just giving off a lot of energy. We call it a solar flare."

Elena looked at him questioningly. "Then how do you explain the lights? They are dancing out of control every night. Surely *that* is the spirits!" she said.

Pablo shrugged and turned to Josh. "I can't teach her science in a day," he said. "And I can't undo all the teaching she's had for the past ten years."

"At least you're with her now and she's willing to stay in the cave with us, even though so many others won't listen," said Josh.

As they watched the sky darken, they saw the lights begin to shimmer and dance on the horizon. It was a clear, moonless night, and the lights were particularly bright and mesmerizing. *They almost look like a city*, Josh thought nostalgically. *Or at least the way cities used to look at night.* Then suddenly, without warning, the sparkling lights winked out and Josh had an intense feeling of déjà vu as darkness enveloped them. *Ten years ago, I was on an airplane when this very thing happened,* he thought. *All the lights went out and I lived to tell the tale. I survived then, and we will survive now.*

Dawn

Troeburg was a thriving city with a functioning hydroelectric power grid that had been restored several years earlier. Yet even a modern power grid could not withstand the onslaught of radiation from this new solar storm and the resulting atmospheric chaos caused by the migrating magnetic poles. When the lights of the two auroras disappeared, the city's power grid failed as well, plunging everyone there into complete darkness.

In their pitch-black basement room, Dawn and Debrak were terrified. They clung to each other, wondering what to do. Alejandro usually slept in the small house directly above their bunker, but he had gone out several hours earlier to visit friends who lived across town. He told them he would be back to check on them before bedtime. They wished he was there with them now.

"What do you think happened?" asked Debrak, his voice echoing in the cavernous room.

"I don't know but I hope my dad, or someone, comes quickly to get us. It's creepy down here," replied Dawn. They waited in silence for a few moments, but no one appeared.

"They tol' us to stay here 'til they figure out how to protect us above ground," said Debrak. "I don' like it here with the lights out but I don' wanna go up there and feel sick again."

"I'm scared," whispered Dawn. She grabbed Debrak's arm, squeezing it tightly. "It feels like we're being buried alive. What if something horrible happened up there? How would we even know?"

They finally decided they had to get out. Slowly they made their way to the stairway. Still clinging to each other, they crept up the stone stairs, step by painstakingly slow step, ready to turn back at any moment if either of them started to feel anything odd. Finally, they reached the landing, and to their relief, they both still felt perfectly normal.

At the top of the stairs they faced a heavy metal door. "Whadya think will happen if we push this open?" asked Debrak.

"I don't know," said Dawn shakily. "But we've come this far. We can't go back down there again without at least seeing what's on the other side. It's the only way we can know what happened." She gripped Debrak's hand like a vise.

"Okay—here goes," said Debrak. "On count of three. Ready? One... Two... Three...."

Together, they leaned against the door. It swung open, revealing a large sparsely furnished room. It was still dark, but not the same stifling darkness as the windowless basement. At least they could make out the shapes of a few chairs. Standing in the doorway, they tried to feel the surrounding air. Were they still being bombarded by little pellets?

"I feel okay," said Dawn, tentatively as they moved further into the room.

"Me too," replied Debrak.

Through the darkness, they smiled at each other, as Alejandro burst into the room.

Chapter 15
Six Months Later

The sun always rose early in West Africa, and Laurie's favorite part of the day was the hour just before sunrise. In that quiet time the world was still, and in that stillness, Laurie always found peace. Getting up early to meditate had long been her habit, and this morning was no different.

On completing her meditation, she reflected on how much things had changed in her life since the night over ten years ago when the power suddenly went out. Some people might say they had lost everything, and in a certain sense, they had. They had lost their house, their way of living, and so many of the comforts that material things could bring. Their entire life had been turned upside down. Without electronic gadgets and robots to do their chores, life was challenging and difficult, and yet they rose to the challenge. They survived. More than that, they adapted, and in some ways, she could say they were better off for all the struggles of the past eleven years. What they had lost in material things, they had more than gained in relationships. Never again would she look at strangers the same way. She had been on the receiving end of strangers' generosity countless times, and she felt like they owed their survival to the kindness of these people.

For sure, Earth was different now. The polarity had shifted— magnetic north and south were still migrating, and probably would continue moving for many years. But as far as anyone could tell, here at least, they were safe. Scientists predicted that years from now, the poles would settle in their respective places and most of the Earth would be habitable again. But that was well into the future.

Laurie liked to continue her long-standing habit of recording what she was grateful for each morning, and today, she took out her notepad and pen, and wrote down a few lines:

I am grateful Dawn and Debrak seem healthy again.

I am grateful Diego found his way and seems to be thriving

I am grateful for food, water, power from the sun and shelter.

I am grateful to the people of this village for accepting us and showing us how to live in a way that is connected to the land and to each other.

I am grateful for little Benjamin.

She looked at what she had written. She was amazed at the number of things on her list. Yet as much as she had gratitude for so many things in her life, she couldn't shake the feeling that something was still missing. *What happened to Josh?* She wondered for perhaps the thousandth time. *Did he survive this as well?*

Just then, she heard a loud shout coming from the shed behind their tiny house. That was George's workspace where he continually tinkered with his radio. About six months ago, shortly after the last solar flare, he had gotten the radio working to the point where he could do short transmissions but was frustrated in his attempts to connect over long distances. He often lamented this, remembering the days when he could communicate around the world with a press of a button. Now, though, they weren't even sure there was a greater world out there.

"I've done it!" he shouted. "I may have reached South America! People are speaking a different language! I'm not sure who I'm talking to, but I think it's across the ocean!"

Brendan and Stan came running, talking excitedly. There were people alive, outside of Africa, outside of the little bubble they had lived in for so long. Even the more powerful radios in Troeburg hadn't been able to confirm this.

"It must be there's been a shift in the ionosphere," George exclaimed. "We always used to be able to communicate across the ocean by tropospheric ducting. That's something that allows radio waves to travel long distances if atmospheric conditions are right. This is huge!"

"Can you figure out who you're talking to and where they are?" Brendan asked.

"I'm not sure yet," replied George. "Damn! I wish I knew foreign languages better! I don't even know what language they're using!" The radio cackled, and a voice came across in clear English.

"Hello, is anybody there?"

"Yes!" cried George excitedly, giving his call sign. "Where are you located?"

"I am in Brazil. My name is Fernando," said the voice. "What about you?"

"Africa, the country of Loscoaya," George quickly replied.

"So… there are other people out there, across the ocean," whispered Fernando. "We weren't sure."

"Neither were we," said George. "Are you able to talk to others nearby by radio?"

"I am, but usually only short distances. Only now it seems to be expanded. Over the last few days, I have managed to communicate with someone in Ecuador as well."

"Ecuador," whispered Grace. "My brother used to live there. I wonder if he's still alive. Is there any way of finding out?"

"There might be a way, if radio operators managed to organize themselves," said George turning back to the radio once again. For several minutes he conversed with Fernando, who promised to do what he could to locate Grace's brother by relaying messages. It was a longshot, but it was a technique that had worked long ago and was certainly worth a try. They finally disconnected, promising to try to talk each day at the same time if feasible. Now that they had some channels of communication open, there was no telling what might be possible.

Josh

Early in the morning, Josh rose to speak with his newfound radio friend. They were checking in with each other every day at the same time to get updates and learn more about the rest of the world. While Josh had managed to reach a few other local radio operators, this was the first person in a different country. At least they knew there was life—human life—surviving in other parts of the world.

"I have some big news for you Josh," began Fernando when they connected. "Yesterday, I managed to communicate with someone in Africa!"

Josh was stunned. "Africa? That's wild!"

"Yes, it is quite crazy. It seems there have been some changes in the ionosphere, so radio waves can travel more freely. This guy was in a tiny country I never even heard of before. I think he said it was called Lo... um...losacoyo or something like that."

Josh couldn't believe Fernando's words. "Do you mean *Loscoaya?*" he asked.

"Yes! Exactly. That's what it is," replied Fernando.

"My brother lives there," he whispered. "Or at least he did ten years ago. I don't even know if he's still there, but if he is, can you get a message to him?"

"I can try," said Fernando. "The guy I talked to told me of a relay system he used a long time ago, and we were thinking of using it to find a relative of someone he lives with. So, sure, I can give him your message and see if he can locate your brother."

Josh paused for a moment. A completely ludicrous thought crossed his mind. How many people knew of the relay system George had described to him years ago? It was a common thing among radio operators back in the day, but still, he figured he had to ask. "What was the call sign of the guy you spoke with in Loscoaya?"

Once again, Josh was stunned by the answer.

Laurie

The following day, everyone gathered excitedly around the radio at the appointed meeting time waiting to hear what Fernando had to say about life across the ocean. Could he possibly reach Grace's brother? Though George told Grace to be patient, they all anxiously wanted to know if there were any new developments.

The radio crackled to life. "Hello, George! I have some information for you!" Fernando said.

"I'm all ears," replied George, wondering if he could have gotten information that quickly about Grace's brother.

"I sent a few relay messages out about your friend's brother and haven't heard anything back yet," he began, and the mood of the group sank. "But I do have some other interesting news."

"We're listening…" said George.

"Remember yesterday, when I told you I had been talking to someone in Ecuador?"

"Certainly," replied George. "That's why we thought you might be able to locate Grace's brother."

"Well, I think you may know this person I connected with." Fernando recited the call sign, asking "Does that mean anything to you?"

George was speechless. His face went deathly pale. "What is it?" asked Brendan and Laurie at once.

For a moment George ignored them, turning his full attention to the radio. "It does," he said weakly.

"That's the person I've been communicating with. He lives in the mountains of Ecuador."

Epilogue
One Year Later

Laurie and Stan sat on the porch in the early morning mist, watching the activity in front of the house as people went about their daily chores. Yesterday was a sad day, as they had buried their long-time friend George.

"He was such a trooper," Laurie said with a tear in her eye, recalling the day two months ago when George had pulled her aside.

"I have cancer," he had whispered to her. "Now don't go getting all teary on me! I've lived a great life. I survived the biggest existential threat ever to hit mankind and I'm proud of how we all made it through."

"Shouldn't you go to a doctor?" Laurie asked.

"Nah...I don't need some fancy doctor telling me I have only two months to live. I *know*. It's my time to go, and it's okay. Back in the day, maybe I would have seen a doctor and been treated with all sorts of poisons to keep me going a few extra months. But I don't need that now. My time here is up and I'm ready."

"He was right, you know," Stan said now. "We survived the apocalypse. It truly was the biggest existential crisis mankind has ever faced."

Laurie wiped her eyes. "I know that, and I know we're all going to die eventually, but it doesn't lessen the pain of losing someone we loved. George was family to us. If it weren't for him, we never would have reconnected with Josh."

She closed her eyes letting her thoughts drift back in time. She recalled Josh as a teenager spending all his time at George's house as he learned about ham radios. And she remembered George's unwillingness to accept that Josh was gone forever and his perseverance in searching for him.

She thought too of their life at that time, of the house she and Stan had called theirs for many years. She remembered how lights automatically switched on and off as she moved from room to room and how toilets flushed by themselves. In her mind's eye, she saw the enormous kitchen with its automatic, oven, refrigerator, and sink, and all the other conveniences of technology she thought she couldn't live without. It was a stark contrast to the way they lived now. True, they had a working toilet, but they had to pour a bucket of water in it to flush, with water collected from a well with a hand pump. They had no kitchen to speak of. An old cast-iron coal pot sat on the porch, as it had for years. She looked at it gratefully. Maybe it was old, but it had certainly served them well.

She looked at Stan, thinking how much the two of them had endured over the past ten years. She was grateful that he, too, had adapted and managed to make a life here. Along with George and Alejandro, they had all made this place home. And much as she would miss George, she had to agree with him that they had all lived their lives to the fullest.

Why did they survive while others didn't? she wondered now. She thought back to her neighbor Lisa's comment to her years ago. "You're a survivor, Laurie… Mark my words, with your resilience and Stan's resourcefulness, out of all of us in this neighborhood, you and Stan will be the last ones standing."

Was that all there was to it? Was it just resilience and resourcefulness, or was a huge amount of luck thrown in there as well? And what about Diego? Laurie had certainly had her share of doubts about him from the time she met him as a seven-year-old boy. At that time, she would never have called him resilient or resourceful, yet somehow, he developed those qualities and managed to find his way and make a life for himself.

Dimly, she heard a noise behind her and turned to see little Benjamin standing in the doorway with Flamingo, holding the stuffed bear Dawn had brought with her from the States a few years back. Flamingo had slowed down considerably, but Benjamin, now four years old, was a bundle of energy. He ran up to her and she pulled him on to her lap.

"Good morning my love!" she said.

"Morning Gammy," he said. "Can you read to me?"

"I can!" she said. "In fact, I have a brand-new book I wrote. Diego even did some drawings for it. It's about your cousin, Jessica."

Laurie picked up her notebook along with the sketch Diego had made and began reading. "Once upon a time, in a land far, far away, there lived a little girl with straight blond hair and big brown eyes named Jessica...."

"My eyes blue," Benjamin pointed to his eyes, interrupting her.

Laurie laughed. "Yes, they are... blue like your dad's."

"Your eyes brown," he said placing a finger on her forehead. Yes, she thought, my eyes are brown just like Josh's and Jessica's as well.

At that moment, Flamingo nuzzled his gray-haired nose into her lap. The old dog was such a comfort to them, Laurie thought. Benjamin giggled, snuggling up to her and sitting with rapt attention. Laurie read the tale about little Jessica, describing how she rode on a boat from California to Ecuador and now lived in a tiny mountain village near some beautiful caves. Jessica dreamed that one day she might journey to the place where her daddy grew up and her grandma and grandpa had once lived. She knew she had a cousin, Benjamin, and she dreamed of meeting him sometime in the future as well.

Benjamin's eyes widened. "She want to meet me?" he asked.

"Yes, she does," said Laurie, closing her eyes and giving Benjamin a tight squeeze. She felt oddly satisfied. Now that the shock of learning Josh was alive with a wife and child was wearing off, she felt an enormous sense of relief, like a giant weight was lifted off her shoulders and her life had come full circle. She wished she could see Josh again someday, and meet Marguerite and especially Jessica, but sadly realized that probably wasn't meant to be. She was here, in a tiny African village that was now her home and would be for the rest of her life. She was here with her family and extended family. With Stan, Brendan, Grace and Benjamin. With Alejandro, Diego and Dawn. She missed George, and she ached for Josh, yet in her imagination, she could envision a scene where her descendants might meet, as the world became more connected once again.

Acknowledgments

Writing is a solitary endeavor, yet this book would not have been written without the help of so many people. First and foremost, I wish to acknowledge the members of SIPA, my writer's support group. Seeing you all at those weekly meetings inspired me when I least expected it and kept me on track when I lost sight of where I was headed. I also want to recognize Nancy Burns, coordinator of the Merrimack Valley Medical Reserve Corp who gave me an overview of community emergency preparedness and connected me with PART, our town's local amateur radio club. PART members patiently explained ham radio operations and answered my many questions about the role of their organization in emergency response situations. Thanks also to Michael Polia, who provided me with more information about ham radios and helped me understand the physics of solar flares and their effect on Earth.

I was fortunate to have several Beta readers who gave me excellent feedback along the way. Thanks to Steve Glines, Cam Finn and Laura Fedolfi, for reviewing drafts of this book, and a special shoutout to Joanne Hyatt who spent countless hours reading, re-reading and meeting with me. You helped transform this book from an interesting story to a living, breathing work of art.

Thank you to Indu Shanmugam Guzman for your expert advice and editorial work and to Barbara Yocum who painstakingly went through the manuscript word by word. I am a better writer now because of both of you. And to Joanne Kenyon, thanks for patiently working with me on the interior design of this book and designing a beautiful cover.

Finally, I could never have accomplished this without the incredible support of my family. I imagine there were times when you thought I was living in an alternate universe. To Andy and Scott, I appreciate you putting up with my constant musings and "what ifs?." And to my husband, David, thank you for giving me the freedom to pursue my dream, and for spending innumerable hours listening to me as I attempted to sort out the story line.

Critiquing something your spouse has written can be a tricky process, yet you managed to navigate that with ease. Your advice and encouragement throughout kept me going and allowed me to see it through to the end.

Thank you from the bottom of my heart.

Discussion Questions

1. How would you describe Laurie's life when we first meet her?

2. At the beginning of chapter 2, "Laurie pushed thoughts of her younger son aside." Did you wonder or have a prediction about what might have happened to cause her to think that?

3. How does Diego's obsession with his electronic gadgets resemble or differ from Laurie's reliance on her electronic gadgets?

4. Contrast Brendan's life/home in Africa vs life in Connecticut.

5. What are some of the original effects of the power outage? Did any of the effects surprise you? What are the difficulties/dangers of the outage? Are there any benefits of the power outage?

6. Imagine a world without technology. What would you miss the most? What could you live most easily without?

7. Do you think we rely too much on technology? Why/why not? Is that good or bad?

8. Do you think the Northern Lights were important to the story? Why/why not?

9. Magnetic North is actually shifting. Do you think we should prepare for the possibility of the poles shifting? Why/why not? What should we do?

10. What are some of the coincidences in the story?

11. As a result of the power outage, life has changed for Laurie, Stan, Brendan, and Josh. Could you put yourself into any one of the characters' shoes? Which one? How would you have reacted?

12. Which character showed the most growth?

13. What does Laurie mean in chapter 13 (seven years after), when she says, "Yet now...I see how little we had then and how much we have now."

14. Does the story have a villain? Who/what is it?

15. In chapter 12 (five years after), when Josh and Pablo are traveling west the author writes, "Automation had allowed the world population to grow and evolve in specific ways, and without that technology, civilization, as they knew it, was doomed." What does the author mean?

16. Does the author have a message? What is it? Do you agree or disagree?

About the Author

Becky Bronson has a PhD in Biochemistry from Boston University, and worked as a research scientist before raising two boys and opening a yoga studio which she ran for 15 years. She has co-written a book with her sister, Phyllis Bronson "*Moods, Emotions, and Aging: Hormones and the Mind-body Connection*" and compiled her mother's memoirs after her mom passed away "*A Life Well Lived: Memoirs of a Woman who Loved Life.*"

In 2018, Becky traveled to Africa to visit her son, a Peace Corps volunteer living in a remote African Village. "When North Becomes South" was born out of that trip and is Becky's first work of fiction.